Dead Handsome

by

Laura Strickland

A Buffalo Steampunk Adventure

Dead Handsome

Cover Art by *Diana Carlile*

The Wild Rose Press, Inc.
PO Box 708
Adams Basin, NY 14410-0708
Visit us at www.thewildrosepress.com

Publishing History
First Fantasy Rose Edition, 2015
Print ISBN 978-1-62830-764-1
Digital ISBN 978-1-62830-765-8

A Buffalo Steampunk Adventure
Published in the United States of America

Chapter One

Buffalo, New York, the Niagara Frontier
November 1880

"He's dead fresh," Ruella said, and slung the man's corpse onto Clara's worktable. "Cut down from the gallows not an hour ago. That's what you said you wanted, innit, miss? One that was fresh, fit, and in good health when he died?"

In theory, it was. However, Clara Marian Allen, faced suddenly with the concrete evidence of her request in the form of a strapping and soaking-wet dead man, discovered theory did not always correlate completely with reality.

"Why is he so wet?"

"Raining outside, innit?" Ruella had been in Buffalo for almost ten years, but her speech retained the flavor of her birthplace, London's East End—just one of her colorful attributes. She growled, "I had to get him 'ere in a barrow through the streets. Covered him up like a load of manure in case someone saw me, but nobody did."

"You're certain?"

"Sure as pudding after Sunday dinner."

Clara strove to pull her gaze from the dead man sprawled on the table, and failed. He looked so large. A hulking fellow he must have been in life, and alive was how he still looked: sleeping, perhaps, or drunk and unconscious. She thought of the dark maze of streets and alleys between her house on Virginia Street and the county jail at the foot of Delaware, from whence Ruella had dragged her prize, and drew a hard breath. By God, what had she started?

"And you say nobody knows he's dead?"

"Only those what murdered him—those at the jail—and few enough they let in on their crimes. This is the third one since August. Dragged him out into the jail yard and forced him up on their makeshift gallows, didn't they? Hanged him proper."

Clara cast Ruella an uneasy glance. A former cook in Clara's household, Ruella had been constrained to go out to work when the family fortunes declined, and now held sway over the prison kitchens. "Why was he arrested?"

Ruella twitched, her version of a shrug. "Why are any of them arrested? Thieving, brawling—who knows?"

Who, indeed. In the Buffalo of 1880, there might be a thousand reasons. The city, a rough and tumble place, included both mansions like that occupied by Clara's wealthy grandfather and hovels on the waterfront. Clara's house, with its now-reduced means, teetered somewhere between.

"Thought you'd be pleased," Ruella huffed. "You said you were desperate and needed one of these soon."

"So I did."

Both women continued staring at the corpse.

"I figured I'd better grab him while I had the opportunity."

"You did well, Ruella, very well. How long was he

strung up, do you know?" A purely practical question rather than a morbid one. Clara couldn't use him if he had too much damage at the cellular level.

Ruella shook her head. "Just long enough for him to kick his last. Nobody stood around watching, with the rain pelting down. Took him a while to die—thrashed about a good deal. That's how I knew he'd suit you, mistress. You said you couldn't use one with a broken neck, and the ones who snap their necks in the drop die right quick."

Poor bastard, Clara thought with dispassion. Ruella was right; the fortunate ones broke their necks. Choking slowly was no way to die.

"Dead handsome he is, too," Ruella put in.

The remark, completely out of character, made Clara withdraw her gaze from the corpse for the first time and eye her companion in surprise. Strapping at nearly six feet tall, and muscled like a wrestler, Ruella could not be called a fanciful woman. But she stood now with her head tipped to one side, regarding the man on the table intently.

"That," Clara said dryly, "is not a consideration."

"Isn't it? I thought, seeing what you intends to do with him—"

"His health matters, and to a lesser extent his age. And the degree of corruption."

Ruella waved a beefy hand. "He's not rotted yet. Far too soon. A few hours ago he was up and walking around."

And a few hours hence, he would be again—if all went according to plan. "I'm very grateful, Ruella. You're sure no one saw you?"

"No one."

"Who cut him down?"

"Tim Jeffers, the prison sexton. I had to bribe him. Five cents, and a bottle."

"You're certain he won't tell?"

"I'm sure. He was already half drunk when he turned up—probably why he did a rubbish job with the noose, and this poor bloke suffered for it—and won't remember anything after he finishes that tot of gin."

"Didn't he think it strange you wanted the corpse?"

"All he was thinking about was the bottle." Ruella stole a look at her former mistress. "You sure about this? Know what you're doing?"

Clara drew a breath. "Yes."

"Want me to stay and help?"

A tempting offer. Clara could definitely use Ruella's brawn when it came to shifting the fellow around. But she shook her head. "Georgina will assist me, as always."

"That little slip of a thing?"

"We'll manage, thank you."

"What if he's stroppy when he wakes up?"

"Don't worry about that. We'll strap him down first."

"Well, and that's sure to improve his temper when he comes to! What a night—hanged, choked, dragged through Buffalo in a barrow, and then he wakes up tied down. Maybe I should stay."

"Well, then, help me strip him before you go. Those clothes he's wearing will have to be burned. They're no doubt full of pestilence from the jail."

Swiftly Clara stepped forward and laid her hands on the corpse for the first time. He felt chilly from the cold November rain, but only as might anyone who'd just come in. With quick, careful touches she examined the abrasions on his throat where the noose had bit deep. Ruella was right; his neck remained whole—a fortunate thing. A snapped neck would have rendered him useless.

And Ruella was right about one other thing, as well. He must have been a handsome brute in life. Even now, lying like an effigy on a coffin, he had a kind of rascally attractiveness. Dark hair, almost black, waved back from a broad and noble forehead. His features, strongly made and elegant, were emphasized by a prow of a nose, and two deep lines that might have been dimples bracketed his lips. His eyes—decently closed—showed twin fans of black lashes. Color still mottled his cheeks, along with residual swelling, products of the strangulation he'd endured, but that would fade. Cleaned up, he would make a passable gentleman.

He had some Spanish blood, perhaps, or possibly Welsh. Neither would nullify the backstory she'd prepared for him.

"Yes, Ruella," she murmured, "you've done well, indeed. Let's get to work."

The next few minutes proved awkward and difficult. Clara had never before handled a corpse this size, or this male. She quickly became grateful for Ruella's brute strength as well as impressed by the musculature of her prize. He must have been a laborer, to be so fit. Well-developed muscles marked his chest, along with an interesting pattern of dark hair, and he had shoulders like a bull. Callouses roughened both hands, and his nails were filthy, but that might well have been from being in the cells.

Clara was daunted—even more so when his trousers came off. Ruella stood back, then, with a grunt.

"Well!" she exclaimed, precisely as if she couldn't help herself. "Ain't he pretty?"

He was, inescapably. But Clara didn't partake in this exercise for the sake of enjoyment or titillation. With a dangerous experiment, and a desperate one, she could not allow herself to be distracted.

She requested of Ruella, "Help me wash him down before you go."

Ruella rolled up her sleeves, revealing forearms nearly as well-muscled as those of the corpse. "I have to confess I don't half want to stay, now. Don't know when I've got my hands on such a fine piece of male, even if he is dead."

Clara knew she certainly never had. Granted, her upbringing at her father's hands had been unconventional, to say the least. Her father, himself a physician, had not hesitated to develop her talents once he discovered them. Not another young woman of twenty in all New York State had done the things Clara had, but none of those things extended to encounters with the opposite sex.

Indeed, Clara thought wryly now, the only way she had of procuring herself a husband was to snag one freshly dead.

She defied all the standards of the day, even to her appearance. She had long ago lopped off her tawny locks, considering them an annoyance, and she went clad in a practical manner for the work she did in plain linen shirts, men's trousers, and a leather corset. Her eyes, as her father had frequently remarked, were unusual, a shade of greenish gray that fairly defied description. As might be expected of one who had the power to raise the dead.

Of course, she'd never before attempted to raise a creature of this size—or this sentience. The first had been her own dog, Mollie, and that an act born of pure love. Since then, she'd practiced on rabbits, chickens, and on one horrific occasion a Christmas goose that had returned to life and run, headless, around the dining room. Two serving girls had passed out.

The power, as her father had also been quick to assure her, was hereditary among the women of her line and went straight back to an ancestress with Native American blood.

"You are your ancestresses, in essence," she could still hear him say. "Do not ever forget that, whilst those who have bought into this society which surrounds us try to make you feel a misfit."

But a misfit she was. And her father was gone, dead these eight months, and with him any protection he lent. His body, riddled with disease, had been too frail and too ruined for her to bring him back.

She blinked now as the dead man's handsome face blurred before her eyes. No time for weakness.

"They say," Ruella observed in her rough growl, "these fellows grow a right hard prong whilst they're hanging. A stiffy, if you know what I mean. No evidence of it now, more's the pity. I can't deny I wouldn't mind—"

Clara bent a fierce look on her companion. "Ruella! That is a shocking observation."

"Just honest," Ruella puffed.

"Never mind, now. Help me wash him and strap him down."

"With pleasure. I'll just take the bottom half, shall I?"

Clara increased the intensity of her glare. "I think I had better do that, don't you? Since he's meant to be my husband."

Chapter Two

"So it's true. Clara, I can't believe it! I didn't think you'd really go through with this."

The whisper came from the direction of the workroom door and spun Clara where she stood. Georgina Jackson's horrified face peeked around the door, her dark eyes wide as those of a child on Christmas morning.

Clara relaxed just a hair. "Come in and shut the door. Where are the children?"

"In their beds. At least that's where they're supposed to be. You know what they are."

The "children" consisted of a parcel of ragamuffin street urchins that had come to Clara by one route or another and now lived under her protection. The first had arrived when Clara's father was still alive. The child was a bootblack from the same abusive household where Georgina had once served—hell on earth, Georgina always called it, the household of a Justice, no less.

"I wouldn't leave a diseased rat to suffer there," Georgina had declared when she found Jimmie weeping on a street corner with livid weals across his cheek.

Clara's father had agreed. The others had come piecemeal, and all with that kind man's approval. Anson Allen had been, above all else, a kind man. But now his protection had ended, and only Clara's ingenuity, determination, and talent stood between the children and ruin.

That didn't mean she wanted any of her charges to see what went on in this room.

Georgina tiptoed to her side. Clara, herself not a tall woman, always felt a giantess beside her diminutive friend. Deprivation in youth would do that to a person.

"Sweet merciful Jesus," Georgina exclaimed. "Ruella told me on her way out she'd brought you what you'd been seeking, but—he's a big one, ain't he?"

"He is that."

"Where'd she get him?"

"Off a makeshift gallows, fresh. No putrification yet."

"Who is he?"

Clara shrugged. The man came with no name, and once she resurrected him he wouldn't remember who he'd been—at least, that had been her experience with animals. Even Mollie hadn't known her but had learned her affection all over again. Of course it might be different with a human.

"So dangerous," Georgina whispered. "Sure you can handle it? What if he's angry when he—er—wakes up?"

"He should be a clean slate, only knowing what I tell him."

"I'm not sure about this, Clara. Maybe you should have Ruella cart him to the graveyard now, while it's still dark out."

"And then what? I need a husband at once, if I am to meet the terms of my grandfather's endowment and keep a roof over all our heads."

She referred to Randolph Van Hamelin, not her

father's sire but her mother's. The old man, still alive at ninety-nine, held the strings of the only purse in Clara's family that contained any money. Even this grand house—lately fallen to far less than grand—had come via Clara's mother, as well as any monies to maintain it.

Randolph Van Hamelin had not approved of his daughter's determination to marry the young doctor Anson Allen. Even though she was his fourth daughter of seven and well down on his list of potentially advantageous matches, he had his sights set higher than a struggling physician who had clawed his way up from the gutter, as Grandfather put it. But Clara's mother, Penelope, had been a forceful young woman, not unlike Clara herself. And when she came up carrying Anson's child, she got her way. The scandal had been legendary, at the time.

That child had not survived infancy, nor had the next two who came along. A punishment for disobedience, so Randolph declared. Clara alone had thrived, and that only because her mother had brought her back to life on the birthing couch, having discovered her own talent in her refusal to lose another child.

So Clara had in essence died and come back again.

I know how you'll feel, she silently told the man now lying before her. Of course, an infant had little to forget, so it hadn't mattered much. And of course, being but a toddler four years later, she hadn't been able to return the favor when her mother died of a seizure in her father's arms.

Father had always blamed himself. "What sort of doctor am I," he asked more than once, "who couldn't save the woman he loved?"

From that day sixteen years ago, Grandfather Van Hamelin had done his best to drive his son-in-law from the house and into ruin. Under the terms of the entailment, however, any child of Penelope's was entitled to live here until the age of twenty-one. After that, in order to hold the property she must be wed.

And Clara would turn twenty-one in less than a week, which meant if she didn't want those who were dependent on her tossed out on their ears, she must conform with the edict as soon as possible.

So why not just find a proper husband—one still breathing? Someone off the street, perhaps, a dockworker or a ruffian who would provide her the pleasure of shocking her grandfather's sensibilities? The answer was that Clara had no wish to answer to such a man, or any man. This fellow would know— would be—only what she told him, her own creation.

"If you wish to stay and help me," she told Georgina softly, "then stay. If you don't, then leave now. I'm ready to begin."

Georgina gave her a searching look. "I'll stay. But what if it goes badly?"

"It won't."

"Are you sure he's strapped down well enough?"

"Yes. Ruella did that job before she left. Flip on the steam generator for me, will you?"

The room needed to be warm—she had learned that during past experiments. It helped if the subject awakened in an environment that was moist and heated, akin to the womb. And the breath of life was more easily received by warmed flesh.

Georgina walked to the corner and switched on the generator, which came awake with a rumble as the boiler lit. Immediately the familiar clatter started, the gurgle as water began drawing through the system. Once it got going, the system thudded like a heartbeat. Appropriate somehow—that would be the first thing her subject heard when he awoke. If he awoke.

Still obviously uneasy, Georgina rejoined Clara at the table. "You know you're going to have to touch him."

"I've already touched him. Ruella and I stripped and washed him down."

"You're going to have to kiss him."

"It isn't a kiss. It's a resurrection."

"You're mad, Miss Clara. Stark raving."

"You think I don't know that?" Wasn't it why she could allow no one—other than these lost waifs and misfits who already surrounded her—into her life? How could she expect an ordinary, sane man to accept the woman she was? Either she created her own husband, or she took none at all.

The room had warmed quickly. Now clouds of steam billowed and surrounded the table, lending an unreality to this thing she undertook. It blurred the edges of her vision and her reason.

Did she do the right thing?

She did the only possible thing.

She rested her fingertips lightly against the corpse's chest and closed her eyes. He no longer felt cold, but he did feel quite dead. She'd learned the difference over these many months. Against all the distractions she quieted her mind and reached for the power within.

It slept much the way the man's flesh did, resting in oblivion. Like a separate entity within her, it mellowed and simmered until she called upon it, when it flared to life, bringing life.

She whispered a prayer now in her mind, none learned in any church but one that seemed to have passed down with the power itself—for protection, for rightness, for the one she sought to raise. She did not know him but she would, in the most intimate way possible.

She let the power grow and flare and burgeon inside her because she would need a great quantity of it, more than ever before. When it threatened to overspill her like hot water in a steaming kettle, she opened her eyes.

Everything looked different. The room had disappeared behind the billows of steam, and the light took on a golden hue. She could sense but not see Georgina beside her. Golden radiance seeped through the tips of her fingers, which still rested against the man's chest.

She felt full; she felt ready. She drew a deep breath—deep, deep, deeper than ever before—leaned down, and placed her mouth upon that of the corpse.

His lips, like the rest of him, no longer felt cold. His mouth lay open slightly, but she sensed nothing in him—no breath, no life. Yet her lips seemed to fuse to his and warm them further; a curious thing.

In the past she had breathed life into the mouths of lambs, cats, dogs—even chickens. Never, never a fellow human. Instantly she knew this felt different, but the life force filled her now, rampant and overwhelming. She could do nothing but breathe it into him.

She exhaled, an impossibly long breath that flowed

over his tongue, down his throat, and into his lungs. She continued breathing—not air now but life itself—her eyes pressed tight shut so she couldn't see.

His lips twitched beneath hers, just the faintest movement, and her heart leaped painfully. By God—or by Satan—it was working!

At this point she usually stopped and let the subject regain itself. Yet this time the life just kept flowing out of her until she wondered if she might not lose herself, pour all of what she was into him through this portal where their mouths fused. She felt his lips move more strongly beneath hers and the resurrection, unexpectedly, turned into a kiss.

She had already flowed her power into him. Now she thrust her tongue into his mouth as well, searching for something in him, some response or essence that should not exist. Her saliva passed into his mouth, and he twitched violently on the table as he tasted her.

And still Clara could not end the kiss. Helpless now and held fast, she stroked his tongue with hers and he answered, responding with a vigor that shook her to her toes. His tongue parried hers, danced, and then thrust into her mouth in turn, where he tasted her, searched her, drank deeply once more.

At that moment, conviction blossomed in Clara's mind: she was not sure who he was, even what he was, but he was *hers*.

Chapter Three

Darkness. Steam. His heartbeat pounded in his ears. A rush of sensation, and lips on his—soft, soft lips burning, giving. Who was she? He wanted to open his eyes but hadn't the strength. Yet he could feel her, oh, lord, he could, her essence flowing from the contact point of their mouths through every part of him. Down his throat and through his lungs, wrapping round his heart, which took up the rhythm he heard in huge, shattering beats. Across his shoulders and down his arms to his fingertips. Down through his stomach and into his bowels, pooling hard in his cock.

He wanted her; he wanted her like he had never wanted anything.

He thrust his tongue into her mouth even as the warmth continued to travel down his legs, making them tremble, and into his toes.

He could not speak; he could barely think. He could only kiss her, taking and giving in equal measures, letting the fervor of his mouth do the talking for him. He could only claim her.

Mine, forever more.

She jerked, spasmed against him, and he felt her strength wane. He stroked her tongue with his, a reassurance. *I will uphold you. I will defend you.*

The pressure of her mouth on his ceased abruptly, but his heart kept beating. He felt stronger now, filled with vibrant life.

He opened his eyes.

Light. Confusion. Billows of cloud and the inability to move.

A face hung above him, that of a child. No, she was a woman with a curiously elfin face. Soft ruffles of light brown hair framed a wide brow that narrowed to a pixie's chin, a sweet mouth—still wet from his mouth—and a pair of eyes so unusual he could barely fathom them. Yet he couldn't look away. Green eyes. No, gray like the clouds that surrounded them, or, no—

He must be in heaven. A curious thing, that, for he'd never expected to get there, not given the way he'd ended. For he remembered being hanged—that awful moment when he'd been forced up on the wooden box with his hands bound, struggling, feeling like his bowels were going to let loose, fighting against the hands that held him while someone put the noose around his neck. The box was kicked away, and—

He thrust the rest of it from his mind. He refused to contemplate the memory of his limbs thrashing, the endlessness of the ordeal, the growing pain and darkness. Who would have thought it would culminate in heaven?

Yet she had to be an angel, didn't she? He wanted desperately to kiss her again, and he knew he was hard down below, like a railroad spike.

He sought for his voice, which rumbled up through him from an inestimable distance and came out in an agonizing croak. "I can't move."

She jumped back from him like a scalded cat, but her gaze did not leave his.

"That's because you are strapped down."

Who would have thought angels spoke like proper ladies? Her voice wasn't low class, but neither was it high. Educated. His sluggish mind supplied the word.

"Why? Why am I—" It hurt too much to complete the question.

"Sweet Jesus," said another female voice from behind the clouds, "you did it!"

"Of course," the angel replied, and he saw her lips move. Lips, tongue, warmth—*kiss me again.* His lashes fluttered as he willed her to it. He wanted to spend eternity so, with her mouth on his.

But she did not kiss him again. Instead she told him, "You are strapped down for your own safety. How do you feel?"

A good question. He wasn't sure how he felt. Physically pained, yet not connected to the pain, if that made sense. But it didn't. As evidenced by his cock, he felt aroused. Yet nothing seemed terribly familiar.

His brain ticked over slowly, struggling against the weight of the retreating darkness. "Untie me."

"Not just yet."

"Untie me!" Rage gathered inside him like rising steam.

"Calm yourself." She touched his brow, and he did calm. Perhaps she was his personal angel, assigned to him here in heaven.

"What do you remember?" she asked.

He shook his head. He recalled nothing before being forced up on the wooden box, and the noose. It felt much like it did after a brawl or a bender—he usually couldn't remember what had come before.

"It will come back to me," he said. His voice sounded like the scrape of a saw on rough wood, and speaking felt very nearly unbearable.

Soothingly she said, "I am sure you have many questions, such as why you are here and why you are naked."

"We go out of this world bare as we came into it." The words appeared in his head, from whence he couldn't tell.

"You are Irish." She turned her head and spoke to someone beyond the reach of his vision. "Irish."

Did it matter? Had he ended up by some error in the English heaven? And so would they toss him out? Made sense, that. Bloody English barely tolerated the Irish anywhere.

"If he was not born here," the other, unseen woman replied, "you may run less risk of him being espied by family later on."

"True." His personal angel returned her attention to him. He felt her awareness curl through him like a balm and drew a long, shuddering breath.

"Untie me."

This time she ignored the request.

He rasped, "Please."

"A few more minutes."

"Are souls tied up in heaven, then?"

"My good sir, you are not in heaven."

"No?" Confusion gripped him, dark and terrible. He strained against his bonds.

She bent closer.

"Miss Clara, be careful," said the other woman.

"But the angel—Clara—disregarded her. Gaze fixed on his, she demanded, "Do you remember your name?"

He shook his head.

"Tell me," she said again, very slowly this time, "exactly what you do remember."

Very hoarsely now he said, "Noose. I died."

"Yes," she told him implacably, "and I brought you back to life."

'Twas just a terrible dream. Surely he'd got hold of some bad liquor somewhere. Half the fellows who ran these saloons made their own drink in a shed out back. A man might have some wicked dreams after drinking that. Because the lass with the pixie's face—Clara—could not possibly have claimed what he thought.

"Shut the boiler down, please, Georgina."

When she spoke, he could hear so much in her voice. She sounded calm, yet she wasn't. False calm, as if she schooled herself fiercely. Yet she was but a wee slip of a thing. Not an angel, then.

The pounding in his ears that he'd taken for his heartbeat ceased abruptly. But his heart carried right on thudding in his chest.

Alive, sure.

He asked, making certain, "I'm not in heaven, then?"

"You are not." Her face swam above him, all he ever wanted to see.

Very well, so he'd been on the makeshift gallows in the jail yard—murdered—and had ended up here stripped down by two women and tied up. One of *those* dreams, then.

Would she kiss him again? He focused his gaze on her lips, willing it. But nay, dreams never went the way a fellow wanted.

And what of the other woman? He'd not yet seen her, but if it truly was that sort of dream, she should lay hands on him down below, and he'd wind up having both of them.

"You must be wondering where you are," Clara said. "You're in the back room of my house on Virginia Street."

"In Dublin?" he asked, his throat a mass of pain.

"Buffalo—America." Something flickered in her eyes. "You won't remember much. The process does not allow for retention of anything but immediate memory. A bit like birth itself, in that—we rarely remember where we have been before."

Process? What the bloody hell was she talking about?

"Just try to remain at ease. You are safe here. And I will tell you all you need to know."

He tried to clear his throat, but the pain remained. "Would you be at ease, then, if you woke up tied down and—?" He flicked his gaze down his own body and left the rest unsaid. Mixed company, after all, and she wasn't a harlot. Was she?

"Probably not." She touched his brow again, just the lightest brush of her fingers, but the sensation went through him so intensely he had to close his eyes for a moment. "Please, just be patient."

He doubted patience had ever been his strong suit. He didn't know for sure, though, because a great wall of blackness loomed just back of being forced up onto that makeshift gallows. He thought he'd been good with his fists and with winning arguments. Clever with his tongue, as well.

At the thought, he relived the sensation of her mouth on his, her tongue encountering his. He wanted it again, so badly it made him breathless.

But his brain was beginning to hum faster now, his wits—if not his memory—returning to him. Cunningly, he said, "Thirsty. Throat hurts."

"That will be from the force of the noose. I am afraid it will pain you for some time. You will need to heal—there is little I can do for you."

"Water? Please."

"Of course. Georgina, bring me the pitcher, if you will."

He heard someone move about, and Clara turned away from him. When she turned back, she held a cup in her hands.

He wanted that water very much. But he wanted his liberty more.

"Here." She tipped the cup to his lips, but he lay flat on his back, and it took little effort to let the water dribble down into his ears.

"Blast," Clara said, clearly annoyed.

"Untie me so I can sit up to drink."

"Not a good idea." The other woman came into view, a little brown lass, very pretty. Nay, he would not mind her hands on him. But she scowled, cautious and troubled. "It's dangerous."

"Perhaps just the first two straps," Clara said, "so he may take the water. We will leave his legs bound."

Aye, and he would have no trouble overpowering them—a slip of a lass and Clara not much larger. Did they not think that once his arms were free he could throttle them and untie his own feet?

And escape. Where? Out into some city he did not even recall?

Georgina had large, dark, almond-shaped eyes set in a delicate face, and hair that frizzed all around her head. "You can't tell what he'll do."

"I can hardly leave him strapped down forever. I shall need to explain things to him, reason with him."

"Better to do that while he's still under control."

Clara bent a stern look on him. "If I help you to sit up and take some water, can I trust you?"

He allowed his lashes to sweep down to cover his eyes, hiding the deception within. "Oh, aye, you can trust me, sure."

"Very well, then."

He felt her fingers work at the straps and looked down. Four straps—two across the top half of his body and two below, with his cock trapped between. They looked precisely like leather belts and had buckles, with which she now fumbled. When the first across his chest came loose, he drew a big breath. The second had cut into his stomach muscles, very tight.

Play at being weak and fool them, the deceptive part of his brain urged. So he lay meekly until Clara put both her hands behind his shoulders to urge him up.

"There now. All right?"

Truly, no. His head swam, and he hurt all over, likely from all the thrashing about he'd done after that box got kicked away. But he blinked and nodded.

"Water," he pleaded.

She reached for the cup. The tiny lass— Georgina—stood at the other side of the table on which he lay, still frowning.

Clara raised the cup to his lips, and the sweet water burned a path down his throat. He drank greedily—all of it—and begged, "More."

She turned away again, and he flexed his fingers surreptitiously, and then his hands. God, how he hurt!

But he felt greater strength begin to seep through him.

When Clara turned back he moved, quick as a snake, reaching out and seizing her by the shoulders. She felt fragile beneath his hands, beautiful as a bird, and desire struck him hard again. He fought it down somehow, even as her curious, greenish eyes flew to his, and held.

"There now, little lass," he addressed Georgina, even though he did not look at her. "Unfasten those last two straps, unless you wish to see me strangle your mistress where she stands."

Chapter Four

Clara caught her breath hard when the subject's hands closed on her shoulders in a bruising grip. Who would have thought he could move so quickly in his debilitated state? She cursed herself for a fool—how could she have trusted his intentions?

And he made no idle threat. If his hands could move that swiftly, there was nothing to keep them from sliding up around her throat.

She stared into his eyes, and by all the stars in heaven, what eyes they were! From the look of him— the tanned skin and the slightly Spanish features—she'd expected dark eyes, but his were clear-water blue, uncanny and intent, fringed by black lashes. They screamed aloud of his Irish blood.

"Georgina, wee lass," he said, the lilt in his voice almost overriding the gravel left by the noose, "unfasten those straps, I tell you—now." His eyes never left Clara's as he spoke. And oh, she could feel him, a backlash of the power she'd poured into him only moments ago, striking wild at her and then sliding through her blood from the contact points of his hands.

Like arousal, hot and sweet.

She held his gaze without wavering and said, "Georgina, do as he asks." Would he kill her? She didn't know, but this felt akin to bringing a wolf to life on her table.

"I don't think so."

That captured Clara's attention, and his as well. Georgina's voice quivered, but her hands remained steady as she clutched the small pistol Clara's father had always insisted Clara keep handy.

"Let go of her now, big Irishman."

He froze but didn't comply. He seemed to measure Georgina where she stood, and Clara almost wanted to warn him, *Don't underestimate her*. Georgina was one of the toughest individuals Clara knew.

"Well now," the subject said, "is this not interesting?"

"I will shoot you if you harm a hair on her head." Georgina's nostrils flared.

Still he did not release Clara. The imprint of his fingers seemed to penetrate through her flesh.

Georgina stepped closer. Something flickered in the man's eyes, and Clara parted her lips—to warn Georgina this time. But he moved before she could speak, in a rapid blur, and had the pistol out of Georgina's hands before anyone could blink.

Clara, released suddenly, staggered back. The pistol looked absurdly small in the subject's hands.

Georgina threw Clara a look of agonized apology.

A half smile crooked one corner of the subject's mouth. "Now, let's try this again. You unfasten those straps, wee lass, and we'll all sit down and talk like the civilized people we are."

****

"You will need some clothes." Clara barely knew where to look. With the man upright—at well over six feet in height—he made an impressive sight. No matter where she turned her gaze, it seemed somehow to glimpse his genitals. "My father's clothes will never fit. And yours, from the jail, are fit only for burning."

He tipped his head to one side, and the dark hair, very nearly black, slid against his bruised neck like silk. He wore it long, and it held a gleam like the wing of a blackbird. More dark hair clustered on his chest and trailed downward to the nest of curls at his—

Blast, she'd looked there again.

Georgina suggested, "Your father's old robe, maybe? Something—something to cover—"

Was Georgina's gaze drawn there too? Almost impossible to avoid it. He had an impressive set of equipment.

At least the appendage in question no longer stood at attention like a battle weapon.

"Yes," Clara said gratefully, "go and fetch the robe, Georgina, if you will."

Georgina fled, and silence fell. The subject still held the pistol casually, dangling from one finger, and they faced each other with the worktable between.

"So you've a father, then," he said abruptly. He raised his hand to rub at his throat, exploring the abrasions there. "Does he know what you get up to?"

Clara shook her head. "He's deceased."

Again something flickered in his eyes. It was as if she could sense his emotions on some visceral level.

"What, you couldn't resurrect him?"

"No." He was sharp, this one, with quick wits, even hampered by what he'd just endured. She wondered suddenly, sickeningly, if she was in over her head. How was she to control him? She'd expected him to be weak as a child, confused, debilitated. But there he stood, dangerous as a whetted knife.

"When my father died, his body was riddled by disease, ruined. Not—" She waved a hand at him, pointing out his vigorous condition. "I could not bring him back only to let him suffer more."

"Ah." His gaze moved over her, head to toe, in a minute examination. "And how is it you can bring anyone back to life at all? What are you? Angel? Demon?"

What are you? That question had prevented her, always, from revealing this ability she harbored. Only Georgina knew, and Ruella. Her father had known, but no one else. Now this man held the knowledge that would allow him to judge her, condemn her, brand her a freak.

She shook her head. "Neither angel nor demon. Just a woman with a very ancient talent, one usually kept well hidden."

"I can see why. Could get you burnt at the stake, that, in bygone days."

What did he remember? He shouldn't recall the past at all, should be a clean slate upon which she might write her demands and requirements.

The workroom door whispered open, and Georgina came in carrying a brocade robe. The garment had always been overly large on Anson Allen, but when the subject struggled into it, shifting the pistol between his hands as he did so, it barely covered his wrists and gaped across his chest. At least it covered the pertinent area below.

Clara strove desperately, perilously, for calm. "Please sit down." She nudged a bench out from the wall, and he flinched. "What is it?"

"Wooden bench," he said cryptically. "Last thing I

heard was the scrape of wood. I could use a drink. Any liquor in the house?"

"Georgina, go and get a glass of my father's brandy."

"Is that a good idea?" Georgina bent a hard look on Clara. "He's only just—you know."

"A drink cannot harm me, lass." The man smiled at Georgina with devastating effect. Ruella had not lied: he was dead handsome, this one, something on which Clara certainly hadn't bargained. "Especially brandy. Run and do your mistress's bidding now, there's a love."

Deliberately, he laid the pistol on the table. "I'll not harm her whilst you're gone."

Georgina shot another agonized look at Clara before darting out of the room once more. The subject sat down; Clara remained standing, her fingers resting lightly on her worktable.

"So, now." His eyes met hers. Despite the roughness lent his voice by the punishment of the noose, his accent sounded smooth as warm honey. "We've a great deal to discuss, Miss Clara."

"You're sure you don't remember your name?"

He appeared to think about it, and then shook his head. "Nay. 'Tis as if I should be able to remember, as if 'tis all waiting for me, but I can't quite get through this damned black wall and grasp it. How do I come to be here?"

Clara drew a breath. How much to tell him? When planning this she had prepared a speech of explanation: you have been through a long illness that stole your memory. You are to take up a new life here, with me. I will look after you, and you will reciprocate as I request—

That would never do, now. He knew he'd been hanged and that she had resurrected him.

"Do you know what sort of life you led?"

He raised both his hands and examined them. "Laborer, I should say. I know I boozed. And brawled. I don't know how I know."

"You've been held in the county jail." Probably for brawling; a common enough offense on Buffalo's waterfront, where taverns were endemic. He might have killed someone in a fight. "The jail warden is corrupt. He accepts a stipend to support those incarcerated there, but some of those in his charge disappear and are never seen again."

Georgina reentered the room, a brandy snifter in her hands. "Should you be telling him all this?" she asked at once.

"He needs an explanation. I thought the truth best."

The subject reached out and snagged the glass from Georgina's hands. The poor girl started like a frightened pony.

"This is what I'm after needing, lass."

Both women watched while he drank deep, and Clara questioned herself anew. This might be like giving a bulldog red meat. She did not want to admit the situation had got away from her, or that she might indeed be in over her head. But she could feel the water lapping around her ears.

"Easy," she bade. "No telling how that will affect you after having been—"

"Dead?" The crooked smile curled his lips again. Definitely devastating. Oh, what had Ruella brought her? "Water of life, this. Your mistress, Clara," he addressed Georgina directly, "was just getting to the interesting part, I believe—how I came to be here."

Georgina wrapped her arms about herself and held tight.

"How do you know all this," he asked Clara, "about the crooked warden?"

"I have a friend who works at the jail. She has suspected for some time what's going on there. This evening you were taken into the prison yard and hanged. You were then supposed to be dumped in the river, but my friend intervened, bribed the prison sexton, and brought you here instead."

"Ah." He buried his face in the snifter again. Clara could sense his thoughts teeming. Unexpectedly, she felt it all again—his mouth on hers, his tongue invading her, indescribably intimate. How would he taste now? Like brandy, heady and hot? "Now we come to the truly interesting bit. Why? Why should a slip of a lass want her friend to bring her a corpse on the sly? 'Tis on the sly, isn't it? No one knows."

"No one knows." He was too sharp by half. "Only my friend and the sexton, who was drunk at the time."

"So these others that murdered me think me safe in the river?"

"They do."

"Aye, so." His gaze took on a faraway look as he contemplated it. Georgina shot Clara another doubtful glance. They had not bargained for this when they formed their plan. They'd been fighting for their survival, and that of those dependent on them. They'd thought he would become a participant by necessity, but not an active one.

Suddenly his gaze sharpened and captured Clara's;

his eyes burned bright and clear as sapphires. "And so, lass, it comes back to the grand question: why? Why would you want a corpse brought to your home and why bring him back to life?"

Chapter Five

The bedroom had clearly belonged to the witch-lass's father. It still contained his things, including clothing and a set of razors. A fine, large room it was, far better than any he had ever before inhabited.

Curious how he did not know how he knew that; he just did. It was as if *knowing* rather than specific knowledge had come back to life with him. He knew he came from Ireland, but he did not remember the place. He knew—or sensed—what kind of life he'd led, though he remembered none of the particulars.

The explanation Clara had given him made no fit explanation. She must have a powerful reason for resurrecting him, if indeed it was what she'd done, but she refused to disclose it. Did he believe anything she'd said? Cursed, but he did. He sensed an honesty about her, and he had this great, painful wound about his neck.

He walked to the dresser on the other side of the room and regarded himself in the mirror. The image shocked him even as it teased him with familiarity. So, he thought, that's me, is it? The *me* who had swung from a makeshift gallows at some bugger's bidding— he needed to settle that score, sure—the *me* who had been dead for how long? An hour? More?

Handsome blighter he was, fine and tall, with a crop of black hair and wicked eyes. The women would like such a face.

Clara would.

Now, why had that thought come to him? Again he remembered her kissing him. If she could be believed, it had been no ordinary kiss but a resurrection. He knew he'd never imagined being kissed like that. The effects of it still flowed through him, and he wanted more.

He ached for her mouth on his again.

But he wasn't stupid. He had waked from some mad, terrible dream and now found himself walking a tightrope.

She had fed him some line of bull about bringing him back in the interest of justice and requiring his assistance in return. She would not say what sort of help. Did she require a servant? An assassin? A stud for her bed?

He realized he was up and hard again, just thinking about her. Another curious thing, that, for she was not the type who usually tripped that wire. He didn't know how he knew that either, but he did. He tended to choose buxom women generous with their favors and with some experience behind them, not girl-child pixies innocent as the day was long. Then why did just picturing those uncanny gray-green eyes of hers affect him this way?

He stared into his own eyes and wondered about his name, which of all things seemed an awful belonging for a man to lose. He wondered if there might be a record of it at the jail from which Clara said he had come.

Clara.

Or if, given his ending, all such evidence had been destroyed. He must ask the witch girl about his clothes.

They might contain a scrap of paper or other clue to his identity.

When the wee lass, Georgina, had showed him to this room, she'd told him to rest, and he did feel the need for it. The brandy had taken the edge off and relaxed him, and he was weary to his bones. But his neck and throat hurt too much to let him sleep.

Curse it, he wanted a name.

He walked to the window and looked out. The light from the wall fixture reflected back at him, and he saw himself again in the glass, wearing the foolish robe. Outside lay pure darkness; he glimpsed no clue to his surroundings. Irritation seized him. He went to the door and flung it open.

At least they had not locked him in, which would have annoyed him further. The broad, carpeted hallway met his gaze. The house slept—no, not quite. Far distant he could hear high-pitched voices. Children?

He frowned, swept the skirt of the robe about him like an emperor, and sallied forth.

A great, well-established house, this, if a bit fallen into ruin. The hallway led to a landing and a broad set of stairs. He could no longer hear the voices, making him think they came from a different part of the house.

The wee lass, Georgina, had brought him up these stairs from yet another corridor that led from the back of the house. Now he descended to a marble floor and hesitated, listening to some inner instinct.

Closed doors lay to his right and left, the outer door directly ahead—freedom, presumably. But he could not seize that freedom wearing only a borrowed robe.

Clara had told Georgina to find him some clothes come morning. "Miller's will have something." A shop, presumably.

Clara.

Unerringly, he chose the right hand door, opened it, and leaned in.

And she sat there alone before a smoldering fire that did little to warm the room. She turned, startled, when she heard him, and then froze, hands gripping the arms of her chair.

"I was just after wondering about my clothes. I know you say they are fit only for burning, but I would like to look through them first if you have not yet disposed of them."

"They are in the workroom."

He entered and shut the door behind him, and she got to her feet. Ah, but she was a curious wee thing—not as tiny as Georgina, but scarcely taller than a girl of thirteen. He felt, again, her mouth on his. No child, this.

"I was hoping to discover me name. 'Tis not a good feeling, being without."

"I can imagine. But you know you would no longer be able to use your real name anyway. The man you were is dead."

"Nay, but I would have it to hold to me, even if in secret. My father's name, like. Happen you would not understand."

She eyed him up and down, her gaze personal as a touch. Aye, well, and she'd already seen all of him. She said, "I might. Georgina already went through your pockets."

"I would like to do that myself, or have I not the right?" With an aggressive edge, he asked, "Have I given up all me rights to whatever magic you've wrought upon me?"

Emotions stirred in her curious eyes. He took a step closer and lowered his voice; it hurt to speak, damn it. "Do you suppose you own me now that you've planted that kiss of life on me?"

The breath caught in her throat. "I own no one."

He tipped his head. "Then I would be free to leave here if I choose?"

"That would be most foolish." She waved a hand at his attire.

"Fair enough. But I—"

The door flew open and two children ran in. One was white and one was brown, nearly of an age and both male, clad in nightshirts with their thin legs bare. What in hell? Perhaps this truly was all a mad dream.

"Miss Clara, Miss Clara, we can't—" They stopped abruptly, both of them, as if connected by a string, and stared at him, wonder in their eyes.

Clara took advantage of their sudden silence to say, "Jimmie, Roscoe, what are you doing out of bed? You should be fast asleep."

"Couldn't sleep, miss," the brown lad replied. He had the face of an imp, all mischief, and at second glance looked healthier than his companion, whose skinny limbs appeared pasty and wizened. "Who's he?"

Clara laid a hand on each of their shoulders. "Never mind now. Go back to bed."

The pale boy asked, "But what's he doing here, miss, in the middle of the night and dressed like that?"

The thoughts moved visibly in Clara's eyes, her mind ticking over like a well-maintained steam engine. "This is a good friend of mine, come to help us save the house."

The brown lad gave a sudden, wide smile. Charm

fairly danced off him. "That's a good thing." He thrust out a small and not overly clean hand in introduction. "Roscoe Jefferson. Pleased to meet you."

The lad's hand felt tiny in his when he shook it. Courtesy demanded he introduce himself in turn. He shot Clara a look.

She said, "This is Mr. William Fitzgerald. Mr. Fitzgerald, Roscoe and Jimmie."

The second lad, clearly wanting no part of introductions, scowled and put his hands behind his back.

"Miss, why is he in his night robe?"

"Had a mishap with me clothes, didn't I? Out in the rain."

Jimmie's pale eyes widened. "And what's wrong with his throat?"

"Part of the mishap, isn't it?" he answered before Clara could. "Accident with a carriage." Clearly neither lad believed him, so he added, "Miss Clara's right, you should be in your beds. Run along now."

Jimmie looked at Clara, a protective glance betraying his doubt as to whether he should stay and defend her.

Were these two lads servants? And what sort of servants ran about the house like heathens in the middle of the night? It was a strange household, sure.

He clapped his hands. "Off with you, back where you belong. Or do I need to put you there meself?"

Jimmie backed up a step. Roscoe's grin widened. A kindred spirit, Roscoe might well be, and cute as sin.

"Go back to bed like good lads," Clara put in. "I will explain everything in the morning."

They went, Jimmie tugged by Roscoe's insistent

hand. He could hear them nattering together all the way back up the stairs.

He straightened and raised his eyebrows at Clara. "'William Fitzgerald'?"

"I had to tell them something."

"I will not be called Fitzgerald!"

"Why?"

"I do not like the name."

"Why?" she asked again.

Damned if he knew. Damned if he knew anything at this point, save he wanted to kiss her.

"It has bad connotations for me." He waved an arm in a helpless gesture. "I cannot say why. Who are those lads? Servants?"

"No, members of the household. They, and some others, have found refuge here."

"What sort of refuge?"

"Buffalo can be a hard city for those who get tossed out of their master's house or flee abuse, especially children. My father was a doctor, and when he treated someone in need, he also offered them a place to heal." She shrugged delicately. "Some never leave."

"A queen of mercy, are you?" He heard the sneer in his own voice.

"Hardly that. But those children, and others, now consider this place their home. That is why you are here—to help me keep a roof over their heads. That's why you need to cooperate with me."

Laura Strickland

Chapter Six

He slept like the dead and awoke with no concept of where he was. He lay for a moment, eyes stretched wide open, and took in the place where he was: fine, high-ceilinged room, burgundy-colored draperies at the window and heavy, dark furniture. Faint sunlight seeped in from outside, showing him he lay in a bed that had four high posters, finer than any where he'd ever laid his head.

Panic clawed at his belly, like the band of pain that encircled his throat. He didn't know this place or how he came here. He didn't know his name.

Clara.

He sat up so abruptly his stomach lurched and he had to fight down the urge to vomit. For an instant he thought his brain would explode. Beneath the satin-edged covers he was naked. A robe—brocade, gold and red—lay across the foot of the bed.

Did he remember the robe?

God, but his throat hurt. He put up an exploratory hand and encountered a wide abrasion. It hurt both in and outside. What did he recall?

A slip of a lass. Gray-green eyes. She'd kissed him.

His panic calmed somewhat but didn't dissipate. He fought his way out of the covers and went to the window. Below lay a street, an ordinary street with houses—fine, big ones. The street lay wet, though it wasn't raining now. Dimly he remembered it had rained. Now light bled from his left. Morning.

The house directly across, built of red brick, had a steamcarriage out front. Two lads tossed a ball back and forth.

Two lads.

Did he know them?

As he watched, a lass came out of the house door directly below and called to them, a tiny, brown beauty.

His belabored brain supplied a name: Georgina.

The lads followed her into the house.

Why was he here? Why couldn't he remember? By God, he needed a drink.

The room door behind him whispered open. He caught a glimpse of an elfin face before it shut again, abruptly.

He snatched up the robe, shrugged into it, and yanked the door open, catching her with wide, startled eyes.

Her gaze skittered from his face to his throat, down across the muscles of his chest and, as if she could not prevent it, lower still.

Clara.

Deliberately, he left the robe hanging open. *Want some of that, do you? Come on in—the bed's just there.*

"How do you feel this morning?" she asked politely.

Better, for seeing you. "Well enough, except for my throat." The pain there burned, worse than it had last night, and soreness radiated across his shoulders and down his back.

"I may be able to do something for that. Come to my father's surgery for a moment."

With a crooked smile, he tied the robe closed, then followed her down the main stairs and through the door on the left.

Aye, and he had been in places such as this before, though he did not know where or when. A high couch covered in leather occupied the center of the room, and a strong smell of cleaning solution stung his nose. A desk stood in the far corner and shelves filled every other available space.

Clara turned immediately to one of these and nodded at the couch. "Sit there, please."

"You know what you're after doing with all these vials and implements?"

"I frequently assisted my father here." She turned about to face him, and he found himself struck again by the impact of her presence. Bright light flooded through the front windows, making her eyes look more green than gray. Her light brown hair gathered like a cap of feathers around her head, and she looked fragile as a bird. A fey creature, sure.

She approached him, a jar and a bundle of cloth in her hands.

"I will just bathe and soothe these abrasions, and wrap your throat to keep you from frightening any more children."

She meant to touch him. *Glory be to God.*

She poured clear liquid from the jar onto a folded cloth.

"What is that, then?"

"Witch hazel."

"Good name for you, that."

"I am not a witch, Mr. Fitzgerald."

"Don't call me that. 'Tisn't my name."

"What else am I to call you?"

"What was that first name you gave me last night?"

"William."

"Liam, then. Call me Liam."

Her eyes met his for a brief instant that rendered him breathless. She stood, now, virtually within his arms, and him wearing almost nothing.

"I hope this will ease the pain of those abrasions; I will also apply some of my father's special unguent. He left a small quantity upon his death."

"How long's he been gone, then?" He fought against the sensation her hands made against the skin of his throat. She had better not look down, for he was hard again. Christ, sure and only green lads were constantly in this condition.

"Eight months. We were not in particularly good straits even then. My father tended to donate his services to those in need more often than he charged for them." Her touch felt far too gentle and careful to affect him this way. He was about ready to burst into flame.

She laid aside the cloth and left him, to search for a second jar on one of the shelves. Devastation assailed him until she returned.

"So," he said, striving mightily to sound sane, "you've no finances, then?"

"There is some money tied to the house, and various small amounts coming in, barely enough to feed all the mouths we have at present."

She dipped her fingers into the jar and then ran them over the skin of his throat. He nearly came off the couch, the pleasure felt so intense.

"Ah!"

"I'm sorry, does that sting?"

He wouldn't be able to tell if it did. His blood roared in his ears and obliterated any pain.

She continued calmly, "And even that funding will end, and we will lose the house very soon, when I turn twenty-one."

"How is that, then?"

"It's a complicated matter, Mr.—Liam. This house never actually belonged to my father but has been in trust to me since my mother died. It was settled upon my mother by her father, a wealthy man in this city. He never approved of my father, you see, but granted Mother's request by including a proviso allowing him to remain here throughout his life with a small, extremely stingy income. And I am to inherit it after, provided I'm married by the age of twenty-one."

"That seems a strange set of circumstances."

"My grandfather is a very strange man." She sighed, a small sound he felt all through his body. "He came to Buffalo as a youngster, when the Erie Canal opened, and made his fortune shipping lumber back east. The wealth he made he invested in the city, buying a great deal of property. He has a good eye and managed to snatch up and build on parcels that later proved valuable. He has become one of the richest men on the Niagara Frontier."

"Aren't you a lucky girl, then?"

"No, Liam, I'm not."

"But the old bugger will kick off one day, and you're bound to inherit, right?"

Her gaze met his in a long look. "No, I will not. My grandfather had other children, who did not defy him and marry outside what he considered their station. I have many cousins of whom he approves. He settled this house on my mother as a dowry, but I expect nothing else from him. And I highly suspect he would enjoy nothing more than snatching this place away from me."

"Aye, well, you are in a bit of a fix."

"I am." She finished fastening the cloth bandage around his throat. Her fingers stilled, but she didn't withdraw them. He remained all too aware of them resting lightly against his skin.

And, sweet Jesus, he could catch her scent, an enticing fragrance like herbs and pure woman. "Can you no' break the terms of this will?"

"We've tried. Out of concern for me, my father attempted just that before his death. And I have spoken with a lawyer, a friend of mine, since. No hope, I'm afraid. As I have said, my concern is not so much for me but all those dependent on me—Georgina and the children."

"So, then, you've only to get married." It should be easy enough for her, uncannily lovely as she was, and with a property promised to her.

"I intend to."

His stomach dropped. Before he could speak, she continued, "But I will tolerate no traditional marriage. No man will ever tell me what to do, nor make me vow to obey him. Just so you know that. And you should also know that the money attached to the house—that I'll come into when I turn twenty-one, provided I'm married—should be enough to keep us all, I hope, at least modestly."

He lifted a brow. "Why do I need to know that?"

Her gaze seared him, burning green. "Because you are my intended husband."

Chapter Seven

"You've told him everything?" Georgina whispered, while Clara and she stood examining the clothing she'd purchased for Liam. Clara would be much happier if he allowed himself to be called William, a dignified name that, in her opinion, carried some gravitas and implied, well, less *Irishness*. But she would be much happier were any number of things different.

The situation—which she had planned out so long and carefully—was very nearly out of her control. She had never bargained on the subject retaining a personality after his resurrection. She had expected him to be a clean slate upon which she, and she alone, could write. A puppet husband, not to put too fine a point on it. A convenience.

Liam Fitzgerald was proving anything but convenient. She had not guessed when Ruella procured him that he was Irish. Ever since the construction of the Erie Canal the Irish had been scorned as brawlers and boozers—if hard workers. Her grandfather most certainly would not approve.

And Liam definitely did have a personality. Also enough sex appeal to knock down a brick wall. He seemed clever, as well. Should she scuttle the plan? But what to do with him then? He was here, alive and dependent on her. Besides, she had no time to find another potential husband. And if word got out that she could resurrect the dead…

She scowled, and Georgina said apologetically, "These things were the best Mr. Miller had, for the money. Not exactly a gentleman's clothing, and I know you will need him to look the gentleman husband."

"Do you think him capable of looking the gentleman?" Clara returned. Liam had something basically rough-and-tumble about him—a brawler, no question.

"He's very handsome." Georgina kept her voice low. Liam was safely in the dining room, stuffing his face with breakfast, but this house was filled with small ears.

"I don't know what Ruella was thinking." But Ruella had understood how desperate Clara was— hadn't Clara said she'd take virtually any male corpse?

Liam wasn't just any male.

"These clothes are fine for now. At least they appear the right size." And Clara would be relieved to get him into proper clothing. "I suppose we'll need to dip further into our savings and take him to a tailor, eventually."

"I was able to trade in those things of your father's, so these didn't cost much." Georgina gave Clara a wide-eyed look. "So you did tell him? How did he react?"

"He said very little." Liam had shot her a shocked look—and she didn't imagine much shocked him—and buttoned his lip. "He's dealing with rather a lot right now, on all hands."

"You didn't expect him to be—like this?" Georgina asked.

She had not. "I thought he'd be meek and biddable. He still has a sense of himself."

"But he remembers nothing before being hanged."

"It wasn't this way with any of the animals."

Georgina pointed out, "He's not an animal. Are you going to carry on with the plan?"

Clara shrugged uncomfortably. "I must. The story is in place, and you know my grandfather is just waiting, poised like a vulture, to ruin me."

The workroom door eased open, and Ruella's face appeared. Clara always thought her friend and former cook looked like one of the personality Toby jugs that also hailed from England, her features slightly overemphasized, with bulging cheeks and a large, protruding proboscis. But Ruella was large overall, a strapping figure of a woman now crammed into a uniform complete with a stained apron, her blue eyes gleaming. She'd come straight from her job at the jail, no doubt ridden by curiosity.

Her gaze swept the table in the center of the room, now empty, and her face fell.

"Where is he, then? It didn't work, eh? Ah, never mind, miss. Wait till dark, and I will cart him to the river for you."

"Come in and shut the door, lest someone hear you. You will not cart him to the river."

Ruella eased her bulk into the room and shut the door as bidden. "Why not? That's where the prison sexton would have dropped him, after all."

"The procedure was successful."

"Blimey!" Ruella eyes glowed. "I'll confess I didn't half doubt it. That was a lot of cold man to resurrect."

Clara thought again of the feel of his mouth beneath hers, his tongue stirring, and a shot of pure desire arced through her.

"So where is he?"

"In the dining room eating breakfast, clad in nothing but my father's old robe."

"This I have to see!"

Before Clara could protest, Ruella took off. Clara caught up the clothing and followed, with Georgina in her wake.

Even before they reached the dining room, she heard voices raised in conversation—Liam's, recognizable by its deep timbre and the gravel lent by his injured throat, and—children?

"Oh, no," she breathed, and pushed past Ruella to enter the room first.

There she stopped like a pole-axed steer. Liam reigned supreme—she had no other term for it—at the head of the table, the lapels of her father's robe open on his magnificent chest, his attitude that of a beneficent king. His dark hair spilled in a tumble over his forehead, and his bandages made a bright patch against his tanned skin.

Clustered around the table—around him—were what appeared to be all the children of the household, and there were ten who lived beneath this roof. Liam seemed to be conversing with the two eldest, Fred and Woodrow, while the others, including little Petey with his brace on his twisted leg, hung on his every word.

"Yes," Woodrow said as she came in, "we go out to work at a proper trade—contribute to our keep, we do. Fred and I are skilled laborers."

Liam slid a glance at Clara and the two women at

her back before returning his gaze to Woodrow. "I am glad to hear it. What sort of work do you do?"

"Repairing boilers, and we're good at it. I was in training at Montgomery's boiler works until there was a mishap."

Yes, and that didn't half tell the tale, but the scars splashed across Woodrow's maimed hand and arm did. He'd been apprenticed to a cruel master, and when the boiler on which he'd been working leaked, the man had left the boy to suffer the ensuing burns without care. By the time Anson Allen heard of his plight and had him brought to the surgery, he was nearly beyond help. When queried, his master told Clara's father that without two good hands the lad was no further use to him.

Woodrow had been beneath the Allen roof ever since. His companion, Fred, to whom he'd taught his trade, had suffered the woes of a drunken father, now deceased, who alternately beat and neglected him.

Now Liam shot both boys respectful looks. Clara knew he must see the scars mottling Woodrow's skin, but he gave no sign. "That's a valuable skill to possess in today's world. Our society and our manufacturing both run on steam. There must be no end of jobs."

"Yes, well"—Fred shot an uncertain look at Clara, his basic honesty winning out—"it's more the small operations will hire us, just lads as we are. And we can't charge as much as the licensed boilermen."

"What goes on here?" Clara interrupted with some haste.

Liam turned those sky-blue eyes, fringed by spiked black lashes, on her. "Breakfast, and I am becoming acquainted with your household," he purred, "as befits your future husband."

Both Georgina and Ruella gasped. Clara's heart seemed to seize for an instant and then start up again, double time.

She was saved the necessity of a reply by Fred turning to her. "I told you, miss, I'd marry you if you needed a husband."

All his heart lay in the declaration, and this wasn't the first time it had been made. Truth be told, Clara adored the lad who was all fight despite his fourteen years and the fact that he stood no taller than she.

Gently she told him, "Fred, we have spoken of this before."

"Yes, and I don't understand—" He directed a clearly resentful look at Liam, who went on eating.

As kindly as possible, Clara said, "I am afraid my grandfather would never take you seriously as my husband."

"And you think he'll take *him* seriously?" Fred jerked his head at Liam.

Ruella pushed her way past Clara into the room. She ruffled Fred's hair.

"No matter, sprog. You know I am only waiting for you to grow enough to marry me and take me away from the hell of the jailhouse kitchen."

Fred smiled, and Ruella thrust a beefy hand across the table at Liam. "Ruella Whedon," she introduced herself. "I brought you here last night."

Clara hissed in annoyance. Nothing like announcing it in front of all the children.

Liam sprang to his feet; he and Ruella were nearly of a height. He took Ruella's hand and bowed over it. "I should say, then, I owe you a debt of thanks. Liam

McMahon, at your service."

McMahon? Clara's eyebrows ascended. What of Fitzgerald, with which she had christened him?

Ruella stiffened. "I did not know you were a bloody Irishman when I dragged you in."

"And under the circumstances, I guess I need to overlook the fact that you are a loathsome, treacherous Englishwoman."

Georgina laughed. Or was that a smothered groan?

Ruella raked Liam with an outraged stare from her slightly protruding eyes, lingering a little too long on his bare chest. "Well, I suppose no one is perfect. I just hope, bog-jumper that you are, you intend to do right by the mistress of this place."

"I can scarcely do otherwise."

Clara elbowed Ruella aside. "Mr.—er—McMahon, we have much to discuss. And Georgina has brought you some suitable clothing, so if you've finished your breakfast—" She eyed his plate.

"Not quite yet." He sat back down and resumed plying his fork in a leisurely fashion. "The other members of your household, here, were just filling me in on how matters stand."

Little Jimmie asked Clara plaintively, "But where did he come from? And will he beat us?" A former servant in a household on Bryant Street, Jamie had been all too well acquainted with his master's fist.

Liam answered before Clara had a chance. "Never. In fact, I hunt down those who abuse women and children, and give them as they deserve."

"Truly?" Pippin, along with the other children, brightened. For Liam, seated there at their head, looked perfectly capable of carrying out the assertion.

Ruella sat down at the table and rested her chin on her fist, staring at him. "An Irish avenger, is that it?"

He shrugged. "I detest bullies, and all those who take advantage of folk weaker than themselves." He waved his fork at Woodrow and Fred. "Remember that, lads—no one who will not stand up for another has a right to call himself a man."

Oh, sweet heaven, what had she done? Clara wondered. But even now, gazing around the room at all these dear ones dependent on her, she did not know how she might have acted differently. They had come, most of them, from the streets. She could not see them cast out there again.

She made a shooing motion with her hands. "Go, children. Off about your chores now. Fred and Woodrow, Mr. Baker will be wondering where you are. Udina, please help Lillie get dressed." Lillie, their smallest, who had been run down by a cart horse, also had a mangled arm. "Mr. McMahon and I have things to discuss."

They obeyed reluctantly, most giving Clara a hug in passing. Fred's arms clasped her spasmodically.

"This is for the best," she spoke into his ear. "I'm acting for the good of all."

He nodded. She knew how he loved her. They all did.

When they had gone, the dining room felt strangely empty. Liam laid down his fork and eyed the three remaining women.

"This looks like a delegation. What have I done?"

"For starters, you're bloody Irish," Ruella accused again, but did not stop gazing at him very like a lovesick goat.

"And," Clara put in hastily, "the name upon which we agreed was Fitzgerald."

"No." He looked her full in the eyes. "That is not the name on which we agreed; it is the name you attempted to force on me. I will not accept it. The Fitzgeralds were more English than Irish, and flaming interlopers in Ireland."

"And," Clara challenged, "how is it you remember that?" He shouldn't be able to recall any such thing.

His expression went suddenly blank, like that of a stricken man. "Damn me, lass, but I have no idea."

Chapter Eight

"So, how do I look?" Liam McMahon asked.

Clara struggled to school her expression and not reveal her true feelings as he turned in front of her, displaying his new clothing. He looked—well, sinfully attractive.

"Not bad, eh," he continued smugly, "for a dead man?"

"Not dead; recently dead," Clara corrected hastily. They were alone in what had been her father's surgery—the one place the children were sure not to intrude. Clara felt unaccountably nervous, a state she despised in herself. She had planned all this, rehearsed the details *ad nauseam*. But she hadn't bargained on Liam McMahon.

Instead, she'd imagined some fellow dragged from the depths of hell, recovering from his resurrection in a darkened room, knowing only what she told him—malleable and dependent on her. Not one who insisted on finishing a breakfast fit for a king, and who clearly had enough confidence to take over her household.

"Please sit down. We need to talk." She indicated the visitor's chair and seated herself behind her father's desk in what she considered the power position. She always felt closer to Father here: the very scents of the room comforted her.

Liam nudged the chair out with his knee and sat in

a lordly fashion. His eyes gleamed at Clara. "You look prepared to call me to task. What is it?"

She folded her hands on the surface of the desk. "I would have appreciated a chance to introduce you to the children myself, and prepare them properly."

He shrugged. "As soon as I sat down to me breakfast they came flooding in, the whole flock."

"You needn't have identified yourself as my future husband."

"Why not? 'Tis the truth, as I understand it. And the way you've explained things, their livelihood depends on us foxing this grandfather of yours."

"Yes, but…" Panic fluttered in Clara's chest. *She* should be in charge. That was how she'd planned and imagined it. "Mr. McMahon, much plotting and consideration went into your resurrection. I wish you to let me decide how it should play out."

His eyebrows lifted. He sat back in his chair and regarded her with a new expression. "Well then, and that may be a bit of a problem. I'm a man used to making his own decisions."

Clara leaned across the desk. "That's just it—you should not be aware of any past personality traits, whatsoever. You shouldn't remember enough of your life to know what sort of man you were. I don't understand what went wrong."

"Ah, so you wanted a puppet, is that it? So many stone of flesh you could raise up, put in his place, and tell what to do? When to fart and when to breathe? Is that how it was with the others you've raised?"

Clara bit her lip. "To tell you the truth, I've never before resurrected a man."

"Is that so?"

"It is."

"Well then, I'm a first." She saw the quick thoughts move behind his eyes. "So how do you know how it's supposed to be?"

"I have used my skills before."

"How many times?"

"It doesn't matter how many—"

"I think it does."

"—because it was on animals."

"Animals!" The dark brows ascended nearly through his hair.

"In theory, there should be no difference. When I resurrected my own dog, she no longer knew me. And every other creature with which I have worked retained no familiarity with past training."

"Aye, well, I retain little enough. I don't remember much before the noose went round me neck." Again he lifted his fingers to his throat and his gaze became distant. "No name, no real memories—just the things I know in the bone."

"You should know *nothing*."

"Are you saying I should not have a sense of meself?"

"I am."

"But what man could live so? Don't we, as babes new born, have a sense of ourselves?"

"Yes, but one that is not oriented." That was how it had been with Mollie. Clara had even needed to housetrain her all over again.

"Well, I'll be damned if I feel oriented," he retorted with a touch of anger. "And do not tell me how to feel, unless you're inside my head."

They stared at one another for several moments in

irritation.

Then Clara drew a breath. "The thing I am trying to say, Mr. McMahon—"

His lips quirked. "There's one thing: you don't like the fact that I chose my own name."

"I do not," Clara agreed with some heat. "I believe the name Fitzgerald carries some gravitas and will succeed better in persuading my grandfather to accept our story."

"Sounds like less of a bog-jumper, is that it?"

It was, but Clara did not wish to admit it. She abhorred prejudice and welcomed anyone in need, of all backgrounds and colors, into her household. "You have not met my grandfather. He is not easy to impress."

Liam reared back. "Need you impress him? Or just present him with a husband, job done?"

"In essence, the latter. But the whole of it will go better the less fault he can find."

"Well, so, Miss Clara, did you truly expect to drag a man home from the jail and end up with someone to impress this paragon?" Not giving her a chance to reply, he went on, "And as for that, I will need the name of the jailer."

"Why?"

"I've a score to settle with him, don't I? Corrupt sod—taking money to feed his prisoners and then doing away with them." A spark ignited in his eyes. "He will know my name, will he not? My true name."

"I do not think that is a good—"

"And, begging pardon, Miss Clara, I don't care what you think."

Now they glared at one another with some heat.

"Look here, Mr. McMahon. We have an

agreement."

"We have not! Did I ask you to bring me back to life?"

"Would you rather be dead?" Again she drew a breath. "We do, in fact, have an implied agreement, since my sole purpose in returning you to life was so you could be of service to this household."

That seemed to arrest him; he inspected her slowly, in a manner that brought the heat to her cheeks. "Service, eh? Just what will this marriage involve?"

"Not *that*," Clara said hastily. "This is purely a marriage of convenience. You play this role on my behalf; I will provide for you to the best of my ability."

Did he look disappointed? Hard to tell, with that wicked light filling his eyes.

"Provide for me, how?"

"A roof over your head, food in your belly. And, need I reemphasize, the enjoyment of your life?"

"So I owe you, is that what you're after saying?"

"I hoped to keep from putting it that way, but in essence, yes."

He let those words hang in the air while he continued to examine her. Clara did her best not to squirm in her seat.

"How do you know," he asked then, "that I am not already married?"

Clara lowered her gaze abruptly. She'd hoped he would not ask that question. "I do not," she replied honestly.

"Bigamy—is that not what they call it?"

"I will confess I have contemplated it at length and concluded the true ethical dilemma rests upon the fact that this will be a marriage only in name, to be terminated after a certain span of time. Even if you are married, you will not in fact be committing adultery."

"What 'certain span of time' would that be?"

She lifted her gaze again and measured him with her stare. "Once my grandfather dies, we can dissolve the marriage and go our separate ways."

"What makes you think he's going to die soon?"

"He is ninety-nine years old and quite frail—he cannot possibly live forever."

"An unpleasant bugger, you say?"

"Extremely unpleasant, with very few redeeming qualities."

"Are those not the sort who tend to live the longest?"

Clara widened her eyes and leaned toward him. "That is one of the things of which you should not be aware. You should have virtually no knowledge of past or present, or any surmises in your mind."

"I have little enough, believe me. I'm not a patch on a clever lass like you."

Clara didn't feel very certain of that. She had the feeling he played her even now. She spread her hands. "If you wish to walk away from this, I cannot prevent you. But we are in a terrible fix here, and it is the children who will ultimately pay the price. They are completely dependent on me, aside from Woodrow and Fred, who do contribute in some small measure to the solvency of the household."

"Not that you would wish to make me feel guilty, or any such thing."

"Of course not."

"So then, Miss Clara, what sort of story have you cooked up to feed your grandfather? Will he not think it odd you should turn up with a husband right before your birthday?"

"You are the son of one of my father's former colleagues with whom he went to medical school. We have been corresponding via letter, and you have agreed to marry me."

"What city?"

"Well, I gave that some thought. I could not make it somewhere too easy for my grandfather to trace your background, should he try. I thought Montreal."

"An Irishman from Montreal?"

"I did not expect you to be an Irishman. Many people of all nationalities are funneled through Montreal via the St. Lawrence."

"And what does this fantastical betrothed of yours do for a living?"

"Well, I had thought you should be at loose ends, which would make you likely to relocate. I thought perhaps a failed business such as a gentlemen's haberdashery."

"A what?"

"Hats of high quality."

"Can you see me selling hats?"

"No," Clara admitted. "But when I envisioned all this I did not, in fact, see you at all."

"A livery stable," he said decisively.

"I beg your pardon?"

He rubbed his hands together. "Tell him I ran a livery stable that was forced out of business by these damned steamcarriages. That will explain why I am a bit rough around the edges, will it not?"

Clara drew a breath. "Does that mean you agree, you'll go through with the plan and marry me?"

He gave her a crooked smile that sped her pulse unaccountably. "Damn me," he said, "but I guess it does."

Chapter Nine

The house had at last fallen quiet, and Liam—he supposed he should now think of himself as *Liam*, since he owned no other name—lay on his back in the bed, straining to catch any stray sound. Sleep eluded him; his thoughts ran rampant, like an enraged rat in a trap, over the same matters again and again. Throughout this endless day, while he'd been agreeing to marry a stranger and trying to sort out the details of the household, two things had battled for predominance in his mind.

He had been dead.

And the little lass with the uncanny eyes had brought him back to life.

How could anything else that happened really compare with either of these truths? How had she done it? She spoke so casually of an ability, but surely this smacked of sorcery. He had been dead. For how long? An hour? Longer? Could a man hope to rationalize that?

His heart now beat strongly in his chest; he could feel it as he lay here in the dark. Air billowed in and out of his lungs. He could hear, see, taste…

He could desire a woman. No question he desired Clara Allen. Every time he so much as looked at her it hit him like a physical blow.

Helplessly, he probed and prodded the wall in his

mind, striving to remember something before the noose. He must have performed a job, in order to keep himself. There would be a reason he'd been hauled off to jail, where some unknown bastard of a jailkeeper had decided to murder him.

Anger flared inside at that thought. He would identify, locate, and settle that bastard. He always did—how did he know that? He would give the fellow a good look at what should be a dead man before doing the world a favor and finishing him.

How did he know the things he knew about himself, then? That he was a man who chose revenge, that he was a laborer who worked with his hands. That he loved horses. That he was a brawler who'd likely been arrested for just that reason.

These pieces of *self* clung to him even though all else had evaporated in his return to life. For he supposed he must believe Clara had returned him to life. She did not seem capable of speaking a lie. And anyway, he remembered that part of it sure enough—her mouth on his, her essence flowing into and filling him.

Suddenly restless, he got out of the bed, went to the door, and cracked it open. Breath caught, he stood listening. Nothing. He pictured Clara in her bed and wanted to be there with her so badly he ached. Which room was hers? At breakfast, the children had confided most of them slept on the third floor, but Clara and Georgina must have rooms on this corridor. What would Clara do if he appeared and demanded his husbandly rights?

But they weren't yet wed, and besides, she said it wasn't to be that kind of marriage.

He cursed long and low, under his breath. He needed out of here.

He tiptoed to the main staircase and looked down. The parlor door stood open and light spilled out. Clara must still be awake, then. He'd never make it past that doorway.

With another muttered curse he turned back for his room. The window would have to do.

****

"Put another in the glass, there's a good man."

The bartender eyed Liam questioningly but not as if he recognized him. No one here seemed to recognize him. The bartender was merely trying to gauge his level of intoxication. The tavern, which sat right on Buffalo's waterfront, hopped with activity, voices raised in laughter and argument, accents of every description. This area teemed with taverns and brothels both.

Liam carefully placed another coin on the bar. He'd lifted the purse from a fellow outside—part of a crowd, all of them inebriated—and thus discovered another of his latent talents. He'd already lost count of how much he'd had to drink.

The bartender nodded and filled the glass with whiskey. The purse Liam had lifted still felt plump, and he considered leaving here and visiting one of the brothels, if just to get some relief.

Might not work, though. He wanted Clara Allen, and no one else.

"Listen to me," he said to the bartender. "I have a question." The man gave him a dubious look. Liam tossed back his drink in one gulp. Maybe if he drank enough this dark wall in his mind would open and he'd remember.

"Who's the prick that runs the jail in this city?"

The bartender looked surprised. "The county jail, you mean, on Delaware?"

"I expect I do." Liam realized he wasn't even sure where he'd died.

"Why do you want to know?"

"I've a score to settle with him."

"You've a score to settle with someone but you don't know his name?"

"Aye. Strange world, is it not?" Liam wagged his head. "Strange life."

"Listen, Mick—"

"Don't call me *Mick*. That's an insult, that is." Liam's mood instantly turned ugly.

"Look, buddy, I can tell by your voice you're a Mick, and a drunk Mick, at that."

"I am a respectable member of the Irish race, and I'll take apart with me bare hands anybody who says differently. Now fill the glass again."

"You've had enough."

"Not your job to say." Liam felt himself growing enraged. "Fill the bleedin' glass."

"Look, sir, you keep this up and you'll be hauled off to the clink, and you'll meet the warden personally."

"Warden, is it?" Liam went suddenly still. "Don't that sound all high and official, the bastard."

"I'm going to ask you to leave. There are plenty other places to drink. I don't want you in mine."

Liam reeled outside. As soon as the cool air hit him, his head began to spin in slow, sickening circles. A stiff breeze blew from his right, and he could smell the river. The street seemed crowded with other fellows—laborers, like as not, bent on spending their wages as quickly as possible.

For an instant he felt so lost it nearly brought him to his knees. Who was he? What had become of all the things a man ordinarily held in his mind—the sound of his father's voice, the memory of his mother's face, the touch of his first lover's hand?

An image of Clara swam before his mind's eye. Annoying, irresistible, fey lass. Not the sort that had ever attracted him, but he was hooked now, like a salmon on a gaff. He should go home to her.

Nay—he should go to the next tavern and get an answer to his question.

****

Something brought Clara awake—she never later knew what. She'd been drowsing beside the parlor fire, which had gone out, her chin upon her chest, after trying to think through the maze of difficulties that surrounded her, and roused abruptly as if someone called her name.

Was it one of the children? Sometimes they had nightmares; then she or Georgina would go to them, hold them if necessary, and let them weep. But no, now she heard only silence, remarkable enough in this household.

Liam. His name and the idea of him blossomed in her mind. No question but most of the problems that plagued her revolved around him. She fought the desire to be with him and then convinced herself she should just look in on him and make sure he was all right.

Following the irresistible urge, she tiptoed up the stairs and eased his door open. For an instant her eyes refused to believe what they saw: a rumpled, empty bed.

Hastily, she glanced about her father's room. The window stood wide open, curtains fluttering in the chilly breeze. Her heart dropped to her feet. He was gone. Wandering out in the city, in the night, not knowing who he was. The fool. Breath caught, she hurried to Georgina's room, where she awakened her friend. "He's gone."

****

"This is madness, the two of us down on the waterfront in the dark," Georgina lamented, not for the first time. "We'll be robbed, or worse."

"I brought my father's pistol," Clara said, feeling for it in her pocket.

"If it will still fire, and if you dare use it." Georgina tugged the hood of her coat more closely around her face. Already one inebriated gentleman, taking her for a doxy, had propositioned her. She added unhappily, "What makes you think he's here?"

"Where else would he be?" Clara returned. She just knew, as if a string connected her and Liam, and he—or his activities—now tugged on it. "He's here somewhere."

"In this maze of boozers. Does this city ever sleep?"

"Not this part of it."

Men—and a small number of women of doubtable virtue—wandered everywhere, talking, laughing, arguing, staggering. It truly made a quite distressing scene, one into which Clara had never before ventured even for the benefit of her children.

Georgina edged closer to her. "Which—?"

Bedlam abruptly broke out two doors down, where bright light spilled into the street. Cries arose, and

68

people fled the doorway before two men tumbled out, engaged in an intense bout of fisticuffs.

"Oh, my sweet lord!" Georgina exclaimed. "That's—"

Indeed, it was. Clara recognized his hair even before she glimpsed his face, fixed in a snarl, and the white bandage affixed to his throat.

What to do? The brawl had spilled onto the doorstep. Folk gathered round, some exhorting the combatants and some, by the look of it, making wagers. Liam grappled with another brawny fellow, whose red hair made a splash of color. The sound of fists striking flesh assaulted Clara's ears.

Another man emerged from the tavern. He was large, wore an apron, and had his shirtsleeves rolled up over brawny forearms. He carried what Clara recognized as a portable steam cannon sidearm, all heated up, by the look of it, and ready to fire.

One of those could blow a man's head off—or leave him looking worse than poor Woodrow. How many steam burns had her father treated?

"All right, you two," the bartender cried. "I've called for the cops. Stop now, or you'll wind up in the hoosegow."

Clara's stomach wobbled. The last place Liam should be. If the warden saw him there again, she'd be undone.

"Wait!" she cried.

Somehow amid all the fuss, Liam heard her. He stopped whaling on his opponent and looked up. His gaze found her with an almost audible click.

Clara drew a breath and, fingers clutching the pistol in her pocket, waded in.

Chapter Ten

Liam's opponent looked dead. Blood trickled from one corner of his mouth, and he lay unmoving as a sack of spuds.

Liam hurt all over but especially his hands, which felt as if he'd been busy pounding them against a brick wall. He shook his head, trying to clear the confusion.

Clara stood over him, arguing with the barkeep in clear, even tones. Her voice penetrated Liam's ears and seemed to seep into his soul.

"I assure you, sir, this man is my husband. He has been unwell. The last thing I wish to do is involve the police."

Liam slid his gaze up her body to her face. She stared at the bartender in appeal, an earnest lady beseeching reason. He fixed his stare on her eyes, which glowed uncannily green. She had looked at him once—a burning glare—and then dismissed him completely.

By God, what had he done? Details came back to him through a whiskey-induced haze. Gone looking for information, found an argument instead. One thing had led to another.

The coppers were on their way.

That was a terrible bad thing, though he could not quite remember why. If he got hauled off to jail—

Jail. A noose. This blank wall in his mind.

Clara.

He reached out slowly and grasped her wrist. The backs of his fingers were smeared with blood. She flicked her gaze to him and away again.

"If it's a matter of damages," she told the bartender, "I will be happy to pay."

She couldn't afford to pay—at least not given that vile grandfather of hers. He, Liam, should go and smother the grandfather in his bed. Ninety-nine was an indecent age.

Anything to make her happy.

It occurred to him she wasn't happy now because of him.

That thought sobered him as much as anything could at this moment. He struggled to his feet.

"Listen to me."

"Hush, please, Liam."

"I can explain."

"I think you've said enough, don't you?" This time her glare scorched him to his soul.

"Put your purse away. I'll pay." He dragged the stolen wallet from his pocket and fixed the bartender with a stare. "How much?"

"You smashed the bar, at least a dozen bottles of whiskey."

"Just say how bloody much."

"Forty dollars."

Highway robbery. Forty dollars would buy the whole shack that housed the pub. But the coppers were on their way.

He sneered and dug the remaining money from the wallet. It swam sickeningly before his eyes. "There's twenty-nine here—more than what you have coming."

The bartender gave him an appraising look and shot another at Clara, who raised her pointed, little chin.

"All right. But I don't ever want to see you in here again, understand?"

"You need not worry about that." Clara seized Liam's arm. "I will take my husband home and see to it he has his medication."

The bartender snorted. Liam and Clara stepped over Liam's fallen opponent—the man still breathed, so he wasn't dead after all—and turned to the street where, to his surprise, Liam saw Georgina waiting.

He said to Clara, "You never should have come down here on your own, two pretty ladies."

"Clearly." Beneath his arm, she trembled with rage. "What was I to do? Let you be taken back to jail, where—" Words failed her.

"No, not that. I quite see—" His head swam. Ordinarily he suspected he had no trouble holding his liquor, but now he thought he might vomit. Sternly, he said, "But don't ever come here again."

She stopped walking, reared back, and glared at him. "Me? You went out the window. You beat a man senseless."

"He insulted me. I think."

"You are stinking, filthy drunk." She pronounced the words as he imagined his mother might, but he didn't remember his mother.

"You have no idea what 'tis like," he retorted, "being brought back to life with nothing in me head."

"Hush! For God's sake, can you not watch your tongue?"

He wanted to put his tongue in her mouth; he still did, despite how sick he felt. Happen she wouldn't like that.

"Sorry," he murmured. "And sorry for—" He was abruptly and messily sick all over the street.

Clara let go of him and leaped aside. Georgina exclaimed in dismay.

"Let's get him home," Clara cried in disgust. "I swear to God I should have left him in the jail."

****

His head hurt. Well, that was to be expected, considering what he remembered of last night. He pried his eyes open and then narrowed them against the morning light coming through windows set high in a stone wall. Where the hell was he? Lying on a cot, a basin half full of puke beside him. He stank like a longshoreman after a three-day bender.

He sat up and cradled his head tenderly between his hands.

A cellar. She'd shut him in the bleedin' cellar. No question about it. The rafters of the house stretched overhead, shelves of canned food lay to his right, boxes and pieces of boilers lay everywhere else. The lads must work down here, Fred and—what was his name?—Woodrow.

He tried to remember what had happened last night. He'd gone searching out the identity of the man who had murdered him. Fallen into a quarrel or two. And then—

The door at the top of the cellar stairs opened. Clara stood there, framed by light.

"So you're awake. You'd better come up."

"You shut me down here," he accused. "Locked me in."

"Can you blame me? Please come. We have things

to discuss."

He clattered up the wooden stairs, his head threatening to burst with every step. He could hear the weans in the dining room, but Clara led him to her father's surgery and, once they were inside, locked the door.

She looked unwell, her face too pale, her eyes surrounded by dark hollows. Remorse hit him. He was responsible for that. But hell, he was a grown man and not answerable to a slip of a lass.

"You had better sit before you fall down," she advised. Her gaze swept him from head to toe. "Look what you've done to your clothing."

What had he done? Aye, his new duds were torn, and stained with blood. "Ah, Clara, I am that sorry. I know these cost you dear."

"Never mind that now." She stood before the chair on which he sat, arms crossed in front of her little breasts, and tapped her foot. "What were you thinking? Do you realize what would have happened if you'd been arrested? The danger to you—to me?"

He drew a breath to reply. She did not give him a chance. "And where did you get that purse? The money you gave the bartender?"

It was mad, but he wanted to kiss her. Badly. Even though she stood dressing him down like he was a lad—or maybe because she did. She wouldn't welcome it, given the condition he was in.

"Stolen," he admitted.

"Stolen!" She paled further, though he wouldn't have thought it possible. "From whom?"

Liam shrugged. "Some fellow outside the first tavern. He was in his cups and never noticed. Well-heeled, though."

She held out a hand, which trembled, in demand. "Give it to me."

"Why? Empty now."

"Because I need to see if there is any identification. If there is, I will have to pay back every penny."

"Why?" Liam asked again.

"Because it is the decent, responsible thing to do. Because I"—she waved her arm wildly—"unleashed you on the world."

Anger began to gather in Liam's chest. "Look here. You can't talk that way to me."

"The wallet, please."

He dug it out from his pocket and attempted to wipe the dried blood from its surface. She snatched it from him. He watched as she searched its empty reaches in vain.

"Nothing."

"Just as well. You'd have to seek the fellow out. 'Twould be one hell of an explanation."

She closed her eyes like a woman in pain, drew a breath, and said, "I don't think this is going to work out."

"Eh?"

"This arrangement between you and me." She opened her eyes and speared him with that uncanny, gray-green gaze. "It's not feasible. I must have been mad to think it was."

"What?" Liam's anger disappeared into a well of loss so deep it terrified him. "You mean—"

"I'm terminating our arrangement. You're free to go, no obligation to me."

He bounded to his feet. "Just because I went off the

rails one evening, drank a bit too much, got angry over an insult?"

"You climbed out the window. I didn't know where you were. Georgina and I had to go looking for you in a most unsavory part of the city. You almost threw your life away…again."

"Ah, now, it worked out well enough, didn't it? And you can't blame me. I have this great hole in my mind—"

"I don't blame you."

"That I thought might get filled just a little bit by revenge. I only went looking for the name of the man responsible for my murder. You cannot expect me to live with him in the free and clear."

"I don't know what I expected. Not this. It won't do. As I say, I don't blame you; I blame myself. I should have known better."

"But where will I go?" He gaped at her. "I have no place, no life."

"There are other cities. Choose one, and I will try to scrape up the fare to send you. You will be able to get work as a laborer."

"Damned if I will."

"You're strong and fit. In a new city, no one will know you or that you were once—dead."

"I'll know! What am I supposed to do with this great, bloody hole where my past is supposed to be?" And what would he do without her? He did not understand how, but she sustained him. If he lost her, on top of everything else, he might as well cut his own throat.

She shook her head helplessly. "I am sorry. This was an ill-advised scheme on my part. I did not think sufficiently about what it would be like for you. I just thought you'd be grateful to be alive."

"I am, I swear it. Clara, do not send me away." He reached out and captured her hands. As from a distance he saw his fingers clasp her paler ones, his skin marked by abrasions and blood. Maybe she was right; she deserved more than a brawler and boozer. But he could not leave her now.

"Please." The word, torn from his still-damaged throat, sounded harsh. "What will you do if you send me away? How keep the house and the children? You'll never find anyone else before your birthday."

"I'd never be able to trust you."

"But, lass, you can. One small slip that was, a single error."

"It was far more than that."

"I swear 'twill not happen again. I shall be a model husband." He gazed into her eyes. "Must I get down on my knees and beg?"

She bit her lip. "It is a terribly drastic step we contemplate. Marriage, even if only in name—"

"Only allow me a chance to prove myself to you." There on the floor of the surgery he dropped to one knee. "Clara Allen, marry me."

Chapter Eleven

"Before the eyes of God and in accordance with the laws of this state, I pronounce you man and wife." The justice of the peace, who also happened to be an Episcopal minister, hesitated but an instant before adding, "You may kiss the bride."

Clara Allen—no, Clara McMahon now—stared into her new husband's eyes and shook her head slightly, willing him to disregard the instruction. He ignored her. She saw his face, barely healed from the fisticuffs three days ago, swoop in on her, and suddenly his mouth claimed hers. No ordinary, polite kiss this: it searched like a drowning man searched for air, it punished and rewarded, and parted her lips beneath his. She felt the brush of his tongue like fire.

The minister, Mr. Baxter, cleared his throat.

Clara planted both hands on her husband's chest and shoved. He released her.

Her husband. Well, it had needed to be done for the sake of the children. And apart from that flaming kiss, there was nothing in it—a joining in name only, a purely legal matter.

Not to say her husband didn't look sinfully handsome with his hair trimmed—not too short—and in his fine, new suit from the tailor's on Franklin Street. She sighed. She'd needed to pawn her father's best clock to afford that suit, but she had to say it was worth every penny. Amazing what black broadcloth and a starched white collar could do to set a man up. He still looked like a rogue, with that gleam in his eyes—for the kiss he'd just stolen, no doubt—and one lock of black hair tumbling over his forehead. But he looked a gentlemanly rogue.

Behind Clara, Ruella sighed. She'd insisted on being in attendance for this, one of only a handful of guests and witnesses. Georgina was here, of course, and Clara's law advisor, Theodore Collwys.

It had been put forward more than once in the past that Clara and Theodore should wed, but Theodore was betrothed to a society miss, and anyway Clara had not the heart, even for convenience's sake. She had seen the way Theodore looked at Georgina, and she at him.

So now she turned to face her guests, still hand in hand with her husband.

"A toast," Theodore suggested, "to the happy couple."

Clara squeezed Liam's fingers. *Not too much*, her touch bade. He clasped her hand gently in return, a reassurance.

Since she'd dragged him back from the waterfront and locked him in the cellar he'd been a model gentleman, even going so far as to undertake some much-needed repairs around the house. Of course it had only been three days.

"Perhaps just a wee sip," he said.

"You must sign these documents first," Mr. Baxter told them. "Your marriage certificate. Your signatures here at the bottom, please."

Clara froze. Could Liam read and write? If he'd ever learned, could he remember now? Why hadn't she thought of this?

But he turned to the parlor table that had served as their altar and took up the pen readily while she hovered at his shoulder.

Please do not write "Liam," she beseeched him inwardly.

He signed where Mr. Baxter indicated with a bold flourish. William T. McMahon. He handed the pen to her with a slight bow.

Clara A. McMahon, she scrawled beneath his signature.

"There now," he crooned, "it's official. Does that allow us another kiss?"

Those gathered in the room laughed almost as if this were a real wedding. Well, it was real in a legal sense, real enough to meet her grandfather's requirements.

Georgina passed around a tray of sherry glasses and glared at Liam in passing. Theodore raised his glass. "To Mr. and Mrs. McMahon—may their future be filled with blessings."

"Hear, hear!" Ruella chimed in. "And now just let me kiss the groom."

****

"You do realize," Clara said sternly to her new husband some hours later, when the guests had gone and the chaos cleared, "this changes nothing. Between us, I mean."

No reply. He sat in one of the parlor wing chairs with his head back and that unholy light in his eyes, half veiled. She'd been proud of him this day, she had to admit it. He'd taken only the one glass of sherry and behaved as she'd hoped of him. But she feared the worst was yet to come.

"Our arrangement," she added delicately, "is a convenience, no more."

He lifted those sinfully long, black lashes and gave her a look. Something in her heart stirred—or it might be lower down. Still he did not speak.

"Tomorrow you will meet my grandfather." She drew a breath. "I will take you to his house and present you as my husband. I cannot stress strongly enough the importance of this."

The corners of his mouth twitched. "So this would not be a good night for me to go out and get drunk?"

She rounded on him and then caught herself. He teased, no more. "It would not."

"Then a good night's sleep might be in order, instead." He purred the words. When had his throat begun to heal? The very sound of his voice made her tremble where she stood.

"No doubt. We are to be there at ten in the morning. I will need you on your best behavior."

"Like a good, well-trained husband or hound?"

"I am sorry to seem patronizing. It is just—"

"Peace, Clara, I know what's at stake. But if this is to work, your grandfather will expect the genuine article. He needs to meet a man, not a puppet."

"You are right."

"Some verisimilitude may be required." Slowly he got to his feet and approached her, moving like a cat. The corners of his lips curled further up. "Surprised I know that word, are you? Just like you were surprised I could sign my name today—ignorant bog-jumper that I am."

She was, but didn't like to admit it.

She stood staring him in the eyes, her breath coming ever faster as he approached. When he reached out and fondled her hair, it came very quickly indeed.

"You looked so beautiful today," he whispered.

"But I am not beautiful."

"Not perhaps in the fashionable sense. Better than that."

Clara wore her best dress, left over from wealthier days. Now the lace at the bodice stirred with her heartbeat.

"Why did you cut off your hair? 'Tis such a bonny color. Seems a shame."

"It was too much trouble and kept getting in the way when I was busy working or helping the children. I did not like to bother." Her words died as his fingers penetrated her hair to her scalp, where they stroked gently.

"No matter, it suits you—all feathery and fey."

"Fey?"

He stepped closer. She could feel the heat of him now, like a banked fire. He whispered in her ear, "Like a wee fairy, one of the fey folk."

"I—"

She looked up and, just as simply as that, he kissed her. His lips, this time, were as gentle as his touch. They wooed and persuaded, then suggested and beseeched, powerful as a demand and heady as strong wine. Clara gathered all her forces, determined to be indignant, to reject and deny him. Instead, without her permission, her lips parted beneath his and invited him in.

Time seemed to stand still and then to tense and bunch like a lion waiting to spring. Outside the parlor windows, the autumn dark gathered. Inside Clara's heart, darkness seemed to flee, chased by desire.

What was this, then? Nothing she had expected. It was desire, wild and hot: it was an answer to longing.

It was impossible.

She tried to break the kiss after all, but his fingers had crept round to the back of her head, and he held her effortlessly. His tongue plundered her mouth, slow and leisurely, and left fire everywhere it touched, flame that raced through her veins and headed south.

All she could taste was Liam. All she could feel—he filled her, breathed for her, turned her knees to water and her brain to one scream of wanting.

No.

Even as she thought the word she stroked his tongue with hers, testing its strength and texture. She imagined it sliding over the length of her body, laying claim to every peak and valley, setting her aflame. She had never conceived of wanting anything so.

He broke the kiss unexpectedly and breathed a gust into her ear. His arms gathered her against him, where she felt very small, helpless, and yet empowered and strong. He was hard down below. He hid nothing but thrust himself against her, making his desire plain.

"No," she said again, aloud this time. "That was not part of the agreement."

"For God's sake, Clara. We're married. Why not?"

She repeated doggedly, "That was not part—"

She broke off when he kissed her once more, his hot mouth swallowing her words. His hands began to move, roved up her back, and left trails of heat behind. One slid around to cup her breast. His thumb stroked her through the fabric of her gown; she gasped, and his kiss swallowed that also.

Oh, and she had never dreamed of such desire. What if she gave in? What if she took him to her bed?

The damage could be irreparable. But his hands still moved. Somehow he had drawn the fabric of her bodice down and got inside, his flesh hot against her own. She felt a sudden spur of shame. She had a girl's body, not a woman's.

He didn't seem to mind. He bent his head, trailed his lips from her mouth downward over her cheek, along the side of her throat, across her collarbone. His black hair, incredibly soft, brushed her chin as he bent still lower and lifted her up so her breast met his mouth.

And then Clara died and went to heaven. Except she couldn't be dead because her heart pounded in her ears and her breath came short and fast. Incredible images flashed through her mind: herself with her legs spread, right here on the hearth rug. Liam without his trousers, all magnificent strength. The two of them coupling with abandon, all of it so real it seemed as if it had already happened.

She whimpered. He freed her second breast from her bodice and made a wet trail to it. Her entire breast fit inside his mouth. His tongue did unimaginably magical things…

"This was not—" Damn. All rational thought seemed to have fled her brain. His mouth left her breast, and he set her down gently. His eyes gleamed at her, so blue their color encompassed all she could see.

"Please," he said.

This, Clara thought, was seduction at its most potent—and by her legal husband, of all things. He licked one corner of her mouth and then the other.

Desire kicked her like a mule, deep in her belly.

"Do you not want to present a convincing picture when we face your grandfather tomorrow—with a successful bridal night behind us?"

Clara whispered, "It would be disastrous."

"It would be sublime, I so promise you."

She believed him.

"Please," he repeated. Then he was on his knees again, moving down her body. His hands slid up under her skirt, skittered up her legs, stroked the inside of her thigh, and stopped only when he touched her where no one ever had before. *Ever.*

She looked down, trembling badly, and met his eyes gleaming deep blue in a gaze so intimate it seared her to her soul.

Somehow her skirts had bunched up around her waist. She stood bare to him, devoid of even her bloomers. Here, in her own parlor.

Her heart threatened to pound out through her breast.

He touched her. His black head bent forward. She felt his lips briefly, and his tongue, swirling.

He looked at her once more. "Come upstairs and let me show you," he said.

Chapter Twelve

Clara woke in her father's bed, and alone.

Not at all certain which point horrified her more, she shot bolt upright, the bedclothes clutched to her breasts. Beneath the covers she was quite naked. The sheets beside her lay rumpled, and she could see the indent left by a head on the pillow—Liam's head—but he had gone.

Gone. Scuppered. Fled. Departed out the window again. Taken her virginity and left her.

Oh, God.

What had she done? The very worst of things: slept with her husband. She could remember all of it, every detail, every kiss, every silken slide of his tongue. That tongue had been places she'd never imagined any man's tongue venturing. All of him had.

And she still quivered from the effects of it.

Who would have thought that a woman—that she—could come apart at the seams like that, shatter in a man's hands? Who would have thought she—with a body more child than woman—could feel so worshipped by his mouth that when at last he knelt between her legs and entered her, she felt like a queen?

But now morning had come, and with it the damages. Her virginity gone. Her husband—gone.

The window stood closed. Likely he had not gone out that way. His wedding suit lay strewn across the floor, as did most of her clothing. He had carried her in, still bare-breasted, from the parlor. She could only hope none of the children had seen.

Her chemise hung from one of the posters of her father's bed. Liam had removed it from her body, slid it over her skin with careful hands. She had given way to a kind of abandon of which she'd never guessed herself capable. But none of that mattered now. He was gone.

She forced her fingers through her ruffled hair and cursed herself again. He had plied her with kisses, convinced her to yield to him, and now he was—

The door opened and Liam appeared, wearing nothing but his short trousers, and those unfastened.

They gazed at one another. He entered and shut the door with care. One corner of his mouth quirked. "The rest of the household is astir, but I do not think they will disturb us this morning."

"Where were you? I thought—"

"Sorry, I had to visit the bog. Didn't want to disturb you by digging the basin out from under the bed."

Clara said nothing. She watched him approach, marveling at the breadth of that chest, those shoulders, the supple length of his legs, the fascinating trail of black hair that led into what should be forbidden territory. She had touched it all last night. She'd had it all.

Moving like a cat, he launched himself onto the bed, which creaked in protest. Clara was reminded vividly of hearing that creak last night also. Her cheeks flamed. What if the whole household had heard?

She turned her head and gazed into Liam's eyes. "It wasn't supposed to be like this."

"Do you know how lovely you are?"

Clara felt the impact of those words in her heart. But she denied forcibly, "I. Am. Not. Lovely."

"You can sit there looking like that, and say so?"

"No need to lie to me, or flatter me, either. At best, I am plain. At worst I am scrawny." She forced herself to add, "Barely a woman."

"Ah, if you can say that, you cannot see yourself perched there against those pillows with the morning light in your green eyes and that sheet clutched to your bonny breasts."

"Blarney."

His eyes widened. "Eh?"

"I've no doubt you can spin as pretty a string of lies as any Irishman ever born. You had your way with me last night. No need to keep playing me along."

"Is that what you think?"

Clara lifted her chin. "It's what I know."

He reached out and touched her hair, then cupped her cheek as tenderly as if he thought she might break. "Let me prove it to you."

"No."

He leaned forward and kissed her. At the simple touch of his lips on hers, fire leaped up through her veins. He laid her down on her pillow, his mouth still on hers, and pushed the covers down from her breasts.

When he ended the kiss, his eyes gleamed. "Let me look at you."

"Please don't."

"How can you say that is not beautiful?" He cupped one of her breasts gently, then bent his head and sampled it. Clara nearly came off the bed with pleasure.

"Oh, hell," she said.

"Oh, hell?" His head came up. Blue eyes dancing with wicked laughter met hers. "Why do you say that?"

"Because here it is broad daylight, and we're going to do it all over again."

****

"Now remember," Clara whispered to her husband, "don't say anything about having been in jail. Or having been dead."

"What do you take me for?" Liam shifted uncomfortably inside his suit and adjusted his tie one more time. They stood on the doorstep of a splendid house—a mansion, really—on Delaware at Edward Street, waiting for the door to open. And all he could think about was tearing the dress off his wife's body and having his way with her yet again. As if twice this morning had not been enough. Quite possibly, he could not get enough.

The taste of her still lingered on his lips, the sweetest thing ever to grace them. He remembered the places he had put his tongue and felt half mad to put it there once more. By God, she—

The door swung open, and he found himself faced with a mechanical man. He'd heard of them, of course, but could not remember—for he could remember so little—if he had ever seen one up close.

"I should have warned you," Clara murmured. "My grandfather keeps a number of mechanical servants—the ordinary sort will not stay with him long."

"Good afternoon, Miss Clara. Please come in."

The butler's voice box clicked when it spoke. Its body, made of silver alloy, stood as tall as Liam but was much thinner, and its surface had been sculpted to resemble a suit of clothes. It turned to lead them, with a distinctive puff of steam. Clara knew it had an internal combustion chamber where a human's guts might be.

"Thank you, Max," she said and tightened her grip on Liam's arm. They stepped in.

And oh, the house was like a picture drawn to intimidate, everything perfect and in place, not like walking into a real dwelling at all. A large entry hall opened from the door, with a black-and-white marble floor and flowers on tables so highly polished they gleamed. A double staircase curved in two branching arcs just ahead, but the steam butler led them to a door on the right.

"Miss Clara, your grandfather had us bring him down to receive you in the parlor."

"How is he, Max?"

Liam admired the calm in Clara's voice, but he could feel her tension flowing into him through the contact point of her arm on his.

"Much the same, Miss Clara." The butler hauled the door of the chamber open; they went in.

A vast room, well-proportioned, languished in gloom. Even though the sun shone brightly outside, the draperies on all the windows had been drawn. Liam found it difficult to locate his host at first. But a lamp burned on a table, and beside it sat a wizened figure in a push chair. Clara's fingers dug into his arm again.

Aye, and he would be careful. He understood what was at stake—his right to her bed, for one thing.

"Clara." The voice sounded like air being forced through a broken bellows. It beckoned them closer, and Liam felt Clara's reluctance rise. Curious, he inspected the figure in the chair.

White hair, a face like a hatchet, and a pair of eyes

so sharp they might carve Liam to pieces. Thin, pale hands clutched the arms of the push chair like weapons. But Liam suspected this one's weapon would lie in his tongue.

"Grandfather," Clara said, stopping as far away as seemed polite.

"About time you came to see me. A dutiful granddaughter would be here every day inquiring after my health and seeing to my comfort."

"You know I am not a dutiful granddaughter." Clara lifted her chin, and Liam felt the steel in her. A flash of emotion for her erupted in his chest. Was it pride? Or something warmer?

The old man's gaze turned to him. "Well, girl, make your introductions."

"Grandfather, this is William, my new husband. William, this is my grandfather, Randolph Van Hamelin."

Ah, and there was a moniker meant to impress. Liam put his heels together and bent his back in a bow worthy of a minor lord. "Sir."

"So—you wed at last," Van Hamelin said, "and so conspicuously previous to your birthday. Well, sit down, girl, sit down. And turn up the lamp. Let me have a look at him."

They sat on a small settee opposite the push chair. Clara leaned forward and turned the screw on the lamp. The light filled her eyes and turned them a deeper shade of green.

The old man's eyes were hard and blue, like specks of ice set in the wrinkled desert of his face. Liam saw cruelty there, and no affection. All his protective instincts arose. This old stick would cause Clara grief over his dead body.

Ironic, that.

Van Hamelin inspected Liam slowly, beginning at his feet and working upward. He sneered. "Looks like you found him in the gutter, girl. He reeks of 'common.' "

The sheer rudeness of the comment knocked Liam back in his seat, and him a bog-jumper.

Clara drew a breath. "We were common once," she said coolly. "You were a poor Dutch boy when you came here, so you never tire of telling us. Off the boat in New York and fleeing a cruel master, without two cents to your name."

"That was a long time ago, and we are not common now."

"Neither is William. He is the son of one of Father's colleagues." Clara's voice remained devoid of emotion, but Liam could feel the trepidation streaming off her. "You must remember him speaking of—"

"I recall none of the drivel your father spouted," Van Hamelin interrupted. "My daughter chose badly. It seems you have gone the same road."

Clara had instructed Liam repeatedly on his course of behavior here; speak only when spoken to and as little as possible even then. But now he leaned forward. "You've not shared two words with me, Mr. Van Hamelin, yet you decide to condemn me out of hand?"

The old man reared back in the wicker chair. His nostrils pinched as if he smelled something distasteful. "Irish!" he pronounced. "And straight off the boat, by the sound of you."

Liam lifted his head. "Dutch!" he returned. "And tight as a turned screw."

Clara gasped. The old man looked so offended, it was almost comical. He switched his gaze to Clara.

"Granddaughter, how could you bring a gutter Irishman to my door?"

Clara's voice now trembled. "Grandfather, William McMahon is a businessman like yourself."

"I've not heard of him." Van Hamelin's gaze switched back to Liam. "And I know of every businessman in this city. In what endeavor are you engaged?"

"I owned a livery in Montreal before I came here—sir." The last word sounded like an epithet even to Liam's ears.

"Owned?"

"The business has been dissolved."

"Failed? That is what you mean." The old man crowed. "Couldn't even run a horse barn! Ah, Granddaughter, you have done well for yourself. And I suppose, McMahon, you will expect her to support you now, on my money."

Liam answered truthfully, "I'd sooner starve."

"Well, on one thing we agree."

An interruption came then in the form of a second mechanical servant that opened the door and entered the parlor, a tray loaded with a tea service in its hands. This unit looked rather battered, its suit less lustrous than the butler's and with dents marking the surface, especially near the head. It groaned and emitted a steady stream of steam as it approached.

Van Hamelin said, "I did not know, when I ordered tea, that you had brought me an Irishman."

Clara replied, "I thought you knew everything that happens in this city. I should think you'd be perfectly

93

aware whom I married yesterday."

Van Hamelin opened his lips to reply, but the servant, rolling forward, caught one of its wheels on the edge of the area rug. It wobbled in its version of a stumble and dropped the tray at the old man's feet.

Chapter Thirteen

The crash reverberated around the room. Shards of pottery and hot tea splashed everywhere; frosted biscuits flew like pink-and-white missiles.

Clara's grandfather howled in rage. He picked up a book from a side table and hurled it at the steam unit's head, and followed it with a small porcelain figurine.

"Stupid wretch! How many times have I told you to watch where you're going? You're fit only for the scrap heap, do you hear me? The scrap heap!"

The unit trembled. It bent down with a gust of steam and began gathering broken china, shoveling the pieces back onto the metal tray.

"Out! Get out of here."

Randolph Van Hamelin's face now shone crimson. Clara wondered if a stroke might not carry him off on the spot, but her hopes were dashed when he continued to roar. "You will go to the scrap yard the moment I am finished here. Go and shut yourself down."

"Please, Master." The unit wheezed. "I do not want to die."

"You can't die, foolish thing. You're not alive."

The unit trundled from the room, head hanging.

Liam squeezed Clara's arm. She felt his strength, a reassurance.

"That is what happens when one keeps them too long," Van Hamelin said in an aggrieved tone. "Let that be a warning to you, girl."

"I do not keep mechanical servants," Clara replied. "I find them an abomination, given there are so many honest men, women, and, unfortunately, even children in this city begging for work."

"Like this 'honest' Irishman you have brought me?" Cruelty shone in Van Hamelin's eyes. "Wed how many days before your birthday?"

"Three," Clara answered.

"I suppose now you will expect ownership of the house, and the funds to run it."

"That was the agreement, Grandfather."

"So it was." The old man leaned toward them. "You needn't think I don't know this for a farce. I'll be watching the both of you to ascertain if this is a real marriage. And if it proves false, I will take steps. Do you hear me?"

Clara's heart clenched. "What sort of steps?" She and Theodore Collwys had made very sure they followed the terms of the legacy. She felt certain she had met them all.

"Never you mind." The old man grinned, which made him look very like a skull. "Leave that to me." He switched his gaze to Liam. "You can be investigated. And exposed. Now get out of my sight."

Clara arose, pulling Liam with her.

"Have your lawyer contact my lawyer, Grandfather."

"Go!"

They moved to leave, but Liam hung back for a moment, pulling at Clara's hand.

"'Twas a pleasure to be after meeting you, sir," he said, rolling on the accent. "And you be sure to sleep well, mind—wouldn't want you dyin' in the night."

Clara made a strangled sound and towed Liam from the room. A second figurine crashed into the door as they exited.

"Wicked," Clara breathed, not certain if she referred to her grandfather or her husband.

"I thought that went well." At least Liam did not appear intimidated. "What is this, then?"

The battered serving unit stood before them in the entry hall, the butler at its back. The server trembled so hard it clattered, and emitted a constant trail of steam.

"Miss Clara," it clicked. "I beseech you to save me. Do not let him send me to the scrap yard."

"I'm sorry, Dax." Clara looked at the poor distressed unit with pity. Who said they had no feelings? The thing was clearly terrified. "What can I do? You belong to my grandfather, and you know very well no one can prevent him doing as he wishes."

"The bully," Liam muttered.

The unit waved its hands. "But I have done my best to serve him for many years. I need maintenance! New wheels. A repair to my boiler. He abuses me, strikes me, beats me."

"I do not doubt it." Compassionately, Clara added, "Perhaps in that case the scrap yard will afford you some peace." She glanced at the butler, who stood as emotionless as if it had been switched off. What did it think? Did it think?

"I do not want to die!" Dax protested with a belch of steam. "Please, Miss Clara, save me. Take me with you."

"Oh, lord, Dax, I can't."

And Liam said, "Wait just a minute." He looked at

the butler. "You know, this might be you in a few short years."

The butler shifted but made no other response.

"Max, is it?" Liam asked the butler unit. "Have you summoned the scrap man, Max?"

"I have, sir."

Dax trembled harder.

"Well, then," Liam gestured at the server unit, while still looking at the butler, "this equipment here might henceforth be considered garbage."

"So it might, sir."

"I don't think you could object to us taking a pile of garbage off your master's hands. Here, Max, help me load him into a steamcarriage. Quickly, now."

"Liam," Clara protested, "I don't think that's wise."

Liam looked her in the eyes and lifted his brows. "Come now, Mrs. McMahon. I can't help but feel for the fellow, under the circumstances. Death is so very unpleasant."

****

"Ah, now, no need to fret about it," Liam told his wife. She had discussed their actions in seizing the steam unit all the way home, and Liam had begun to learn that when she talked things up it meant she was worried. He, personally, thought it a great achievement to have stolen a patch on the old toad in the mansion. And anyway, why should the poor clattering server die?

"Your grandfather didn't want it. And you take in every other blessed waif that comes to your door. Why not Dax?"

She stared him in the eyes as they disembarked from the steamcarriage. In the clear morning light, her eyes glowed an uncanny green.

How could she say she wasn't beautiful? She looked like an elfin princess from some magical world. And he wanted to bury himself in her, so much it hurt.

"You're right," she sighed, which made a first. "There is no difference, on an ethical level." She placed her hand lightly on the unit's shoulder. "Come, Dax. Let's get you inside."

"Do not feel well, Miss Clara," the unit complained.

"We'll fix you up," Liam told it heartily. "Those two lads—Fred and Woodrow—will be able to give him an overhaul, right, Mrs. McMahon?"

They clattered into their own entryway only to find Theodore Collwys in close conversation with Georgina. The two broke it off at once, however, and Collwys turned to Clara with a warm smile.

"Greetings, my dear. How went your meeting with your grandfather? I've come to discuss all the details."

Liam tried to decide how he felt about Collwys. The fellow looked like a dandy, dressed in a fine, brown suit with his fine, sandy-colored hair worn in a sculpted coif, and with the kind of features Liam suspected would make women swoon. Liam thought him a little too cozy with Clara. Now he literally felt his back go up.

"No need to worry about her," he growled. "She was with me."

"I was not worried, Mr. McMahon, merely anxious to hear about the outcome. And what is this?" Collwys raised his eyebrows at the serving unit and did not appear to notice Liam had failed to shake his hand.

"My grandfather condemned it to the scrap heap.

You know what he's like."

Liam narrowed his eyes. No, he definitely didn't like the confiding, comfortable way his wife spoke to this man. He wondered why Clara hadn't taken Collwys to play her husband. He looked exactly the sort of which the old fart back on Delaware would approve.

Collwys smiled indulgently. "Just like you, Clara, to let your heart rule your more practical sense."

"'Twas I who insisted we bring the unit," Liam put in. "It didn't want to die. And I happen to believe in second chances."

Collwys gave Liam a searching look. "Fascinating," he murmured.

Liam's back went up still further. "'Tis not a logic problem, but about a life—his." He gestured at Dax.

"So, Mr. McMahon, you feel steam units have sentience? And rights?"

"Everything has a right to live, if it wants to."

Clara closed her fingers on his arm. "We will have time later for esoteric discussion. Let's go into the surgery, where we can be private. Georgina, where are the children?"

"The lads are out working, of course, and the others are in the dining room, supposed to be about their lessons. But you know what they are like."

"Yes." Clara stripped off her gloves. Liam immediately thought about her small, soft hands all over his body earlier this morning, and ached for it again.

She gestured to the door of the surgery and spoke kindly to Dax. "We do not wish to be overheard. Do you feel up to standing guard at this door?"

But Collwys hung back, a hesitant, apologetic look

on his face. "Clara, are you quite sure we should include your husband in this discussion? These are, after all, private financial matters."

Why, the pompous ass, Liam thought. Clara must have been able to feel him bristle, for she seized his arm again in a calming gesture. "Liam is heavily invested in this—"

She got no further. From outside, in Virginia Street, came the squeal of iron tires, screams, and the sound of a collision that rattled the front windows.

Liam had the door yanked open before he knew what he was about. The others crowded past him and then froze at the scene that met their eyes.

The accident had occurred directly in front of the house. A steamcab had swerved, likely to avoid a crowd of children playing in the street. It had then plowed into a parked lorry wagon, losing a wheel in the process. Now steam rose in a cloud from the damaged boiler, but it wasn't that which caught Liam's attention. For the cab driver hadn't managed to miss *all* the children.

He had already leaped from his cab, seemingly unhurt, and gestured wildly as he explained himself. "She ran right in front of me! They all did. Stupid urchins, why are they running wild in the street? She ran right under my wheels!"

The child lay beneath them now, on the bricks of the street, either senseless or dead. Her golden hair spread out in a fan. She looked no more than six years old.

"Oh, God," Clara said in Liam's ear. Her whole heart lay in the words, and Liam's stomach turned over.

"Best not to look," he told her.

She ignored him, pushed past, and hurried down the steps into the street. Helpless, Liam followed.

The steamcab driver still protested to anyone who would listen. "Wasn't my fault, was it? I've two kiddies of my own at home. But I don't let them run in the streets. Where are her parents? Oh, shut up, you lot!"

The last he directed at the felled child's companions, who now stood in a knot, weeping and accusing him. Residents of nearby houses—servants, mostly—and the lorry driver gathered, staring.

"Call the cops!" someone yelled.

Amid the confusion, Collwys moved past Clara and crouched at the child's side. He looked up at Clara with regret in his eyes. "She's dead," he pronounced.

The children wailed louder. The cab driver began to excuse himself all over again. He latched onto Liam and yelled into his face. "She ran right in front of my wheels! You can see I swerved to try and miss her. You understand, don't you?"

Liam ignored him, busy watching Clara. He saw her look at the child, then haul herself up and speak to Collwys.

"Bring her inside."

"Clara, she's dead."

Liam saw his wife look Collwys right in the eye. "I am sure, Theodore, you are mistaken. Bring her inside."

Chapter Fourteen

"She's a pretty little thing." The words came from Liam without his volition. The child looked so small lying on the table in Clara's workroom, her hair gleaming in the garish light of the steam lamps. Blood splashed her milk-white skin.

"Ascertain the damages." Clara spoke to Georgina, not to Liam. He doubted Clara even remembered he was there. He backed off a step from the table and stood quietly. At least Collwys, having carried the child in, had been dismissed from the room.

Liam could still hear commotion all the way from the street—the voice of the steamcab driver, very faint now, the shrill voices of the children, and then a whistle. Was that the police?

The two women worked frantically, their heads bent together—one black, one brown—running their hands over the child's body with gentle persistence. Liam had the image of two huddled witches—two merciful, pretty ones.

"Broken arm," Georgina said. "That's nothing. Crushed abdomen?"

"I feel no bleeding there."

"Lungs?"

"A couple cracked ribs. I think the wheel went right over her. If she's too badly damaged, I can't bring her back."

Bring her back.

A chill of pure, superstitious fear traced its way up Liam's back. Was that what she meant to do? Clara, his wife, who could raise the dead.

For the child, draped on the worktable, did not breathe. And her eyes stared sightlessly.

He swore beneath his breath. He wondered if he should join Collwys outside. Did he want to watch this? Part of him, rooted and helpless, did. Another part wanted to run as from the Devil.

"Open her dress. Look at the damage just here."

"Is it too bad?"

Clara shook her head. She rested her hands very lightly on the child's thin chest, lifted her chin and drew a deep breath.

From where he stood he saw her stiffen in every limb. Her eyes rolled back in her head. Suddenly, she didn't look like Clara. Despite the soft, ruffled brown hair, the fragile, elfin prettiness, she looked strange and foreign. Something about her sharpened. She filled, and changed.

She bent down and placed her mouth over that of the child.

Liam felt the impact of it throughout his body, as if she breathed into him again. He could feel the warmth and intensity filling his own lungs. Not air, but life.

Horrified and fascinated, he stood with his back now pressed against the closed door of the room, repelled, fascinated, and, truth be told, aroused. She was a witch. She was pure magic.

He wanted to follow her till he died. Again.

His vision blurred, and the two of them, woman and child—for Georgina now stood a few steps away—

wavered and melded into one figure outlined in light. Mine, he thought savagely, and then the child's body jerked. Her arms flew out—even the one Georgina had said was broken. Clara continued to breathe into her— long, long—until she could not possibly have any breath left. Then she lifted her mouth from the child's.

The girl began to cry, a weak mewling sound.

Someone pounded on the house door. Clara turned her head and for an instant her eyes met Liam's—they gleamed intensely green. She leaned limply against the worktable, as if too weak to stand. He didn't realize he'd moved until he found himself at her side, his arms wrapped around her.

"Here now, lean on me."

She did. For a blessed, wonderful instant she laid her head against his shoulder; he felt her weariness and elation as if they were his own.

He looked down at the child who lay with her eyes wide open, clearly terrified. Georgina soothed her with kind hands, refastened the front of her little dress, and crooned soft words.

"All right, it will be all right."

Georgina looked up, and in her eyes Liam saw some of what he felt—wonder, horror, devotion. "I know who she is. Her mother works at the laundry on Niagara Street—I've seen them in passing."

"They'll be coming." Clara sounded haunted. "I hear—"

So did Liam. Someone was in the entryway, arguing with the mechanical servant.

"Stay here," he bade Clara, and went out into the fray.

A little knot of people stood just ahead of him at

the end of the hallway. A thin woman wept and wrung her hands, a neighbor he recognized, and a copper, along with Collwys and Dax.

Drawing on every bit of authority he possessed, Liam marched down the hall and into the thick of them.

"There was a terrible accident in front of the house," he told the copper. He looked at the woman. "A child—your daughter?—was run down, but she lives."

The woman gasped and sobbed.

The copper said, "We were told the child was killed."

"No, just knocked unconscious she was, which is why we carried her in out of the commotion. My wife has some medical skill, you see. The girl is awake—sore hurt and very confused, but alive."

Aye, and he remembered how he'd felt when he woke. Confused didn't half describe it.

The woman fell into his arms. "Take me to her, please."

"I'll bring her, shall I?" Clara wouldn't want them in her workroom with all its secrets. "A moment. Dax, please show them into the parlor." The lawyer, Collwys, no doubt wishing to distance himself, stepped back as the others went into the front room.

Liam retraced his steps to the rear of the house and the workshop. Inside, both women and the girl met him with frightened eyes.

"Come, lass." He held out his arms. "Your mother is here for you."

She whimpered and clutched at Clara with her one good hand.

"Here," Clara told her, "I will come too."

They went down the corridor in a knot of three. As

soon as they entered the parlor, the woman flew at them, weeping.

"Oh, Cassie! Cassie, I told you not to run in the street. Are you hurt? Speak to me, love!"

"She was stunned, knocked out." Clara spoke as much to the policeman as the mother. "She has a broken arm, and probably other injuries also. My father was a physician, so I have some knowledge. She'll need to go straight to a doctor, mind."

The mother lifted devastated eyes. "Oh, but I can't possibly afford… What I earn at the laundry barely keeps us. Her pa was killed on the waterfront last year."

The copper shifted uncomfortably.

Clara raised her chin. "Wait here a moment." She slipped out and soon returned with her purse. She thrust a handful of money at the mother. "Here. Take her to Mr. Rogers on Franklin Street. He will not charge much."

The woman wept harder. "I can't accept that. You've already been so kind."

She had no idea, Liam thought.

Clara turned her gaze on the policeman. "Officer, will you carry the child to Mr. Rogers?"

"I would, ma'am, but I'm on duty, and there's still that tangle out front."

"Send Dax," Liam advised. He would go himself, but he could feel how weak Clara was, and knew as soon as their visitors left she was going to collapse.

"Yes." Clara grasped at it. "Perhaps you would allow our servant to assist you."

"I would be ever so grateful, ma'am."

The child was passed carefully into Dax's arms. With the mother virtually clinging to him, they went out.

"All's well that ends well, then," the copper said in parting.

Liam just hoped Dax proved more adept at carrying a child than a tea service.

He shut the door, turned to look at his wife, and was just in time to catch her as she went down. She made virtually no weight in his arms. How could so much strength be contained in this fragile bundle?

He held her silently, and she clutched at him. He could feel her emotions surging, a backlash of what she had spent to bring the child back from death.

"Ah, lass," he crooned, and pressed his lips to her forehead. He carried her to the sofa and sat down with her cradled in his arms like a child.

The storm inside her abated, even as Liam listened to Georgina dealing with the curious children in the house and as he heard the uproar outside subside. The rumble of traffic along Virginia Street resumed. His wife rested against him with her eyes closed.

And he felt connected to her, each breath and every heartbeat. How beautiful she looked with her elfin face pale as alabaster, feathery hair ruffled, brown eyelashes aquiver. He wanted to absorb her into him, protect and defend her.

At last he whispered, "Was that how it was with me?"

Her lashes fluttered and lifted from those incredible, gray-green eyes, and Liam's heart stuttered in his chest. She did not try to prevaricate or misunderstand. She merely said, "Yes."

"It is a"—he struggled for words—"profound thing you do."

"It is a dangerous thing," she whispered. "But I couldn't let her go for a broken arm and a collapsed lung, could I? I couldn't let her mother lose her."

"No." Liam drew her still closer. He wondered what would happen if his wife's strange ability became known. He imagined a fearful mob out in Virginia Street throwing rocks through the windows.

He would die over again before he let anyone harm a hair on her head.

"The wee lass—will she remember her mother?"

"I don't know. She wasn't dead as long as you."

"Does the length of time matter?"

"I don't know that either. She's the only person I've raised, besides you."

"And that money you gave her mother," he began. Money Clara could ill afford. Yet he started to learn about this woman he had married.

She sighed. "We should have the funds we need soon. If Theodore can deal with my grandfather's lawyer, our dire situation should improve. We will not be affluent, by any means, but the outlook will be much improved." She stirred. "You can let me go. I feel stronger."

"No. I cannot let you go."

His lips quested for hers softly and took them without demand. He wanted so badly to give back to her some of what she'd spent in raising the child, and he poured his essence into her like strong drink. What started as an act of mercy soon flared into fire. He felt her catch flame, felt the heat course through him in powerful claiming.

"Clara," he whispered into her, "let me take you upstairs and heal you."

Her eyes gazed into his, touched him on some level so deep he barely comprehended it. "Shocking, Mr. McMahon. It is the middle of the day."

"I don't care." He wanted her fragile body naked beneath him, wanted to give to her, and give and give.

"Is Theodore still here? We must conclude our meeting."

"Blast Theodore. Where did he disappear to when you needed him?"

"I—"

"Listen to me, Clara. Listen." He framed her face with his hands. "I will never forsake you. Never. Do you understand?"

She lifted her fingers to his face and touched him in turn. What did she see in his eyes? The devotion he felt, that coursed through him like his blood?

Slowly she nodded, and he kissed her again.

Chapter Fifteen

"Madam, the child is at the door. Shall I let her in?" Dax wheezed and clacked the words like a defective teakettle. The boys had not yet had time to overhaul him, beyond giving his battered exterior a quick polish.

Clara, still at the breakfast table, paused with her teacup balanced between her hands and turned her gaze on her husband. Nearly a week had passed since Cassie was up on her feet and out of Dr. Rogers' care, her right arm swaddled in plaster. Each day she had haunted the doorstep, a moth to flame.

Liam treated Clara to a forbidding scowl and grumbled, "Again? I swear by all the saints, I barely have you to myself anymore."

How could he say that, when they had only just finished a bout of morning loving before coming down to the table? Indeed, Clara still tingled from his touch.

She lifted both eyebrows at him and turned back to Dax. "Let her in, please. Her mother will not want her out in the street."

Dax trundled off, and Clara shot her husband an apologetic look. Since they were late coming down, all the other children were off about their business. They'd been enjoying a few precious minutes on their own—now ruined. No wonder Liam looked like a thundercloud.

"Can the child's mother not keep her to home?" he complained.

"Cassie's mother is away at work fifteen hours a day, and Cassie is still confused and in need of company."

He said nothing but did not look appeased. Didn't he understand the responsibility inherent in bringing someone back to life?

Cassie slid into the room and sidled up to Clara's chair. The child, so thin and pale as to look almost transparent, fixed Clara with a wide, blue stare. "Morning, miss."

"And how are you today, Cassie?" Clara returned. "Any ache in that arm?"

They had already established during previous visits that Cassie remembered nothing of the accident nor what had happened before. She claimed not to know her mother, either, and called her "the kind woman." But she certainly knew how to find her way to Clara's door.

And, could Clara turn her away when she was Cassie's one touchstone?

"Have you had any breakfast, Cassie?"

"The kind lady gave me some porridge."

"Are you hungry still?"

Cassie shook her head and quietly, determinedly, crawled up into Clara's lap, where she pressed her face against Clara's shoulder and clutched the front of her gown. Clara knew from experience how difficult it would be to pry the girl's little fingers off again.

Liam muttered disagreeably beneath his breath.

"What's that you say?" Clara asked him.

"Child's like a damned limpet. Why do you put up with it?"

"I know what she's feeling—as should you."

"Doesn't mean you have to let her climb all over you." A sudden thought seemed to strike Liam; he stared at Clara with a new expression in his eyes. "'Tisn't how you feel about me, is it, when I want to touch you?"

How could he even ask, with the memory of the intimacies that had passed between them, not half an hour since, still fresh in both their minds? True, when she married him she had not expected that kind of marriage or, in truth, any intimacies at all. Now she wasn't sure she could give him up if she tried.

"Don't be foolish," she told him, but he did not look satisfied.

He parted his lips to reply but never had the chance. The dining room door opened once more. Ruella marched in.

"Still at your breakfast, are you?" she inquired, sweeping Liam with an appreciative stare. Clara didn't know how she felt about the way Ruella looked at her husband, as if she wanted to eat him alive. Of course, Ruella had seen Liam naked, a sight difficult for any woman to forget. "Slug-a-beds this morning, were you?"

"It is barely eight o'clock," Clara replied. She and Liam had been awake at dawn. He had moved above her, and…

He looked at her and his eyes gleamed, almost as if he heard her thoughts.

"And why aren't you at the jail?" Clara asked Ruella quickly.

"Finished with serving breakfast there, didn't I, and came as fast as I could. I have news."

Ruella edged a chair out from the table and sat down facing them. Her gaze settled on Cassie. "What's this, then? A new sprog?"

"This is Cassie." Clara spoke above the child's head. "She had an accident a while ago."

"Ah! I did hear tell of a girl miraculously surviving a crash up this way." Ruella's slightly protruding eyes studied Clara with interest. "Did you—?"

"Hush!" Clara gathered Cassie closer. Liam grumbled again.

"So," Ruella asked, "she lives here now?"

"She lives with her mother, who works very hard at a steam laundry. She just needs to be here from time to time."

"I see. Well!" Ruella shot a look at Liam. "Appears, Irishman, you've some competition for her attention. Bet that puts your nose out of joint."

"What's your news?" he returned disagreeably.

Recalled to her mission, Ruella leaned across the table and widened her eyes. "Only that it's happened again."

"Eh?"

"At the jail—they hanged another man last night."

Clara felt Liam stiffen even though they were not physically touching. She glanced down at Cassie, but the child slept soundly, cheek against Clara's breast.

"How do you know?" Liam asked.

"Well, I got wind of something last evening when I was finishing up in the kitchen. Old Tim came stumbling in—he's the prison sexton—and more than half sober for once. He doesn't show up unless they send for him, and they never send for him unless they've a job. I knew there hadn't been any fights inside, and there was no one ill. So all my suspicions were aroused."

She waggled her eyebrows. "I'd been keeping my eyes peeled so long on your behalf, mind, it's become instinct. I gave Old Tim a meal and pumped him for news. Not difficult to persuade him to say too much. He told me Maynard—that's the warden—had sent for him on the Q.T. Could only mean one thing."

"Maynard," Liam repeated viciously. "Can't say I remember him."

"I never would have thought him on the take," Ruella admitted.

"Are you sure it's him and not the commissioner who's crooked?" Clara asked.

"The commissioner rarely sets foot in the place. He's usually wining and dining with his old-boy cronies. And Old Tim definitely said it was Maynard sent for him on the quiet."

"Bastard needs settling, then, doesn't he?" Liam growled. "Needs to meet with some vengeance in the dark."

Clara and Ruella both stared at him. Clara's stomach tightened. "You will not go there," she told him. "Promise me."

He lifted his eyes to her, and she felt his emotions burgeoning like those of some wild, avenging angel.

"Promise," she pressed.

He shook his head slightly; a dark lock of hair tumbled over his forehead. "I will not make you a promise I cannot keep."

"You *can* keep it! You are out of all that and have established a new life for yourself."

"Have I?" The smile that curved his lips looked

bitter and rueful. "That man stole far more from me than my life. He stole my past, the memories of my mother and my father, all the grief and laughter ever I knew, my youth, and my home. He stole the man I was—for the sake of his greed! Now he's done it again. And you expect me to sit on my arse and be comfortable here?"

The panic Clara felt licked up, sharp and bright. "You'll have to. Don't you see the danger?"

"Danger?" He jerked his shoulder and scoffed. Switching his gaze back to Ruella, he asked, "You sure about what happened last night?"

Looking grave, she nodded. "I hung around after the kitchen was dark, to see, just as I did the night you, er—"

"Died," he supplied the word.

Ruella shot a look at Cassie, but the child clearly slept deeply.

"I heard it, when they hustled one of the men out from the cells and into the yard. I heard the sound when he—fell. There was no struggle. I think this one died clean. Then Old Tim's cart trundled away. He headed to the waterfront. The body will be in the river by now." She added, "You'll not prove anything."

"I don't need to prove anything. 'Tis not as if I'm planning to take him in front of a magistrate."

"You're planning nothing," Clara insisted.

He ignored her. "Where does this paragon of a warden live? Surely not at the jail."

Ruella shook her head and looked at Clara, as if realizing belatedly what she'd done. "I shouldn't have come here with this news. Truly, Irishman, it will do no good for you to hunt him down."

"How can you say so? 'Twill be a balm to my soul, provided I still have one. *There's* an ethical question for you, Mrs. McMahon."

Upset beyond all reason, Clara snapped, "Of course you have a soul."

"Sure about that? I didn't lose it when I died and started over new, like that mite in your arms? What makes up a man's soul, anyway? If it's his memories and all the things he's learned along the way, then mine's surely gone."

"Jesus," Ruella murmured.

Clara covered Cassie's ear with the palm of her hand, as if she could protect the child from the blasphemy and from the emotions now zinging about the room. "Liam, let Ruella handle this. You will handle it, won't you, Ruella?"

Ruella's eyes widened once more. "Me? How?"

"Report your suspicions to the authorities. You're in the perfect position to do so."

Ruella pushed back from the table. "And lose me job?"

"We will be coming into our allowance soon, once Theodore straightens out the legal tangle. You can come back here to live, and work for me."

"You'll barely have the brass, or the room, with all these sprogs," Ruella jerked her head, "and him living off you."

"I can make me own way," Liam retorted. "I'm that sure I must have some skills and abilities."

"And how would that look to my grandfather?" Clara could not imagine why she felt so upset, but her morning crumbled around her.

"Like I'm an honest man of good intentions." Liam

leaned toward her and nodded at Cassie almost viciously. "I'm not that wee lass, wife, whom you can keep gathered up safe in your arms for all time. I'm a man, and I'll live as a man or not at all."

Chapter Sixteen

Moonlight trickled in through the tall bedroom windows and crept across the carpet toward the bed. By its filtered radiance, Liam studied the woman who slept beside him.

How lovely she looked, and how fragile, her slender shoulders bare, the swell of one small breast peeking from the cover. Her feather-soft brown hair, still ruffled from his fingers, clustered on her pillow, and her lips were swollen from the touch of his lips. Just seeing her at his side made him ache to have her all over again.

It would be so easy to act on that desire, place his mouth at the tip of that breast and bring her once more to the peak of passion. How easy to lose himself completely in her and think only of the moment, since the moment was all he possessed.

But what would that make of him? A half man? Less than that, because all he had was Clara—this small portion of his life, since he had lost everything else.

What made a man a man? The ability to satisfy a woman, to couple with her so deeply they both tumbled off the edge of desire's cliff and then flew? Or was it the culmination of all his thoughts, his feelings…his memories?

He reached out and touched her breast very softly, just because he couldn't resist, traced the sweet pink bud at its tip, which immediately hardened for him. Clara stirred slightly in her sleep and sighed, but slept on.

Aye, and he'd worn the lass out quite thoroughly, which made this his perfect opportunity to slip away.

But she held him—she held him there in the bed, there at her side, helpless as poor Cassie, who followed her like a hound pup.

He, Liam, was no hound. He wasn't even Liam McMahon, for God's sake. And if he ever wanted to reclaim any part of himself, he needed to get out of the bed while he could.

He slid from beneath the covers and stood, naked as born, gazing at his wife. What did he feel for her? He must have had women in the past, though they were now lost to him. He certainly possessed the skills necessary to please a woman and himself. As he'd said to Clara at the outset, he might even be married. She'd claimed at the time it didn't matter since theirs would be a marriage only in name.

If he were married, he committed adultery now, right enough. And couldn't wait to do so again.

Aye, for what he felt for Clara was need—deep and almost paralyzing. But he felt tenderness toward her, as well. Love?

Frozen there, gazing at her, he admitted to himself he couldn't tell. Along with his memories he'd lost all experience with his emotions.

Hastily he turned away and donned his clothes, refusing to let himself gaze at Clara again: if he did, he would stay. Out he went through the room door, moving like a shadow, down the stairs, and through the silent house. The entry hall lay full of gloom, and he reached the main door before a sudden clanking sound from behind startled him half out of his skin.

"You need something, sir?"

Damn. Dax stood in the shadows. How could Liam have forgotten the unit didn't truly sleep? Now it stirred, and Liam heard the slight hiss and pop of its boiler heating up.

"Air, Dax, I just need some air."

Dax trundled forward and "looked" at him with its molded, metallic eyes, though Dax didn't actually see anything through them. A device in its forehead let it recognize objects and people.

"Madam will not like it if you go out alone."

And that was a judgment call, wasn't it? Just where did Dax's loyalties lie? He, Liam, had been the one to save it from the scrap heap. Quickly, he said, "But you won't be telling her, will you? You've no wish to upset her that way."

The unit seemed to hesitate. A small jet of steam escaped the joint at its neck and drifted upward like a thought.

"Plus," Liam added, "you will not wish to wake her. I'm sure you never awakened your last master."

Dax trembled. "You will not send me back to him, will you?"

Ah, it would be easy to use the thing's fear—if it truly experienced fear—to insure silence. Liam hadn't the heart.

Instead he said, "Do you prefer me to your old master?"

"Yes, sir."

"Then I think you owe me your loyalty."

"Yes, sir."

"You will keep silent about me going out to catch some air. Just," Liam waved his hand, "go back to sleep."

A cloud of steam erupted, indicating agitation. "I do not sleep. I go on standby."

"Then go back to standby. I'll return soon enough."

"Perhaps I should accompany Sir."

Aye, and that was just what he needed, a rolling teapot steaming after him.

"Go back in your corner and stay there until I return. That's an order, mind. And keep quiet."

Before Dax could argue further, Liam slipped outside into the moonlight. Never was Virginia Street so quiet—all the steamcabs, workmen, and urchins, gone.

A shiver traced its way up his spine. This must have been how it looked when Ruella brought him here in her barrow. Of course, it had been raining then, and no shadows thrown by moonlight.

He thought about his conversation with Ruella as she left this morning. He'd caught her at the back door and laid his hand on her arm.

"This man Maynard—where might he live?"

Ruella had stared at him before she shook her head. "Don't know."

"You're lying."

"You can't say that."

"I can."

She straightened and shrugged away his hand. A strapping woman. Liam wouldn't want to go three rounds with her. But he meant to have the answers he sought.

"Where does he drink, then?"

"He doesn't drink."

"Now, I know that's a lie. He may drink brandy rather than that swill they serve men like me, but he drinks, sure as I'm breathing."

Ruella's expression turned mutinous.

Cunningly, Liam asked, "Attends a gentleman's club, does he? Maybe one of those up on North Street?"

"How do you know that? That there are gentleman's clubs up on North Street, I mean? Your memory ain't returning, is it?"

Liam shook his head, though he couldn't be sure. Occasionally, knowledge just appeared whole in his mind, like a rock dropped into a pool. "I've still no sense of myself," he said truthfully.

"But you mean to find it by way of revenge, I suppose."

He challenged her, "Do you think it right, what that man's doing?"

"Of course not."

"Then give me his direction."

"He might attend a club called Sterling House on North Street. But you can't go there."

"Why not? Don't I look the gentleman?"

Ruella's gaze raked him. "Clara might fit you out in the clothes, but you're no gentleman. As soon as you open your mouth they'll toss you out on your ear." Ruella couldn't quite hide her sneer. "You're no gentleman—you're an Irishman."

"Your prejudices are showing."

"Just stating the truth. And I'm not the only one with prejudices—some of them justified."

"Meaning?"

She leaned toward him and whispered, "He was

another bog-jumper, that fellow they hanged last night."

****

So now Liam found himself tramping through the moonlight seeking vengeance not only for himself but his countryman or countrymen—who knew how many times Maynard had pulled this stunt? He did not doubt this city teemed with Irish, also immigrants from other parts of Europe, such as Ruella herself, as well as former slaves come north like wee Georgina. He could only imagine his fellow Irishmen got into their share, or more than their share, of scrapes and brawls. If Maynard took them in on the prison books, he could charge the county for them and then dispose of them and pocket their keep.

But wouldn't his higher-ups—the commissioner, for one—eventually inquire after these men, expect them to go to trial? Or did drunk and disorderlies not go to trial? Perhaps once hauled in, they served a standard sentence before being released.

Or not.

North Street was a broad avenue lined with upscale businesses and fine houses, most of the latter still lit even at this advanced hour. Liam could only hope the Sterling House would also still be in operation. Of course, that didn't mean Maynard would be in attendance.

As for getting tossed out on his ear, did Ruella think him a fool? He could put on a high-class Limey accent with the best of them.

But he'd need some money before he pushed his way in. And he had no compunction, despite that owned by his wife, about stealing.

The crowd of young bloods he encountered in front

of one of the busier clubs had clearly been carousing—and gambling too, no doubt. They stumbled about on the curb, arguing over where to go next, daring one another to go down and throw potatoes at the police station.

"Damned cops are all bog-jumpers," the nearest said, and whinnied with laughter. "Make 'em feel to home."

"Excuse me, good sir," Liam interrupted, practicing the accent while striving mightily to conceal his loathing. "Would you have the time?"

The fellow fumbled about his person for his pocket watch. By the time he located it and decided it was "damned late," Liam had the fool's wallet in hand.

"Thank you." He ambled off down the street congratulating himself on selecting a mark who must have just won at cards, judging by the dollars bulging from the leather.

The Sterling House boasted a broad façade and an air of staid gentility. Liam was glad to see the lights all burned, including two flanking the doors, and a doorman—a late model steam unit—stood in attendance.

Could he make his way in? How hard could it be to fool a mechanical servant?

He approached with a dignified gait and the doorman stirred. "Good evening, sir."

"Evening."

"Are you a member, sir?"

"I am not, but I'm here to meet a member." Liam took a deep breath and brazened it out. "Mr. Maynard." He should have asked Ruella the blighter's first name. But the doorman gave a polite bow as it contemplated the matter, then opened the door with a gentle puff of steam.

"Mr. Maynard is in the card room, sir. Shall I escort you?"

"No need. I will find my way. Is the bar still open?"

"Yes, sir."

"Thank you, my good—er—man."

Liam sauntered in, feigning ease but with every sense alert. In the foyer he stood for a moment orienting himself. To the left, through an open doorway, he heard the soft clink of glasses that marked the bar. A flight of stairs lay directly ahead, and another doorway opened from the right. The place smelled of floor polish and expensive cigars.

Was the card room on the right, or upstairs? No matter, he was in, and he needed a drink.

The bar, when he reached it, lay dimly lit and, at this hour, nearly empty. Two men sat at a table over drinks. Another fellow in the corner looked as if he was asleep.

Behind the bar—

Liam blinked at a sight he'd never before seen. The bartender was young, female, curvaceous, and apparently naked.

Chapter Seventeen

The sight of the naked, beautiful young woman behind the bar didn't jive somehow with the staid exterior and quiet interior Sterling House presented. Liam imagined he must have encountered such a sight before—in a brothel, for one. But he couldn't remember that now; if he'd visited such places in the past, the sights and pleasures were lost to him.

The only woman he could actually recall seeing naked was Clara, and Clara, while eminently desirable, looked nothing like this.

He approached the bar as if drawn by strings, his eyes busy all the while.

The young woman had blonde hair in a riot of curls piled atop her head and another triangle of curls lower down, just visible when he peeked behind the bar. Her pretty, rosy face owed more than a bit of its color to rouge. If Liam wasn't mistaken, the tips of her breasts were rouged, as well. Magnificent breasts, they sat large, high, and perky, and at the perfect height for a man seated at the bar to admire.

"Good evening, sir. Can I get you something?"

Liam could think of about ten things, and he reminded himself he was a married man. Wasn't he? The ties between him and Clara remained strong and deep, but that did not keep a man from looking. He slid onto a stool and struggled to focus on her face. He very nearly forgot his fake accent.

"Whiskey, please, my dear—the best you have."

She turned to fetch a bottle; her rear was as pleasing—almost—to view as her front. She poured a very small drink and set it on the bar in front of Liam.

"A dollar, sir."

A dollar for one drink? Outrageous. But Liam supposed the whiskey was the least of that for which he was being asked to pay. He hauled out his wad of stolen cash, grateful the fellow he'd robbed had been so flush.

When he looked up, he found the bartender studying him with interest.

"You're new here," she observed. "Did you just join?"

"I'm here to meet a friend." He took a gulp of his drink, excellent whiskey that hit him right between the eyes. Serving drinks this strong, how did they keep the patrons' hands off the server?

She tipped her head and rested her hands lightly on the bar. Her nipples were definitely rouged. They reached for Liam like two tempting rosebuds. "What's his name?"

"Maynard." Liam smiled. "He invited me for a game, but I've heard about the beauties of the Sterling House bar and had to come and see for myself, first."

Her gaze moved slowly from his hair, now tumbled over his forehead, to his face and down his body, lingering in one or two places. It came to rest on his bulging wallet.

"I hope you like what you see."

What man wouldn't? Liam took another quick gulp of whiskey.

"My name's Jenny. And there are fringe benefits

available, for a price."

"How much?" Liam would defy any man to keep from asking.

She leaned on the bar and her breasts bobbed toward him. "Usually these benefits are only available to our members. But it's been a slow night. And sometimes I also like what I see. You say you're a friend of Mr. Maynard's?"

"One of his very closest friends."

She smiled; it didn't reach her eyes. "I finish here at three. There are exclusive rooms upstairs."

"How much?" Liam asked again, just out of curiosity.

"One hundred for my services."

"Dollars?" He couldn't keep his eyebrows from rising.

"Another fifty for the room." She told him dispassionately, "I'm worth it."

An unprecedented amount for a prostitute. A man could work three years and not earn that much.

With a rueful smile, he shook his head.

"Too steep for you?" She looked at the wallet again. "We could bargain."

"I'm married."

"So?" She shrugged, which did interesting things to her chest. "Most of the members are. It's just recreation: doesn't mean anything."

What was the point of engaging in it, then? The question surprised Liam. He thought of Clara lying beneath him, the flare of connection when he touched her, how he could feel her deep inside him and how just a look from her had him up and hard. Tiny, fey witch— she had enchanted him.

Or maybe he was just in love with his wife.

The idea felt like a hot poker in his gut. He straightened where he sat. "Newlywed," he explained.

"Well, that's a damned shame. You'd make a change from all the flabby old geezers who lie on their backs and expect a girl to do all the work. Guess you'll have to keep your money for the card table. You'll need it if you want to buy into Mr. Maynard's game."

"Tell me"—Liam leaned toward her in turn, and switched on his charm—"are these games on the up and up? Because I have a suspicion my good friend Maynard has brought me here tonight in order to fleece me."

"Oh, the games are honest. Just very expensive, Mr.—?"

"Rodney Ellingsworth the Third," he told her, pulling the name out of the air.

"Mrs. Rodney Ellingsworth the Third is a very lucky woman."

"And I'd better go join that game before I change my mind." Liam tossed back the last of the whiskey. "Good night, Jenny."

"Good luck. And if you have a fight with your wife, be sure and come back."

Liam left the bar wondering if he might have persuaded her to entertain him for free. But even now, Clara called to him. He thought of her lying in the big four-poster bed, all warm with sleep, the pale moonlight on her fragile face. The memory of rouged breasts slid from his mind.

Should have asked the lass how to find the card room. Upon the thought, he heard voices from across the hall. He drew a deep breath and went in.

A large room with a sculpted plaster ceiling, it contained at least ten tables set up for cards, three of which were occupied. Cigar smoke floated like a rising blanket and probably kept him from being noticed immediately.

He paused, realizing all at once he had no idea how to identify Maynard. He didn't even remember the face of the man who had murdered him.

The desire for revenge surged up through him like a gout of sickness. The man—whichever he was—needed settling.

Five men sat at the table nearest him, absorbed in their game. The amount of money piled in the middle of the green baize was enough to knock Liam back on his heels. The next table over held only four men, as did the last, back near the corner.

The men spoke in murmurs, but Liam could feel an intensity born of concentration. The stakes were, quite literally, high.

"Evening, Maynard," he said.

A man at the nearest table looked up in response. He had a broad face, well-fleshed, and a thick brown moustache which, at the moment, had a cigar protruding from beneath it. Clad with casual elegance, he looked more the prosperous landowner than the warden of a county jail.

His narrowed eyes found Liam through the smoke, fixed on him for a moment without comprehension and then widened. A dull flush roared up through the skin of his face, and the cigar fell from his lips onto his lap.

He howled like a scalded cat and leaped up. Several of his fellow gamblers exclaimed also, and a mechanical servant—heretofore unnoticed—trundled forward to add to the confusion. Liam stood unmoving and stared.

So this was the man who, for the sake of greed, had ordered Liam's death.

Liam might have forgotten him along with most of his past, but he would know him now, right enough.

"Samuel, what in hell—" cried one of his companions, whose drink had spilled.

Maynard did not so much as blink. He continued to stare at Liam the way he might regard—well, a ghost.

"Sir?" Dismayed by the commotion, the mechanical man waved its hands. "Sir?"

"Mr. Maynard," Liam said, "I believe you owe me the price of one life."

Maynard's flush drained away, followed by a terrible pallor. "You! Bog-jumper."

Deliberately Liam raised his hand to his throat, decently covered by a white neckerchief. Maynard, now on his feet, swayed where he stood.

"What is it?" exclaimed the man seated to Maynard's left. "Who is this fellow interrupting our game? Damn me, I was winning."

Liam had now gained the attention of most of the occupants of the room. Time to scarper.

"Vengeance," he warned Maynard, "shall be mine."

He spun for the door. As he turned he saw Maynard reach for the mechanical servant and say something Liam could not hear. He ducked under cover of the smoke and was out the door onto North before anyone else could speak.

Take that for starters, he thought as he stood drawing in great breaths of the cleaner air. Buffalo might smell like coal and steam most times, but it smelled better than that expensive funk inside.

"Sir?" said the mechanical doorman in inquiry.

Behind Liam, the main door opened. Out trundled the mechanical servant from the card room. "If I might detain you just a moment sir," it said.

Liam ran.

He headed east along North Street, making for Clara the way a foundering ship makes for port, and soon realized not one but both mechanicals came after him. The one from the card room no doubt had orders from Maynard; the other might have joined in on general principle. Liam, not sure how fast they were able to roll, risked a look over his shoulder and saw them closing rapidly, each leaving little trails of steam.

What would happen if they caught him? What order had Maynard given? He could imagine the steel fingers closing on his throat, finishing the job the drunken sexton had boggled.

He dodged a knot of carousers, lungs working like bellows, and pelted on. He heard the carousers get in the way of his pursuers for an instant and took advantage to veer right down College Street, which was darker and less occupied. But he could still hear the mechanicals coming behind him, a wheezing sort of clack, clack, clack. Far too close for comfort.

He pelted down the center of College Street and then, in an effort to lose his pursuers, cut between two houses, through a yard and out into the sudden bright openness of Allen Street. He dashed down the center of the sidewalk, still heading east, angled between two more houses, and leaped over a low, brick wall. The moonlight slid over him, playing games with the tall houses, deceiving his eyes. When he ducked between the next two houses he did not see the carriage house blocking his rear exit until it was too late.

He turned like a stag at bay. The mechanicals were already in the alleyway and heading for him. He wondered if he could scale the wall of the carriage house and go over the roof. But there was no time. The steam units barreled toward him like two runaway engines, and the breath seared painfully in his lungs.

He was going to die. Again.

The unit from the card room reached him first. Moonlight reflected from the indentations that formed its eyes. Liam took one look, turned, and did his best to scale the wall behind him.

The unit seized the back of his coat, which tore. *Damn*, he thought, *Clara's not going to be pleased about that.* And then, *Nor will she be pleased if I'm killed.* Would she even know what happened to him?

He struggled in the thing's metal grip, fought like a singed cat, and registered on some level that the second unit had arrived. They grappled with and held him between them. A silver arm with a clenched fist on the end of it raised up like a hammer and came down on the top of his head.

"Clara!" he thought, and fell like a steer in the slaughter yard.

And just before the moonlight flickered out into blackness, he looked up from the ground and registered not two units standing over him, but three.

Chapter Eighteen

Clara awoke abruptly, as if someone had called her name, and lay in the bed listening to the quiet house. Moonlight crept from the window across the floor like a ghostly presence.

She stretched her ears, but none of the children cried out, caught in a nightmare. No creak of footsteps betrayed them sneaking between each other's rooms for late-night shenanigans.

She sighed and rolled over, reaching for Liam. Her hand encountered nothing but a smooth, cool expanse of sheet.

Her eyes flew open, and her heart began to beat faster. He could have gone to use what he called the "bog." That had happened before. Yet if he'd just arisen, his side of the bed would still be warm.

She sat up, eyes wide in the gloom, and looked at the window. Safely shut. He had not gone out that way. But he had gone. She felt the empty ache of his absence.

She slipped from the bed, donned her robe, and went to open the door, where she stood listening. After a moment she went out and tiptoed down the stairs.

"Dax?" The mechanical servant must be about somewhere. Sometimes he shut himself down to standby in the kitchen, sometimes here in the foyer, which at the moment contained nothing but shadows.

Truly agitated now, she walked down the passageway to the kitchen, which stood empty and silent.

"Dax?" she called anyway.

Mudroom, empty. Her workroom, empty. The door to the cellar still chained.

Hurriedly, she retraced her steps back to inspect the parlor and her father's surgery.

"What is it?" The query came in a whisper. Georgina leaned over the banister, her hair frizzed about her face.

"I can't find Dax." Clara drew a breath. "Or Liam. I fear he's gone out. Damn Ruella anyway."

"Ruella?"

"She was here this morning, speaking of another murder at the jail. What if Liam has gone seeking vengeance?"

"He wouldn't do anything so reckless."

"Wouldn't he? Georgina, this is the man you and I dragged out of a waterfront boozer."

Georgina came softly down the stairs. "Maybe that's where he's gone again. You and I can get dressed and go look."

"Better to send Dax, now that we have him. But I can't find him, either."

"Let me look."

Georgina set about retracing Clara's path, lighting the lamps as she went. By the time she'd satisfied herself of both Liam's and Dax's absence, Fred had come down the stairs.

"What's up, Miss Clara?"

"Dax seems to be missing."

"Your new steamie, you mean? Maybe he's broke

down somewhere. Woodrow and me, we mean to patch him up for you, soon as we have the time."

"I can't locate him, broken or otherwise."

Fred joined the search and looked in the same places as they had. He then asked, "Where's Mister Liam?"

Clara wrapped her arms about herself. "I cannot find him, either."

"Just let me take a look around outside."

Fred ducked out, leaving the front door ajar. Fingers of moonlight reached in, along with a chill.

Georgina came and hugged Clara. "We'll send Fred and Woodrow down the waterfront to look, shall we? Much safer if you stay here. Anyway, he might come back."

Clara shook her head. She felt convinced something had happened—something dire.

Fred reappeared and said, "Not out there, neither of them."

"Fred," Georgina beseeched, "would you please fetch Woodrow, and the two of you go look down near some of the taverns—?"

"Sure thing, Miss Georgina. You leave it to us."

"And you, Miss Clara, go into the parlor and stir up the fire. I will make some tea."

Fred went back upstairs, and Clara took herself into the parlor, but her disquiet grew by leaps and bounds. What if something had gone wrong with Liam's resurrection? That had never happened before. Mollie, for instance, had lived a long second life before both her heart and joints gave out, making it far more merciful—and less selfish—to lay her to rest at last.

But Liam, Clara's first human subject, could well

prove very different. What if she had not breathed sufficient life into him? Granted, he seemed vigorous—to say the least—but she had no experience in this, and—

"Miss, Woodrow and I are just going. Don't you worry, now." Fred stuck his head in through the doorway. "And if the worst happens and you find yourself a widow, like, well, I'll be happy to take up the slack."

"Thank you," she told the lads. "And both of you be careful."

He nodded and went out. Clara had just begun to pace the rug, unable to hold still, when the lads were back.

"Uh, miss?" Woodrow called. "You better come look."

Hurrying in response, she found the two of them on the doorstep, the door wide open. Moonlight, nearly bright as day, cast a milky radiance and glinted off the dented surface of the figure that approached. Clara blinked and then blinked again.

Dax trundled up the street, listing severely to one side and clearly struggling. His head sat slightly askew, and he came with a horrendous clacking that echoed off the dark houses. Draped over his arms like an oversized child was a figure Clara recognized only by the locks of dark hair hanging down.

Liam.

She caught her breath and ran out, pushing past the lads, who quickly followed. The two groups met in front of the house amid a gout of steam.

It took Clara only half a glance to tell the steam unit was in rough shape. Dents far beyond what Clara's grandfather had contributed marred its surface, and half its head had been bashed in. There also seemed to be something wrong with one of its arms, though it still managed to cradle its burden.

"Dax!" Clara exclaimed and switched her gaze to Liam. "Is he dead?"

He looked it. His head dangled at an unnatural angle, and his clothing, torn, was liberally marked with blood. Abrasions covered what skin she could see.

Dax tried to speak but accomplished only a distressed whine. The boys reached to relieve the unit of its burden.

Woodrow said shortly, "Still breathing."

"Bring him into the surgery."

The next few minutes proved anxious and terrifying. The boys laid Liam on the examination couch even as Georgina hurried in, exclaiming softly. Clara had to rein in her rising panic enough to assess her husband's condition.

He breathed, yes, but not much more. His eyes, half closed like those of a dead man, revealed slits of blue, and in the light she could see the number and severity of his wounds.

She laid her hands against his face and he jerked violently, as at the touch of lightning, but didn't wake. Heart thumping hard, she made an inspection. Bruises everywhere, along with abrasions—splayed across his chest, livid on his face, decorating both hands. But she soon discovered the worst of the injuries was to his head, where a gash oozed blood steadily, wetting the black hair.

"What happened?" she asked Dax as she gathered supplies.

The battered unit whirred and clacked, puffed a weak jet of steam, and began to power down. Clara could see that its right arm hung damaged. How had it managed to carry Liam home?

"Can't speak," Woodrow pointed out.

"I need to know what happened, who did this to him." Clara's hands trembled with her distress.

"We'll take the steamie to the workroom," Fred offered, "and see if we can patch him up enough to restart him."

The lads should be in their beds, Clara knew that well enough, but she nodded, and they went out, rolling Dax between them.

Softly, Georgina said, "I'll bring hot water."

And, just like that, Clara found herself alone with her husband, only the moonlight accompanying them in bars striped by the window blinds. Terror rose and nearly choked her. What would she do if she lost him? Panic beat at her, fierce and bright, bringing a wall of devastation. She simply wouldn't be able to go on.

She loved her husband.

The thought appeared clear and whole in her mind. A mad premise, and one from which she should have protected herself. She knew better. He was the last kind of man to whom she should make herself vulnerable. But she loved him all the same.

With a sob, and on a veritable storm of emotion, she leaned down and put her mouth on his.

And just as the last time, it felt like pure magic. Her lips fit his, her heart did, and her spirit.

This time she did not need to give him breath—he still had his own. This time she needed to give him her love.

140

His lips parted beneath hers; her tongue slipped into his mouth. His hands came up and cradled her face.

Liam. She exhaled his name, and he caught the breath and returned it to her. *Clara.*

She began to pull away then, but he prevented it. His hands slid to the back of her head and he drew her closer, kissed her more deeply, and she melted into him, helpless.

Things began to get very warm indeed before the door behind Clara clicked open.

"Oh!" Georgina sounded startled. "He's come to, then?"

Clara withdrew from Liam's embrace, though it hurt physically to do so. She met Georgina's embarrassed gaze.

"Er—would you like me to—" Georgina gestured at the door with the basin she carried.

"No. We'd better patch up this wound on his head."

Liam attempted to sit up, grimaced, and subsided back onto the couch.

"What happened?" he asked.

"I was hoping you'd be able to tell me that. Dax brought you home." Clara swallowed the reproaches she wanted to voice about him having left her in the night.

"Wait. It's coming back to me." Again he tried to sit up and made it this time, though he paled drastically. "Ah—my head. I remember now. The mechanical doorman clubbed me."

"Mechanical doorman?"

"From Sterling House. There were two of them—came after me. Cornered me up against a wall. You say

Dax was there? I don't remember that part."

"He came home carrying you." When had Dax become a "he" rather than an "it"?

"Let me speak to him."

"Not right now. He's damaged, and the lads are working on him. Let's see that head."

The next few minutes were unpleasant for everyone concerned. Liam swore woefully as Clara examined the cut on his scalp, sponged the blood from his hair, and gave him several stitches.

"Now," she said when she had finished and stood washing her hands. "I want an explanation."

Georgina slipped quietly from the room.

Clara fixed her husband with a hard stare. "And don't bother lying to me. Admit the truth—you went out last night looking for vengeance."

Chapter Nineteen

"If you already know the answer, why ask?" Liam wondered disagreeably. He hurt all over, some places far more than others, and still tingled from that kiss they'd exchanged—some places more than others.

He eyed his wife, trying to gauge her mood. She looked like an enraged pixie, greenish eyes wide and distressed, hair still messed from her bed. Just that word—*bed*—in conjunction with her had his cock interested, but he sought mightily to disregard it.

"This is because of what Ruella told you, isn't it? You went out looking for retribution."

"No." Retribution would take some planning and, obviously, greater care than he'd employed this night. "I just wanted to get a look at the man who murdered me." He slid off the examination couch and paced the floor. "Do you know what it's like not even remembering the face of the bastard who took my life?"

Clara backed off a step. "And did you see him?"

"I did." Liam stopped pacing. "And he saw me—and sent his mechanical henchmen after me."

"He recognized you, then."

"Oh, aye."

Clara drew a breath, and her gaze burned on his. "So if Dax hadn't turned up, you'd have ended up in the river after all."

Liam didn't know what to say. He could sense her

emotions surging, anger and a whole lot more he couldn't quite bring himself to identify. And she was right, damn it.

He reached out almost gingerly and caught her shoulders between his hands. She stiffened when he touched her; he knew she would not be easily mollified.

"Clara, I know what I did was risky."

"Risky? It was suicidal!"

"Reckless, perhaps. But what would you have me do? The man's after murdering people for his own gain. My countrymen. Am I supposed to turn a blind eye to that?"

She stiffened further; her chin came up. "And what about me?"

"Eh?"

"No, you didn't give me or my situation a thought, did you? You didn't consider the risks I'm taking in this or how much rests on the success of this charade we play."

Charade? Was that all it meant to her—their marriage, their partnership? Was his presence in her bed just a temporary measure till her grandfather's demands were met? What would happen then to the ties he felt binding him to her? Would she dismiss him, cast him off?

His entire being protested it. Without her, he would be lost—far more so than when he'd awakened on her worktable with nothing.

He doubted he'd ever been a humble man, but he knew he'd get on his knees and beg her now, if it meant she'd let him stay.

"I am that sorry," he told her. "I did not think on that part of it."

"You do realize you may have scuttled our plans? We won't know till Dax is operable whether he was followed bringing you back here."

"Aye, and what can Maynard do? He's not likely to admit he's seen the ghost of a man he murdered."

"To whom must he admit it? He's capable of coming after you in secret. You've endangered this entire household—Georgina and the children."

"Nay, but listen—I know his motive now. That place, Sterling House, it's a den of iniquity. There's a bare-breasted girl in the bar, and Maynard was involved in a high-stakes poker game when I arrived."

"What did you say?"

"Heaps of money on the table. It explains why he's after lining his pockets, don't you see? He must be desperate for the green and living well above his means."

Clara's eyes blazed. "Bare-breasted?"

Liam's brain belatedly caught up with his tongue. "Aye, so she was. Decadent sort of place, as I say, the sort a man couldn't resist—"

"So, you can't resist a pair of naked breasts?"

Liam doubted many red-blooded men could, but he wasn't quite foolish enough to say it. He began to think it would be harder than he'd expected to beguile his wife.

"Ah, now," he dropped his voice, "she was there. I had to look. But," he added with absolute veracity, "she wasn't a patch on you."

"Get away from me." She flung his hands from her shoulders and turned from him. "I should have known."

"Known what? Clara, lass, look at me."

"It's no use crooning at me in that accent of yours,

or making false compliments."

"False? You must know what you do to me." He melted in her arms, combusted almost instantly when she looked at him.

She walked to the window, where she stood rigid, gazing out at nothing. "I thought I did. But it becomes apparent that charm is a deceptive commodity. And you have charm in spades."

"So, you're after calling me deceptive?" Liam's voice rose. "I have not been anything but honest with you, as honest as a man with no past can be."

"Were you honest when you crept from my bed?"

"Well—"

"How do I know anything you have said is honest?" She did whirl to face him then, her stare accusing and her eyes disconcertingly filled with tears. "Yes, I should have known."

Liam swallowed hard. "Known what?"

"That a man like you"—her gaze swept him head to foot—"could have no use for a woman like me."

Liam felt as if he'd been punched in the gut, all the breath knocked from him. If she failed to believe him, then what had it meant all those times he'd rocked her in his arms and whispered in her ear? Through stiff lips he asked, "And what are you like, then?"

She waved her hands in a comprehensive gesture. "Look at me! I'm no beauty. Absolutely nothing to recommend me. I've never cared about my appearance." *Until now*. But those words remained unsaid.

Liam wondered how to convince her she was wrong. "Listen, Clara, what I did last night—creeping away—had nothing to do with you or how much I desire you. Christ! I should think that would be plain to see; I'm fully raised every time I'm near you."

She looked away, her face tight. "I would appreciate it if you do not betray my trust again."

"You don't believe me."

"Not for my sake but for those beneath my roof, for whom I'm responsible. The only point of this farcical marriage was to provide for them. Until Theodore has had a chance to finalize the legal details, I'd rather you didn't leave this house. Once the terms have been satisfied—"

"What then?" he prompted, both head and heart pounding.

"We will dissolve the marriage, and you'll be free to go and pursue whatever revenge you choose."

Liam's mouth went dry. "That's what you want, to be shed of me?"

Still she did not look at him but stared away to the window, her face set. "That's what was always intended."

"Aye but—what of what we've been to each other?"

"And what is that?"

He said hoarsely, "Lovers."

She did look at him then, her gaze a raised weapon. "We are not lovers, Mr. McMahon."

"We sure as hell are."

"Just because we have had physical relations, that does not make us *lovers*. Lovers, in fact, care for one another. They *love*. What you and I have shared is a certain amount of pleasure, no more."

"No more?" he echoed like a damned parrot. He felt suddenly, hopelessly, at sea without a clue how to

Laura Strickland

deal with her. "That's all I've been to you? A fecking dildo?"

"Can I have your promise you won't leave this house again before the legal details are secured? It shouldn't be more than a few days."

"Why bother to ask for my promise, if my word means nothing to you?"

"I would hate to have to lock you in the cellar again."

He squared up. "I would like to see you try."

"You're right, of course. I won't appeal to you on my behalf. But for the sake of those in my care—?"

"I'll go nowhere, since you ask."

"Fine, then. I'll send word at once to Theodore. Until we part ways, I think it best if I move back to my old room."

He did want to fall down then, it hit him so hard.

"Ah, now, Clara, you don't want to do that. I'm sorry I upset you, lass—"

"Hold the blarney. It has no effect on me."

She lied. Something affected her—either him or her own anger; her normally alabaster skin had flushed, and her eyes glittered.

He drew another ragged breath. "Look, Clara— you're right, I never should have gone off that way. It was fecking boneheaded. But it's not been easy, this, taking up a life when I can remember nothing, and it hit me hard that the bastard, Maynard, is still doing the same thing to others and getting away with it. But don't pull away from me. If you do, I'll have nothing."

In answer, she slipped past him and out the door, shutting it firmly in her wake.

Chapter Twenty

Clara's head ached unbearably, but not so much as her heart. She'd arisen from her solitary bed at dawn after a sleepless night and tiptoed out to the door of her father's bedroom—Liam's now—where she stood listening intently. Was he inside? Had he left her after their quarrel, perhaps for good? She stood for an untold number of heartbeats, breath caught, until she heard him stir in the bed, and then stole away.

All through breakfast, getting the children fed and started on their day, and the arrival of Cassie, her mood did not improve. Nor did her husband put in an appearance. She could only assume he remained in the big upstairs bedroom, languishing in the bed, where she ached to be.

At length she sat in the parlor, with Cassie gathered in her lap and clinging like a barnacle. She'd thought contact with the child, who sought her out so determinedly, might help fill the terrible emptiness inside, but somehow it just seemed to emphasize Liam's absence.

She heard the peal of the front doorbell and Georgina's quick steps going in answer. That would be Theodore coming to discuss the legal situation and pave the way for the dissolution of her marriage.

But, though Clara could hear Theodore and Georgina talking together in soft murmurs, Georgina did not announce the attorney.

Curiosity got Clara to her feet with Cassie still in her arms. She crossed to the door, where she opened it a scarce inch and stood listening shamelessly.

"You know it's impossible." Georgina's voice was low and full of certainty.

"Why? I've confessed how I feel—"

Georgina interrupted him. "A thousand reasons. Do I need to number them? You're a smart man."

"Please, Georgie, look at me." Clara had never heard that note in Theodore's voice. "Tell me what you truly feel about me, because I don't think I can go on this way."

Sympathy clutched at Clara's heart. She'd known for some time these two felt an attraction. And she understood all too well Georgina's reasons for refusing to act on it.

"Don't be a fool," Georgina said now. "You want me to look at you? Better you look at me! Only look at the difference between us."

Theodore's voice dropped and throbbed. "I'm a man and you're a woman."

"A black woman. A former servant, living on charity, no education to speak of."

"You're wise and compassionate, the very definition of a gentlewoman."

"I'm not part of your class or your world."

"I don't care. Georgie, darling girl, I love you."

"Don't say that!"

"Should I keep it bottled up inside? I don't think I can much longer. Do you think I care about the ridiculous demands of society?"

"It's impossible, Theodore."

"Why? We can move, start over somewhere else."

"In case you've forgotten, you're engaged to be married."

Those words silenced Theodore as effectively as a blow from a sledgehammer. It took a long moment before he said, "You know I didn't choose that match."

"No, it was chosen for you by your family. You think they'd be happy to welcome me instead?"

"I don't care," Theodore said again.

"Well, I do. Leave me some self-respect. I've no wish to be the 'dirty darkie' you dragged in off the street, your little bit on the side."

"You're none of that."

"It's what they'd call me."

Another silence fell while Theodore apparently struggled with that unpalatable truth. "Ideas like that need to change," he said then. "The world needs to change."

"Perhaps someday people will be allowed to be together on the strength of the feelings in their hearts," Georgina conceded, "but not yet. It's only fifteen years since the end of the war. My people are not much more welcome here in the north than back down south."

"So we'll go to Canada, to Toronto."

Georgina's voice softened. "Would you do that for me? Give up your home and career?"

"In an instant."

"But if I care for you, how can I possibly ask that?"

So swiftly Clara had no time to step away, Georgina made for the parlor door and flung it open, catching her in mid-eavesdrop. Georgina's dark eyes were wide and full of pain.

"Mr. Collwys," she announced briefly, and fled in

the direction of the kitchen.

Theodore met Clara's eyes ruefully. "I suppose you heard all that."

"Come on in."

Juggling the child in her arms, Clara swung the door wide. Theodore entered and shut it carefully behind him. He then sank onto the settee and put his head in his hands, pushing his fingers through his sandy hair.

"I didn't handle that very well, did I? How in hell am I to convince her I need her in my life?"

"Breaking off your engagement might help, for starters."

"I will. I fully intend to. But it will make such a damned hullaballoo in my family. Roanne's the daughter of my father's closest colleague."

"And Georgina's the daughter of a former slave who gave her own life to buy Georgina a better chance—which didn't start out much better than what they knew in Georgia. You know what she suffered in that household where she worked, she and Jimmie both."

"Yes, I know. And if Georgina would just give me an assurance we'll be together, I wouldn't hesitate to tear the rest of my life up by the roots. But what's the point if she won't have me either way?"

"The point is that she has to see you put her first before she'll believe you love her. If you can't understand that, there's no hope for you."

"Why can't she just take my word for it?" Theodore raised a devastated face and looked at Clara. "Your Irishman seems to have no difficulty accepting that you want him."

"Do you think?" Clara stiffened and shifted Cassie, now sleeping, against her shoulder.

Theodore gave her a long look. "Ah, so it's that way, is it?"

"Let's just say we need to get the legal part of things settled as soon as possible so I can dissolve my marriage."

Theodore frowned. "I don't think it would be wise to hurry that. Your grandfather is no fool. If he suspects this marriage is a sham, he will be sure to challenge it in court."

The parlor door opened abruptly, and Liam came in. Even to Clara's prejudiced eyes he looked like hell—far worse than when she'd revived him from the dead—face pale and haggard, with visible bruises, and a bandage on his head. He shot Clara one burning glance before sauntering in with an attempt at his old nonchalance.

Theodore leaped to his feet and gave Liam a comprehensive look that took in his injuries before shooting Clara another stare. "Mr. McMahon." He held out his hand.

"Collwys. I assume this is a legal meeting. Am I not to be included in matters that affect my future?"

His blue gaze returned to Clara in a look so intense she could barely bring herself to meet it. What did she see in his eyes? And what did she feel streaming off him like heat from a kettle? Distress, agony, disappointment—betrayal. How dare he feel betrayed when he had abandoned her?

She said stiffly, "Had I thought you needed to be in attendance, I would have called you."

He grimaced. "But she is allowed to be in your

presence"—he nodded at Cassie—"as she craves."

That set Clara back on her heels. She understood Cassie felt a need created by the bond forged when Clara revived her. She had not paused to consider Liam might feel the same. Did that explain why the sex between them was so consuming? Did it explain also why he claimed to love her?

Nothing but a byproduct of the power that had called him back to life. It had nothing to do with her at all.

She knew by the disappointment that flooded her heart she'd retained a few shreds of hope that his feelings might be genuine. She swallowed the lump in her throat and said, "Sit in, by all means, if you choose."

Liam took a seat opposite her and Cassie.

Theodore cleared his throat. "What happened to you, Mr. McMahon, if I might ask?"

"A run-in with a couple of mechanical servants. I got the worse of it."

"Not Mr. Van Hamelin's mechanical servants, I hope. It would not be wise for you to be seen in the vicinity of his home."

"Not his, no."

"Let's get to business, please," Clara requested.

"Yes. Mr. McMahon, I was just telling Clara it would be unwise to hurry a dissolution of your marriage. Mr. Van Hamelin retains a posse of lawyers, most far more ruthless than I, who will jump on any suggestion your union was contrived and haul the matter into court. I would not be at all surprised if Mr. Van Hamelin has at least one judge in his pocket."

Liam shot another look at Clara. Was that triumph

she saw in his eyes?

"Very prudent thinking," he said. "No need to rush things on my account. I am content to stay put."

"And you, Clara?" Theodore queried.

She gave a grudging nod.

Clara had difficulty following the details as Theodore proceeded to lay out the rest of the legalese. Liam's presence distracted her, as did the way he kept looking at her with unhappy longing, each glance as tactile as a touch. Cassie's warm breath on her neck only served to emphasize the distance between them.

At last she said, "So if all goes well, we can expect the transference of the deed and the first settlement of funds within the month?"

"If all goes well," Theodore emphasized. "But we can afford no mistakes." He looked at Liam. "No more run-ins with mechanical servants."

"That's been made more than clear to me," Liam growled.

Theodore gathered up his papers and returned them to his attaché case. "I'll place the application for deed transfer before the court today and be in touch as soon as there's any news."

Clara nodded. Like any true master of the house, Liam got up to see Theodore to the door. She heard them speaking in low voices before Theodore went out, but she couldn't catch the words.

Liam returned and once more shut the parlor door behind him. "Put the child down, Clara."

"She needs—"

"She's sleeping and won't mind." Without waiting for her to comply, he lifted Cassie from Clara's arms and set her carefully where Theodore had been sitting.

Then he drew Clara to her feet by her hands, and fast into his arms.

"Don't do this to me, Clara," he said, his voice rumbling through his chest and into her ear. "Please don't."

Clara melted. Despite all her doubts, her annoyance with him, and her conviction that his feelings for her weren't genuine, she crumbled like wet plaster. She closed her eyes, pressed her cheek against his shoulder, and just absorbed the feel of him, while the tight knot inside her loosened.

"Whatever you may think of me, and however you might condemn me, I'm your husband. And you heard what Collwys said—we need to stay married a while and make it convincing." His words became a whisper, a croon. "I can't think of anything more convincing than you here in my arms."

"I'm sorry I ever got you involved in this."

"I'm not. And if you'll forgive me saying, that's a damned hurtful thing to say, like telling me you're sorry I'm alive."

"I did not mean that."

"That you're sorry I ever kissed you." His lips stole to her temple.

"No."

"Made love to you." They traveled down her cheek in the direction of her mouth.

Clara ached with want. She longed to raise her lips to his. More, she yearned for the feel of him hard between her legs and the wild abandon that took hold of her when they moved together. But one of them had to remain rational and sane.

"It's just that this is such an emotional tangle," she

began.

His mouth swallowed the rest of her words as his lips captured hers. Pleasure seared, sharp as pain, and reached right to Clara's soul, claiming her once again.

Please don't, she screamed in her mind, but it was too late because his tongue was in her mouth, searching deeply, and all at once she wanted this more than anything. Foolish, precipitous, unquestionably unwise, but she'd take him right here on the parlor rug if he asked.

He broke the kiss and said into her ear, brokenly, "One night apart from you was more than I could stand. Come upstairs with me. Now."

Clara's senses reeled. Already she could feel the weight and heft of him pressed against her. His hands slid up her back, stroking, and then around front to palm her breasts. She knew what he wanted. By God, she wanted it as well.

"Not a good idea," she managed to say.

"Why?"

"We're already much too—involved. And eventually there will have to be a parting of the ways."

He froze and then let go of her abruptly. The look in his eyes when Clara met them made her heart hurt.

"So you'll hold to that, will you? Dismiss me the way your grandfather dismissed Dax?"

Bitterly, his lips twisted. "Perhaps you're more like the old man than you think."

And he slammed from the parlor, not to return.

Chapter Twenty-One

"What do you think of him, miss? We've pounded out most of the dents, mended that arm, and made those repairs to his boiler. He's almost good as new."

Fred sounded proud of his work, and so he should, Clara thought, regarding Dax with amazement. The unit looked so fine she might not have recognized him as the same one that had struggled home with Liam.

"You've done a wonderful job, boys," she praised sincerely.

"More efficient now," Dax contributed, "no longer leak steam."

"He actually helped us," Woodrow put in. "Guided us a bit once we got to his inner workings."

The four of them stood in the entryway where they'd met. Three whole days had passed since Clara's encounter with Liam in the parlor. Estranged from him, she'd found the days difficult and the nights endless.

He had spent his time in his room or making himself useful around the house. As Clara had learned from Georgina, he had already climbed up and patched the exterior gutter work, fixed the back door which tended to swell and stick in damp weather, unblocked the kitchen flue, mended a faucet, and performed a dozen other small tasks. Whatever he had been in his past life, he'd obviously possessed a host of skills.

No sooner had he come to her mind than he

appeared. That, she acknowledged, seemed to happen a lot lately. Now he came down the main staircase focused not on her but on Dax.

"Got him refurbished, then, have you, lads? You've done a grand job."

Both boys glowed. Clara couldn't deny they shone in Liam's presence, sought his company and his approval, as was to be expected, she supposed. Lads their age required a strong male role model.

"Did they not, Clara?" Liam prompted.

"I was just about to say that. Dax is quite splendid."

"Dax splendid," the unit repeated. "High praise. Will be able to perform many more tasks now. Asset to household."

"Indeed, and you are," Clara confirmed.

"Just don't let old man Van Hamelin catch sight of you," Woodrow put in, "or he'll want you back."

"Dax go nowhere!" the unit intoned. "Dax *home*."

A startled silence fell. Clara raised an eyebrow at the boys. "Did you feed that into him?"

"No, we didn't alter his commands at all, just worked on the mechanics. What do you think it means?" Fred asked.

It meant Dax had an at least rudimentary sense of self, but Clara couldn't voice that; it seemed too absurd.

Instead she touched the unit on the arm. "You're staying with us," she told him.

"To be sure," Liam chimed in, "Mrs. McMahon keeps her possessions close, however she may or may not value them."

"Dax," Dax announced, "will shovel the new load of coal that arrived this morning."

"No, don't do that," Fred objected. "You'll spoil your shine. Come along of us, and we'll teach you some things."

The three disappeared to the back of the house; Clara and Liam remained standing alone together.

"Another load of coal," Clara fretted. "I don't know how we're going to pay for it."

"Have you considered sending me out to work? I could probably earn twice as much as those lads."

"No. You are supposed to be"—she waved a hand at him—"a gentleman." He did not look it. At the moment, with his collar wide open at the throat, eyes bright and hair tumbled over his forehead, he looked all rogue. One with whom she ached to go to bed. It was no wonder she couldn't sleep; she spent all her nighttime hours thinking about that, about *him*.

"I'm bored, Clara. I've little to do but think, and there's precious little in my head to think about. You want me to stay here shut in like a damned convalescent. You'll have to give me some way to occupy myself."

"I hadn't thought of that." Her days were so full with the children—especially Cassie—and the household, she hadn't considered how his must drag.

"Do you think of me at all?" He stepped closer and her breathing immediately hitched. "Do I mean anything more to you than that steamie?"

"Of course. Though I value Dax very highly—"

He stepped still closer; she promptly lost her train of thought.

"Clara, I can't stand this. Why won't you come to me at night, if only for the sake of my sanity? This feels like being starved by bits. Do you feel nothing, no want? No need?"

Did she feel nothing? She closed her eyes a moment against the intensity of emotion. He had to know some of what she felt, must feel it the way she gleaned the overflow of the turbulence he experienced.

"Liam, I am trying to protect myself, to protect both of us."

"How? By killing me over again? You must know how it feels, being denied your presence."

"You are not denied my presence. You can be in my company any time."

"Except at night, when I need you most, when I lie there with my sanity in shreds, straining to hold on to myself. You don't turn Cassie away. Why me?"

"You're much more dangerous." The words slipped from Clara before she could hold them back.

"Me, dangerous?" He widened those sky-blue eyes, and Clara's pulse sped up another notch.

She whispered, "Liam, please."

"That's better; ask nicely." His voice dropped still further. He reached out and caressed her cheek, a gentle touch that sent a shiver through her frame. "Where is everyone?"

"The lads, as you see, are busy with Dax."

"Aye?"

"Georgina has taken the rest of the children to chapel."

He leaned closer and his lips fumbled the curve of her ear. "God bless Georgina. And Cassie?"

"As it's Sunday, her mother's at home, and—"

"Ah, Sunday morning. I cannot imagine spending it better than in worship."

"Eh?"

"Of you."

His lips found hers then, and pleasure speared through her, effectively disengaging her brain. His tongue, wild and hungry, plundered her mouth, stole her breath and the last shreds of her self-control.

How had she thought she could live without this?

He broke the kiss long enough to whisper, "Come upstairs and let me worship you." Without waiting for a reply, he swept her up into his arms. She felt instantly light as thistledown and disconnected from reality. He bore her up the stairs and into not his but her old room, and her heart pounded all the way.

No, not here, she wanted to say. If he made love to her here, she would never be able to inhabit the place again without having him in her head.

She expected him to deposit her on the bed. Instead, he set her on her feet and then carefully shut the door and placed a chair under the knob. Next he drew the curtains, shutting out most of the daylight.

"Liam—"

"Hush." He approached her softly, as one might a wild creature. His hands came out and unfastened the leather corset she wore. She stood unmoving but breathing hard as his fingers loosened the hem of her shirt from the waistband of her trousers. He unbuttoned the shirt very slowly, letting it fall open as he worked his way down.

She wore nothing beneath. He drew the fabric down her arms and tossed it to the floor.

"God. Oh, God, Clara."

He sank to his knees precisely like a man at prayer and buried his face in her bosom. She wrapped her arms around him and held him there, where he trembled against her with the intensity of his emotion.

The last of Clara's resistance crumbled, and her bones turned to water—no, to molten, liquid fire. She felt his eyelashes tickle the skin of her breast and then his lips move, seeking. He latched on, and the sheer pleasure of it almost knocked her down.

She stood there in the dim room as any hope of rationality flew away from her and she realized in full her danger. For she felt at once wild and wanton, tethered only to him.

She moaned as his hot, wet mouth abandoned her first breast for her second. She tangled her fingers in his thick, dark hair, and he gave a gusty laugh.

"Like that, do you? Then why do you deny me? Why, precious girl, make both of us suffer? No—don't pull away. Only stand there and let me finish worshipping you."

Stand she did, trembling in every limb, and worship he did, still on his knees and fully clothed while he lavished her with the attentions of lips and tongue, leaving both her breasts wet and tight, and working downward. When his fingers untied the laces on her trousers, she caught her breath.

"Liam—"

"Don't you dare stop me now. If I don't have a taste of you, I'll die all over again."

Couldn't have that, not when she'd spent so much energy raising him. Utterly shameless now, she stood with the cool air of the room pricking her breasts while he stripped the trousers from her and rendered her completely naked and utterly open to him.

Then he began to worship her all over again, pressed kisses all down her legs, onto her ankles, and up again until she quivered like piano wire. By the time she felt his warm breath between her thighs, she would have offered herself to him in public if need be.

He did not have to ask her to open for him. The instant his hands curled round her thighs and eased them apart, she arched into his tongue. And she stood trembling, consumed by fire, while his mouth plundered her into waves of pleasure that seemed to go on and on.

When at last it ended in a brilliant burst of light, he caught her so she wouldn't fall down. Breathing hard, he pressed his face against her stomach.

"Lovely girl, beautiful girl." His breath gusted against her skin when he spoke. "I cannot live without that, without you. Please don't make me try."

Some hard knob of resistance within Clara melted. She did not know who he was—from what life he had come—but they belonged together. "No," she said.

"No?" He tipped his head and looked up at her, his eyes full of light.

"No, I won't deny you again."

"Thank God."

She caressed his hair as she might that of a child, though the feelings burgeoning inside her had nothing childlike about them. "You will need to be eased," she said then. "Let me."

Without another word she slid down through his arms onto the carpet in silent offering. Already she felt her desire for him spark again. She lay on the floor of the room that had been hers since birth and watched while he stripped the clothes from his body, marveling that he could be hers.

But he was, he was.

Then he covered her nakedness with his flesh—hot, burning, ready. His tongue entered her mouth an instant before he plunged into her, where he belonged.

Sanity returned slowly, gentle as the light in the room. He had not withdrawn and remained still inside her. She lay with her arms wrapped around him and his breath gusting against her neck.

"Clara, say it once more, promise you'll never deny me again."

"I promise," she whispered, "I'll never deny you again."

Chapter Twenty-Two

"Clara, some troubling details about Liam have come to light," Theodore said. "Your grandfather's attorneys unearthed the record of a William McMahon arrested for assault last month and taken to the county jail on Delaware. They've also uncovered notations of a man by the same name who entered this country from Canada, via Niagara Falls."

"Impossible," Clara breathed. She had agreed to meet with Theodore in her father's surgery, fully expecting good news from him regarding her finances. Instead, it seemed her grandfather had decided to investigate the legitimacy of her marriage before signing the papers that would bestow her mother's inheritance.

Theodore gave her a serious look. "Didn't you say your husband had lived in Canada, in Montreal? Admittedly, you have not given me much information about him, but I was under the impression he's connected with one of your father's colleagues."

"Yes."

"And he did live in Montreal?"

"For a time." But, Clara thought desperately, William McMahon was just a name they had made up. Or was it? She had chosen *William*, true, and it was common enough. But Liam had come up with *McMahon* off the top of his head, so she'd supposed.

166

Could it have been a memory surfacing?

She asked cautiously, "What else did my grandfather's attorneys discover?"

"I've been able to learn only the bare bones of what they claim, but it is not good, and they're insisting upon withholding finalization of the paperwork for the present. I've sent my own man to find out what he can. Meanwhile, there is indeed a record of a McMahon, first initial W, arrested on October eighteenth, but he never appeared before a judge and, though he's still on the jail books, they're claiming he served his sentence and was released."

"Ah. Wouldn't he have appeared, if he was arrested for assault?"

"The warden—a man named Maynard—claims the charges were reduced to drunk and disorderly when the other party refused to press for injuries."

"I see."

"It seems we'll have to discuss this with your husband. Is he in?"

"Umm—I think he's busy with something."

Inconveniently, Liam appeared then, opening the door and leaning in, his dark hair ruffled. Not half an hour ago, Clara had been busy running her fingers through that hair, and elsewhere on his body.

"Ah," Theodore said, "just the man we need." He got to his feet and extended a hand. "Morning, McMahon."

"Is there a problem?" Liam swept Clara with a look. He could read her all too well.

"Nothing we can't work out, I hope," Theodore told him. "However, we have run into a sizeable snag with the legal side of things. Please sit down."

With another questioning look for Clara, Liam complied. Though he took the chair across from her, she could feel him acutely, feel his need pull at her along with his desire.

"I'd like you to give me some details about your background," Theodore began at once. "You are William T. McMahon, lately of Montreal?"

Stiffly, Liam nodded.

"And before that"—Theodore consulted a paper—"of Dublin, Ireland?"

"Sounds about right." Whatever else he might conceal, he couldn't hide his Irishness.

"Your name has been found on a passenger manifest traveling from the port of Galway to St. John's, Newfoundland in April of 1877. Does that sound correct? Occupation listed," Theodore hesitated marginally, "laborer."

"That may have been me."

Theodore fixed him with a hard stare. "Traveling, so it says here, with your wife and infant son."

****

Clara gasped. Liam turned his eyes on her and beheld the shock in her face, the panic and pain. His head pounded in big, sickening thuds that kept time with his heartbeat as if it flailed against the great, black wall in his mind. Had the wall begun to crumble, or was it just his imagination?

I don't remember. But he couldn't say that to Collwys. A wife and son? How could even death make him forget?

The surgery door opened, and Dax steamed in carrying a tea tray and looking proud of himself.

"Tea, Mistress, Master?"

168

"Thank you, Dax. Just put it down." Clara's voice sounded faint and far away. The tea service clattered onto the table, and the scent of tea assaulted Liam's nostrils; suddenly he feared he'd vomit.

"That has to be a mistake," he told Collwys, forcing the words out. "An error on the manifest."

"You've never been married, then?" Theodore eyed him closely. "Because that would scuttle Clara's chances of attaining her inheritance. I assume you're Catholic, and there's no such thing as divorce."

"Ah—"

The pain in Liam's head became blinding. A wife. The name "Nancy" appeared in his mind. Nancy McMahon. Oh, sweet Jesus. And a son. Thomas Tyrone McMahon.

"'McMahon' is such a common name," Clara put in, "as is 'William.' And obviously my husband cannot be the same McMahon who was in the county jail. He's no brawler, but the son of an upstanding gentleman of business who immigrated to Montreal."

Again Theodore looked at Liam doubtfully. "I'm afraid that's not how your grandfather's attorneys see it. They're attempting to create doubt any way they can."

"Clearly a confusion, or bad recordkeeping at the jail," Liam insisted. "Something very much amiss there. Should be investigated."

"You may be right. Their records are a mess. There seems to be a veritable confusion of prisoners coming in and out."

"Check into that, then. I'm sure the rest of it is just a case of another fellow, besides myself, called McMahon."

"But you did say you arrived via St. John's in the

Republic of Newfoundland?"

St. John's. A deep harbor cradled between two arms of rock and a narrows leading to the sea, and home. Liam rubbed his forehead fitfully.

"Liam?" Clara whispered.

He looked up at Collwys. "That can't be me, though, can it? Not if there's a wife and son."

"Right. Can you give me the date you did leave Ireland? We'll investigate further. If we can find you on another manifest, it will call Mr. Van Hamelin's findings into question."

"Uh—my father and I lived in Montreal for some time. That was how Clara's father knew us, see. He and my father were acquainted during their university days long ago. But I went back and forth to Ireland frequently, visiting relations. I don't recall precise dates." That surely made a reasonable explanation. "I thought I made a trip in August of '77, but it may have been the other way round, sailing to Dublin once the good weather came."

"I see. And your address in Montreal? The location of your father's business?"

"I can get you that," Clara said. "It will be in father's records somewhere."

"Certainly Mr. McMahon remembers," Collwys' eyes had narrowed now. "He's only lately arrived."

"After my father's death, I moved around quite a bit, stayed with friends. I had no fixed address of my own."

"Perhaps you'll be so kind as to make a list of these friends and their situations. If they can verify your identity, we can bring them in as character witnesses."

In deeper and deeper. Liam gave Clara a helpless

glance.

"Look," Clara said to Theodore, "things may not be what they seem." She reached out and laid her fingers on the lawyer's wrist. Despite his current state, Liam bristled, unable to tolerate the idea of her so much as touching another man. "I can trust you, can't I, Theodore? For my sake—for Georgina's?"

"You know you can."

Clara said to Liam, "We'll have to tell him the truth."

"Nay."

"There's no other option. We need his help."

Liam bowed his head into his hands. He sat in silence while Clara said, "Theodore, Liam is the man who was in the county jail. He knew my father, had come to him for care once after a brawl. He came here looking for my father again, not knowing he was dead, and I... Well, I was desperate and enlisted his help."

Tersely, Theodore said, "You enlisted the help of a criminal, a felon?"

"I was only in for brawling," Liam said defensively, playing along. "Nothing so terrible."

"Assault," Theodore asserted, without looking at him. "Clara, this is disastrous." He threw his hands in the air. "I assume the two of you made some kind of deal. If so, I say cut your losses now. Pay him off and send him out of Buffalo at once. If you need to borrow money, I can advance you some."

"No." Liam surged to his feet. "We're married."

Collwys did look at him then. "What good can you do for Clara? For all we know, you're a God-damned bigamist. There are a lot of Irish in Boston, so I suggest—"

Liam stepped forward and loomed over the lawyer. "No one sends me away from her, understand?"

To his surprise, Collwys neither shrank nor flinched. Instead he sneered, "Here's the thug coming out—the vagrant hauled away for assault." He looked at Clara. "You've done yourself an enormous amount of damage."

Liam stepped back quickly, as if slapped.

Sounding badly shaken, Clara said, "Theodore, you don't understand. It's more than just a bargain between us now."

Collwys, whose wits moved very quickly indeed, said, "I suppose you've actually taken him into your bed."

"Yes. But our relationship far surpasses the physical—"

"Please spare me the details." Collwys began gathering up his papers. "I don't need to imagine this wastrel from the gutter crawling over you."

"He's not from the gutter."

"Jail, then. Clara, I know how desperate you were, none better. But you've made a grave mistake this time."

"Perhaps not."

"You know virtually nothing about him. He may well be married. What does that do to the contract with your grandfather?"

"We'll think of something." She caught Collwys' arm. "Promise you won't betray us."

"You know I won't. You can believe I'll continue trying to help you, if only for Georgina's sake."

"Thank you."

"But Clara, you've put me in an untenable

position."

"I have. I'm sorry. But it's done now."

"You're wrong there." Collwys glared first into her face and then Liam's. "The trouble has only just begun."

Chapter Twenty-Three

"What is it? Can't you sleep?" Clara's voice came at Liam out of the dark. She rolled over in bed and slid her hand up his naked chest. The room, full of soft darkness, was very quiet, but that did little to soothe the mayhem in Liam's mind.

"I cannot. My head hurts."

Clara sat up and reached for the lamp. "Let me go get you a draught. There are still some remedies left in the surgery."

"Don't go." He caught both her hands in his. When she remained near him, he could breathe. Her hands felt so small in his; she seemed so tiny to be his whole world.

"I am sorry," he blurted. "I am a disappointment to you. More, I am a liability—as Collwys said."

"Theodore was worried and upset. He'll come round. He knows what it is to love in what others might call the wrong place."

Liam could think of many replies to that, but one chose itself. "Are you saying you love me?"

"I hardly know." She sat there regarding him in the dim radiance of the lamp, her brown hair ruffled around her face. "It feels too wild to be love, too strong, too insistent."

He clasped her hands tighter. "I love you. And I need you desperately. In order to keep living."

Very gently indeed she told him, "We have spoken of this before. What you feel may only be a side effect of the resurrection."

"Aye, because you're so damned unlovable." He released one of her hands, but only to stroke her face. "That's what you insist. But if you could see yourself through my eyes, you'd change your mind."

She turned her head and he felt her lips press into his palm. His heartbeat sped up as it so often did when she touched him.

"Liam, do you think you remembered the name McMahon from your past? Was it, in fact, your name?"

"How can I tell? I thought I snatched it out of the air, but I cannot say for sure."

Her eyes met his, distressed and questioning. "Can you remember anything else?"

He shook his head. "Very little. There's still this great, fecking black wall in my mind. Sometimes I get images—flashes of things. I can't tell if they come from behind it or not."

"Images of a wife? And a son?"

He'd remembered the name *Thomas Tyrone McMahon* at the mention of an infant son, but he dared not tell her that. He shook his head again.

She bit her lip. "Is it possible you are the William McMahon on the manifest my grandfather's lawyers located?"

"I hope not, lass."

Very gently she drew her fingers from his and turned her face away. Her profile looked delicate against the radiance from the lamp.

"So our marriage may be a lie. Well, it was always meant to be a lie, wasn't it?" She admitted bitterly,

"That's what I get for daring such a great and terrible deception."

"Clara, lass, if I've a wife and child, where are they?"

She shrugged. "Living down on the waterfront, or in the streets south of Niagara Square, where most of the Irish have settled. Wondering why you haven't come home. My God, Liam—what if the poor woman thinks you're dead? And here you are in bed with me."

"Stop with torturing yourself. You don't even know the 'poor woman' exists."

"I need to find out, Liam. I need to know the truth. I will ask Theodore to investigate thoroughly."

"I'll bet he intends to. He'd like nothing better than to turn me away out of here."

"If he locates your wife and child, well, they'll need you." Her voice trembled. "I'll have to give you up to them."

Say you need me—he thought in desperation—*and I'll abandon whomever I must.* Instead it seemed he would just draw more difficulty down upon her. Maybe Collwys was right—he should do her a favor and slope off.

"Only say the word, if you want me to go."

She did look at him then, examined him closely, from the hair tumbled over his forehead to his bare chest, lingering overlong on his lips. "God help me, I don't. But I warn you, Liam, if your wife turns up, this alliance between us must end."

****

"I need you to do me a favor, if you will. Trouble is, I don't know how you'll accomplish it."

Clara looked at Ruella where she stood full in the

sunlight pouring through the parlor windows. The woman wore a pair of men's overalls and a red-and-white checkered shirt with the sleeves rolled up to reveal her brawny forearms. Her brown hair, gathered in two bunches at the sides of her head, made her look like a Toby jug version of a mastiff.

"Leave the ways and means to me, Miss Clara. Only name what you need."

"Is there any way you can get a look at the prison records? I need to know Liam's real name."

Ruella pursed her lips and widened her protuberant blue eyes. "Well, now, that might be a steep order. Records, if there are any, would be either in Maynard's office or in the main day room. I might find some excuse to visit the day room, say, if I brought round something for the lads to eat, but Maynard's office? Never."

"What kind of arrest records might exist?"

"In an ideal world, every arresting officer is supposed to write up a report. With the way things are there now, who knows? Even if a report was made when your man was brought in, it may have been destroyed—or altered—when they hanged him."

"They must have him on the books, though, if they're charging the county for him."

"Maynard is playing some daft game. A proper kettle of stinking herring, innit? Anyway, miss, I don't see as how I could get near any such paperwork even if it did exist."

"What we need is a friend on the police force, someone willing to help us."

"Well now, I might know just the fellow. One of our most zealous coppers, he is—the one who brings most of the prisoners in to jail. Big, strapping lad. And get this—he's Irish."

"You, Ruella, friendly with an Irishman?"

She shrugged. "It's different here than back home, innit?"

"Do you think you can persuade him to help us without saying why?"

"I might. The lad has a weakness for me scones."

Clara reached out and touched Ruella's arm. "See what you can do, please. It's vital to me. My grandfather's investigators have discovered a man they're insisting is Liam. They claim he's married, with a son."

"Crikey! That's not good news."

"Far from it. If they can prove my marriage is a sham, we'll all be out on the street and Liam probably locked up for bigamy."

"I'll see what I and young Fagan can do. But I wouldn't pin too much hope on it, miss." Ruella hesitated and then asked, "Might be better just to send him on his way, mightn't it? I mean, for his sake—before he gets caught."

"I hadn't considered that." Much struck, Clara did so now. Since the start of all this she had given Liam far too little consideration. He'd been an anonymous weight of dead flesh when Ruella brought him. Clara hadn't truly paused to imagine how it would feel for a man brought back to life without a past, and with little to which he might cling. She'd thought of him as a temporary convenience, someone she might use as she now used Dax to perform tasks. But it became evident Liam possessed feelings in plenty, and she possessed feelings for him. She had to provide him some peace, but for the life of her she didn't know where that lay.

Surely not in separation from her.

"Just, please, bring me what information you can, Ruella. You've never failed me. I know you won't now."

"I'll do my best, miss. And you take care. No sense you getting too attached to him now, under the circumstances."

"You're perfectly right," Clara said. But it was far too late for such sense and caution.

Chapter Twenty-Four

Liam thrashed wildly, caught in a dream of fire and darkness. The inky black of an early spring night it was, in a place he knew—familiar yet now full of terror and discord. He stood surrounded by the pulsing night while flames rose like the tower of a bonfire and lit the scene.

Garish, bright, destructive radiance, and someone screaming, "Tommy, Tommy, Tommy—" A woman's voice, and then that of a man beside him, so close it made Liam jump.

"Never say he's in there still? I'll get him out."

"Nay—" Liam tried to seize the arm of the man at his side, someone dear to him, he felt sure, but missed as his companion raced toward the flames, nothing but a dark silhouette bent upon sacrifice.

And a woman stood there also—his flailing mind supplied a name, *Nancy*. She waved her arms as Liam's companion pelted past her into the fire.

Leaden steps took Liam forward to where the woman stood and the impossible heat beat at him.

"Nancy," he said.

She looked at him. Her wide eyes reflected the madness of the flames, and dark patches marred her milk-white skin. He realized, with a sick twist of his stomach, those marks were burns.

"Tommy's inside?" he barked. Tommy, no more than six months old, the smallest McMahon.

"In his cot."

The child would never survive.

No sooner did that thought possess Liam's mind than Nancy clutched his arm with both hands. "'Twas an accident," she wept. "I was angry, but I never meant—"

"Never mind that now." Liam denied the rage that flared inside him, hotter than the flames. Foolish woman! Could she not be trusted to watch her own child and keep him safe? But nay, all that mattered now was the child inside and the heroism of the man who'd run in after him.

If only Liam could remember his name.

He came awake even as the black wall crashed down in his mind, shutting away the bright and terrible scene. He lay in the quiet of his bedroom, flat on his back, like a dead man, and concentrated on just breathing. What had that been? A scene from his past, unquestionably—a memory. A communication from beyond the barrier death had left in his mind.

A woman called Nancy. His wife? And an infant son.

He drew another shuddering breath, this one deep. But then who was the man who had run into that conflagration? And had he come out again with the child, alive or dead?

The child must have survived, if the manifest old man Van Hamelin's lawyers had turned up contained any veracity. They said he had traveled with his wife and infant son.

From Dublin, via Galway.

Yet he knew to his heart the scene he had just witnessed had taken place somewhere out in the countryside, at a place he both knew and loved.

No matter, he told himself sternly. If this memory had returned to him, surely more would come.

And that meant he had to tell Clara.

At the thought of her he reached out in the bed, but encountered only empty bedclothes. He started up, a sick feeling gripping him.

He saw her at once. She stood at the bedroom window gazing out, motionless as a woman carved from alabaster. Only the faintest radiance filtered in, making a soft nimbus of her ruffled hair and rendering opaque the simple white nightgown she wore.

Liam's heart clenched. What if it all proved true? What if he had a wife, a son, other claims upon him? He believed Clara when she said she would end it with him. But if she did, he would never survive.

He rose softly and went to her where she stood, enveloped her body with his from behind, and looked where she did. Outside, dawn filtered over the streets and rooftops from the east, flowing toward the river. All lay gray and quiet, nearly formless save for roof slopes and chimney pots, the lines that denoted streets. For what could she possibly look?

He wrapped his arms tight around her and she tensed for a moment before relaxing against him. She felt so small and fragile to contain his whole world. He bent his head and nuzzled her ear, just for the way it made him feel.

"What are you doing up? You're chilled to the bone. Here, let me warm you."

She said nothing, merely continued to gaze at whatever she saw. But he could feel the discord inside her, like lead in her heart.

The light outside strengthened, fluid as music. A figure appeared in Virginia Street, a hawker with a cart.

"Come back to bed," Liam persuaded. "'Tis no good standing here in your bare feet."

"Did you ever wonder if any of it is real?" she asked, and her voice traveled through him the way pleasure did when he loved her. "Maybe it's all just a dream."

Dream. The word echoed in Liam's mind. Did he even have to tell her? Did she somehow know?

"If I'm to live a dream," he told her, heartfelt, "I want it to be this one, with you." He ran the palms of his hands up her body, felt easily through the thin material of her gown. Her emotions kicked through him, and when he reached her breasts he paused to cup them. She leaned back into him then, but didn't stop gazing.

"Blarney," she said.

He didn't like that response. "You think that all it is?"

"You have a magic tongue and magic hands—whoever you are."

Ah, so that was what rode her, was it?

He found her nipples with his thumbs and stroked them. Into her ear he crooned, "I am the man who needs you in order to live. You didn't bargain on that when you brought me back to life, did you? That it wouldn't be enough to breathe the revival into me—you'd have to keep feeding it to me with your presence."

"I did not."

"Do you want shed of me, Clara? Do you?"

She sighed. Both her nipples now stood at attention, ripe for plucking. For him, only for him.

"No, I don't want rid of you. But I'm wondering just how selfish I can be."

"Selfish?"

"As you just pointed out, I barely considered you before I began this. I thought it nothing to use you—a man with a blank slate for a mind—as I needed. Except you weren't blank, were you? Not quite. And now you have a past following you, and I—"

"You?" he prompted.

She began to tremble. "I want you so very badly. What a tangle."

It was, that.

She said abruptly, "Ruella thinks I should send you away before you're arrested for bigamy or fraud."

"Damn Ruella." He pressed his warm mouth to the cool skin of her neck, just the place he knew she liked. God, but he needed the taste of her. "I'm going nowhere."

"I should perhaps cut my losses before it all comes crashing down. Vacate the house before we're thrown out, find smaller quarters. The lads are earning a fair wage. Georgina and I could go out to work also."

"Doing what?" He stiffened indignantly.

She told him almost dreamily, "Doing as other women in this city do, earning their way. Georgina is a fine seamstress. I could take on manual work."

"Where? At one of the laundries, like Cassie's ma? Working yourself to sickness or worse? What about me?"

"You, Liam McMahon, are dangerous. I should have seen that at the outset. I never should have started all this."

He ignored those words. "You think I would see

you ruining yourself at labor when I've two hands and a strong back? I'll work for you, Clara. I'll—"

"You'll be gone. I think Ruella and Theodore are right. Boston's the place. I can borrow the money from Theodore for your fare."

Liam had no doubt Collwys would contribute the funds, just to be rid of him. But he said, stubbornly now, "I'm going nowhere."

"It's best."

"No. Listen to me." He turned her about to face him and got a glimpse of the troubled look in her eyes. "You just got done saying you were wrong not to have considered my feelings. Yet you want to do it all over again and send me away like a servant?"

"Because"—disconcertingly, her lip trembled and her eyes filled with anguished tears—"because I care."

Liam's heart melted in his chest.

"I can't see you taken into custody, perhaps back in Maynard's hands, at the very least facing prosecution. My grandfather won't make any mistakes with it, Liam. Then we'll be torn apart anyway. It is more," she concluded with dignity, "than I think I can stand."

"Och, darling." He caught her up in his arms, light as a child, and carried her back to the bed. "Nor will you need to," he promised rashly. "We'll find a way."

"How? It's hopeless."

He held her close while she wept against him, a veritable storm that left his chest sodden. Ah, how could he tell her now what he'd dreamed, and add to her distress? Instead, he kissed her all over her face, blessing away the tears, and then fixed his mouth to hers. She clung to him, trembling badly now, while he ran his hands up under the thin fabric of the gown and brought her alight. He already stood for her, helpless and utterly unable to prevent it.

"Please," he begged into her open mouth, "let me take the hurt away. And the fear, let me take that also."

"It is no answer," she protested. "Just a temporary—"

He silenced her with his tongue in her mouth, stroking wildly. He let his love and need pour into her. He let his hands do the wooing and his fingers, between her thighs.

When she next broke the kiss, gasping, it was to beg in turn, "Liam, please."

"Trust me," he bade even as he surged into her. "Trust me to take care of you."

And as he loved her with all his devotion, he thrust the memory of Nancy McMahon from his mind.

Chapter Twenty-Five

"Where is Liam?" Clara demanded of Georgina, even as she denounced herself for fretting. She grew weary of asking the same question over and over again. Keeping track of Liam was like trying to leash a wayward hound.

Now she stood at the parlor window with Cassie beside her, the child's hand in hers. Cassie hadn't been by in several days; her intense need for Clara seemed to be waning as her attachment to her mother reformed. Clara wondered whether it wouldn't be the same for Liam, if he would eventually be able to move away and separate from her, if the mad rush of physical need would die away.

The very prospect left her feeling stunned and breathless. He might be able to live without her, but she without him?

Georgina paused at her shoulder and peered outside. "I've not seen him since early this morning when he had his breakfast. Speaking of which, Clara, I need some money for eggs, bread, and sugar—tea, as well, if we can afford it. We're just about cleaned out of everything."

Clara sighed gustily. "I thought we'd be in the money by now. There's very little left in my purse. Do you think Meyers would give us credit?"

Georgina shook her head but said, "I don't know.

Maybe if I take Jimmie with me. Mrs. Meyers has a weak spot for him."

Clara rubbed at her forehead fitfully. "I've not paid for that last load of coal yet, and winter's breathing down our necks." And Liam made another mouth to feed, one with a healthy appetite. "See what you can do in the way of credit, Georgina. But get at least a small measure of tea." Liam did enjoy his tea.

"I will." Georgina went out into the hallway, where she called to Jimmie and then took up her hat and coat. Clara accompanied her to the door, still yearning for sight of Liam. Virginia Street bustled with life, horsedrawn wagons and steamcabs both rattling by, and the man who sold fresh vegetables from a barrow on his usual rounds. Children ducked and played; wan, cold sunlight shone down.

Georgina turned away to help Jimmie don his jacket, and Clara asked Cassie, "What time does your mother leave work today? Is it her half day? You'll want to run home to her then."

When she straightened, her eye became caught by a figure coming along the street at a swagger. Tall and broad, he had a cloth cap pulled well down over his forehead and wore a workman's clothes the way another man might a finely-tailored suit. Her pulse leaped even before she recognized him.

"That's Liam."

Georgina and Jimmie looked where indicated. Georgina's eyes widened. "Is it safe for him to be abroad in daylight?"

"Most certainly not." The man whistled as he came, all self-satisfied nonchalance. When he saw her, he stopped whistling and grinned.

"Good day, ladies," he bade them when he reached the walk, and doffed his hat. "Lovely weather for the time of year."

Georgina rolled her eyes.

Clara demanded, "Where have you been?"

He did not answer at once, but stepped up to Clara and gave her a glance, mischief bright in his eyes. "Did you know, Mrs. McMahon, you talk in your sleep?"

"I do not."

"Ah, but you do, most definitely." He smiled at Jimmie, who beamed back at him. "Perhaps you've heard her, lad?"

Jimmie shook his head, and Clara cried, "What are you on about? What have you done?"

In answer he dug in one of his front pockets and produced a wad of cash. Jimmie spoke a word that ordinarily would have brought censure down upon his head. Now Clara barely noticed. She stared, blinked, and Liam stuffed the money into her hand.

"There should be enough for our immediate needs and a good bit toward the bill owing for the coal, as well." He added to Georgina in a charming aside, "She was after fretting about it last night."

"Was I?" All Clara remembered was lying in his arms and waking at dawn to his kisses. When she fell back asleep after, he must have left her.

She stared from the money overspilling her hands to his eyes.

"Where did you get this?"

"Found me a job, didn't I?"

"What?"

"Earned that right and proper, and there'll be more coming."

"But you can't go out to work."

"I can't have my wife worrying in her sleep, either, because I can't provide. What sort of man would that make me?"

Hastily, Georgina took Jimmie's hand and then pried Cassie away from Clara's side. "Come, Cassie love, I'll take you to your mother on our way. Let Miss Clara and Mr. Liam talk now." She shot Clara a meaningful look. "But not here on the doorstep, I would hope."

"She's right," Clara told Liam. "Come inside."

He strolled behind her, still all confidence. Clara deposited the money on the table in the parlor and struggled to identify her emotions.

She turned to face her husband. "A job? Why didn't you tell me? Why go off that way? You know how I worry when I wake and find you gone."

"Sorry, darlin'." He pulled off the cloth cap and tossed it onto the sofa; his dark hair spilled over his brow, giving him a rakish look. "I didn't think I'd be able to find work so soon." He measured her with his gaze. "You're not best pleased."

"I'm not."

"But, Clara love, you can't expect me to sit on my arse in this house day after day while I've two good hands and can earn a decent wage. I'll not have you worrying over bills when I can provide."

"You can't provide!"

"I most certainly can." He nodded at the table. "I got that in one morning."

"How? Where?"

"Down the waterfront, helping unload a freighter just come across the lake from Fort Erie."

"Out in the open? In broad daylight? What if you were seen?" Clara's voice rose without her permission.

"I wasn't. The place is teeming with people. Who's going to notice one more body at work? Besides, if it's Maynard you're worried about—"

"It is."

"He's not likely to be lounging down on the waterfront looking for me, is he?"

"Someone else might see you."

"Who? The steamies from Sterling House?"

"Liam, you had a life before you were hauled off to jail. Presumably you had acquaintances. You probably drank at those taverns on the west side. Any number of former acquaintances could see and recognize you."

"'Tis a chance I must take," he said airily.

"Are you mad?"

"No, but I thought about it, sure, lying there beside you in the night. This scheme of yours, Clara, it wasn't best advised. Now, I'm not criticizing you or saying I'm sorry you launched it; I'm that glad to be alive." His voice dropped to a throb. "Even gladder I've met you. But you will admit you bolloxed the details, and it hasn't come out the way you hoped."

"True."

"Part of that's down to you, and part's down to me, but the way I see it, we're together in it now. I have my role to play, and I mean to take it up. If something in my past has spoiled you getting your inheritance, I'll do what I can toward the keep of this household."

Clara drew breath to reply, to protest again. He didn't give her the chance.

Still sounding self-satisfied, he went on. "There's no end of work for a man with a strong back and some

191

skill in his hands. And it seems I've talents to spare—some coming back to me." He gazed at his own palms in calculating wonder. "I can work wood with these. I spoke to a man on me way home—a coffin maker. I believe I could make a very good wage working for him." He shot her another bright look. "So if you balk at having me out in the open, I'll take the job he's offered, instead. No one will see me in the back of his shop, making cradles for the dead. And there's a certain poetic justice to it, isn't there?"

"I don't want you endangered at all." She wanted him near her, within reach of her hands and her mouth.

"Ah, well, Clara, you can't expect me to idle about when you're in need. I intend to look after my wife."

Clara's heart clenched in her chest. What if he already had another wife for whom to provide, the mother of his infant son? What had become of her now? Clara's interference had effectively stolen the woman's husband from her. Of course it might be argued the warden, Maynard, had stolen him first.

The parlor door opened, and Dax trundled in. Without taking her eyes from Liam, Clara told the mechanical servant, "Not now, Dax, please."

"But, Mrs. McMahon, the tradesman Black is at the door, seeking payment for a coal delivery."

Clara's gaze flicked to the money on the table. Liam drew himself up and asked Dax, "And how much, Dax, would we be owing him?"

"One dollar ten cents, the man said, sir."

Liam gave a low whistle, went to the table, and counted out a sum. "Coal's as costly as gold, it seems. Here—give him this. Tell him the rest will be paid after the next delivery. Need to keep him coming, sure. We have to make certain all these wee ones stay warm, eh, Dax?"

"Yes, sir."

"Go now, and let us talk."

But Clara discovered, once the steamie had departed, there wasn't too much left to say. She buried her face in her hands and fought for composure.

"And here was I thinking—hoping—you might be proud of me." Liam's voice crooned, warm, low, and very Irish. He stood so close she could feel the heat of his body; he pulled at Clara's every sense, but she struggled for rationality.

Slowly she lifted her face from her hands and gazed into his eyes. "Did you really earn all that money this morning, and not steal it?"

"Steal it?"

"As you did before, that night on the waterfront."

Something flickered in his eyes, moved like the shadow of deception. At that moment she wondered what she really knew of this man and the secrets behind those eyes.

"You wound me, Clara." He laid his hand over his heart.

"That's no answer." Pulse pounding hard, she held his gaze.

"Aye, well, I might have lifted part of it from a fellow. You would have done the same, in my place."

"I would not!"

"He was abusing a servant at the time, and never even noticed when I relieved him of his no doubt ill-gotten gains." He added, unrepentant, "But I earned the rest."

"I don't want it in this house." She began to

tremble. She wished she could add that she didn't want him, but she had not the strength.

"Ah, now, you don't mean that. Anyway, 'tis already gone. That's the bit we gave the man for the coal."

What have I done? Clara wondered quite suddenly and clearly. *Brought this man—this unprincipled rascal—into our lives. I should send him away now, cut my losses, and have done.*

But her body craved him, her flesh did, her lips and her fingers. More, her soul craved him. She could no more chase him from her than bar him from her bed.

"Sure, when you think about it," he crooned, his voice curling through her consciousness, "me stealing that money's no different than you scheming to wrangle that settlement from your grandfather with your deception of a marriage."

Just so must the devil whisper, Clara thought. Sweet, low, and convincing. Because she couldn't deny he was right.

Chapter Twenty-Six

Clara, at work straightening her father's surgery, heard the front door open and Georgina invite someone into the hall. She paused to listen, and the murmur of voices caught her ear.

"Where's the big Irishman?" Theodore, and not sounding very pleased.

"Out at work," Georgina replied.

"What?"

"These past three days. Left early this morning."

"Yes, well, I have news for Clara. But first, Georgina, darling girl, we need to talk—you and I."

"We've said all we need."

"We haven't. I broke off my engagement last night."

Silence fell in the foyer, like a heavy curtain. Clara, now just inside the surgery door, listened shamelessly.

At last Georgina breathed, "You never did!"

"It's torn my family apart, and my life, but I don't care. I should have done it months ago. Can you forgive me being a coward so long?"

"You're mad! Go home and make it up with your family. Likely your fiancée will take you back."

"No."

Georgina's voice, usually so soft, rose sharply. "You think this changes anything?"

"I hope so."

"It doesn't change who you are—who I am."

"I'm the man who loves you. Georgina, say you'll consider my suit."

"I should say not! A black wife? It would ruin your career. The world—"

"I don't give a damn about the world. I know who you are—the kindest, sweetest, gentlest, and most beautiful woman—"

"Theodore, no."

"I love you."

"And," Georgina's voice carried the weight of heartbreak, "I love you. That's why—"

Georgina's voice broke off. Clara, frozen with her hand to her mouth, ached for her friends.

"Georgie," Theodore whispered, barely audible.

Georgina stumbled on, now sounding desperate, "Just think how hard you've worked to establish your clientele. Would you throw all that away?"

"In an instant."

"We'd be ostracized."

"So? There's work in plenty to be had in this city. I may not make a fortune, but I can take the cases other lawyers won't touch, like the worker who loses an arm in the mill and can find no one to represent him, the mother who's intimidated by an unscrupulous landlord, all those disenfranchised who need someone to speak for them in the courts. I'll live what I believe, with you at my side."

"You paint a real pretty picture, Theodore, but—"

"Not just a picture, Georgie. It's the life I choose for myself. For *us*."

Clara, her ear now virtually pressed to the door, heard what might be a sob from Georgina. "I can't do that to you, Theodore. I just can't!"

Georgina fled, her soft steps retreating toward the kitchen. When Clara opened the surgery door, Theodore stood with a wry look on his face and anguish in his eyes.

"You heard all that?"

"I'm sorry." Clara gestured to the surgery. "I—"

"It doesn't matter. She wouldn't listen."

"She's overwhelmed, Theodore. She'll come round."

"You think so?"

"She'll reason it out in her head the way she always does."

"It's not her head I want to win, but her heart."

"With Georgina, I suspect you'll have to win both. Come in. You have news for me?"

"I do, and I'm afraid it's not good."

Clara's heart sank. She pulled out a chair at her father's desk and indicated a second. "About Liam?"

Theodore nodded. He seated himself, pulled some papers from his attaché case, and reached visibly for composure. When he lifted his eyes to Clara's, she saw his regret.

"My agents have been working to trace the movements of William T. McMahon from the ship's manifest forward, here to Buffalo. They've located his wife."

****

"She's alive?" Had Clara truly wished otherwise? She gripped the edge of her father's desk so tightly she half expected her fingers to snap. She knew if she didn't grasp hold of something, she would tumble down.

"She is, though it seems the infant son perished during their journey—most likely in Montreal. They're still investigating that detail."

Detail. Surely a child's life proved more—a son, Liam's son.

"How unfortunate," she said, her voice distant as a stranger's. "The wife is still here in Buffalo?"

"Yes." Theodore scowled. "Surely you see what this means, Clara? He lied to you. He never told you he had a wife, and he has obviously been running his own con, trying to fleece you out of your inheritance. I'm sorry," he added. "I know you've become...attached."

What to say? Dare Clara confess all the truth to Theodore and involve him in her mucky vortex of doubt and secrecy, perhaps watch the liking for her she saw in his eyes fade? Would he think her a freak, a witch?

"Tell me about his wife," she said instead.

He consulted his papers. "One Nancy McMahon—age twenty-four. They've been in Buffalo less than a year, entered the country via Niagara Falls. During that time they had a number of residences, both in South Buffalo and near the waterfront."

Nancy. Liam's wife, mother of his child. The woman he slept with, the woman who had a right to him.

"Where is she staying now?" The poor woman must be frantic, believing her man still imprisoned, or dead.

"The women's hospital on Porter Avenue. It's a psychiatric facility."

"What?"

Theodore raised his eyes to Clara's. "She was

committed two months ago."

Clara lost all her breath in a gasp. "Are you sure?"

"Very. My investigators spoke with the landlady at her last residence, a boardinghouse over on Carolina. She says Nancy was out raving in the street before being hauled away. They also spoke with the administrators at the hospital. The woman is definitely there."

Clara parted suddenly dry lips. "Where was Liam? When she was taken in, I mean. Why didn't he try to get her out of that place?" She'd heard tales of the hospital on Porter, and the kinds of things that went on there. Everyone had.

"Landlady, a Mrs. Kraus, says Nancy's husband was seldom home, worked a job and spent most nights at the boozers, drinking and brawling. Failed to pay the rent. Typical Irishman, so she said."

Clara stiffened with indignation. Could that be the same man who even now insisted upon working to support her?

She drew an unsteady breath. "I want to see her."

"What?"

"Nancy McMahon. I want to meet her face to face."

"Oh, Clara, no. Not a good idea."

"You don't understand, Theodore."

"I think I do." Theodore glanced at the door, beyond which was Georgina. "You've fallen for him. Don't try to deny it. I suppose it was inevitable, but the fellow's a lout, and you're a smart woman."

"The man I've come to know isn't the man you describe. That's why I need to see her, Theodore, and ask her—"

"What makes you think you'd get any sense from the woman? Raving, the landlady said."

"Surely she'll be better by now."

Slowly, Theodore shook his head. "It would be irresponsible of me to allow you to enter such a place."

Clara clasped her hands and leaned toward him. "It would be irresponsible of you not to accompany me. Because if you don't, I'll go, with Dax, on my own."

****

As soon as they disembarked from the steamcab, Clara could hear the screaming. It trailed through the sharp air of the cold afternoon the way one of the new fire sirens might, and sent a frisson of horror up Clara's spine. The building, large and with a corner turret, had many windows, all of them barred.

She looked at Theodore uneasily. He responded with a wry grimace. "These places should be shut down," he said, "and many will be, now that the new psychiatric facility on Forest Avenue is up and running. State of the art, that is—unfortunately, they don't allow women there yet. Perhaps someday."

Clara made no reply. Pedestrians passed by in both directions on the busy thoroughfare, none sparing so much as a glance for the place, and she shivered. Were such screams so commonplace that they attracted no attention?

"I still believe this to be a bad idea," Theodore pronounced in a grim tone.

Quite suddenly, Clara's courage flagged, and she agreed with him. She didn't want to enter that place of potential misery, but need must take her even there.

She reached out and clutched Theodore's arm. "We're here now, and I have to know."

The front steps were steep and led to an ill-lit hall that smelled of boiled turnips and something else Clara couldn't immediately identify. The screams were louder here, much louder—they echoed through the building and were accompanied by other sounds: moans, plaintive cries, and hysterical laughter. Clara faltered.

It was Theodore who led her through the doorway on the left, marked with a placard that read "office."

Inside, behind a desk, sat a woman of late middle years, gray hair pulled into a pile atop her head and spectacles perched on her nose. She looked up at them in surprised inquiry.

"May I help you?"

Theodore spoke. "We're here to visit one of your patients, a Mrs. Nancy McMahon. We're acquaintances of her husband."

Chapter Twenty-Seven

Liam, hard at work polishing the outside of a plain pine coffin, heard voices in the outer shop and wondered if Mr. Hengerer had another commission. Liam's new employer dealt fairly with his customers and kept his prices so reasonable he already had a large backlog of orders. But the old German and Liam agreed on one thing: no one, rich or poor, deserved to be laid to rest in a shoddily-constructed coffin. That was why he kept smoothing the pine surface with loving hands even while what sounded like an argument erupted between Hengerer and his unseen visitor.

When the discussion ended at last and Franz Hengerer appeared in the doorway of the dusty workroom, Liam looked at him in inquiry. He liked the man with his gray hair and large, drooping moustache and, after only three days, trusted him. He hoped Hengerer felt the same.

"Someone asking after you," Franz announced abruptly in his heavily-accented English.

Liam stiffened. How could that be? He'd spent the past three days squirreled away here among the tools and wood shavings. The only people he'd seen, besides Franz and his plump wife, had been dead.

"For me? You sure about that?"

"*Ja*, sure." Franz eyed him with shrewd, hazel eyes. "Called you by name. Also told the look of you."

Liam straightened slowly and dropped the linseed-soaked cloth he held. "What did you tell him?"

Franz leaned against the door jamb and eyed Liam frankly. "Are you in some sort of trouble, William?"

Liam hesitated, and Franz went on, "Because he had the look, this man, of a *hund* after a brock. To tell you truly, I did not like the appearance of him. I have seen men chased down before, in old country. I did not like that either."

"My situation is complicated," Liam said simply. "Let me just say I would rather not be found by that man, or anyone."

Franz nodded decisively. "I must ask you one thing: you have not sinned against your *Gott*?"

"That's a big question." Was bigamy a sin? Adultery definitely was. What of loving a woman more than life itself, when married to another?

"I've killed no one," he told the old man, "if that's what you're asking. But I may not be who I seem."

"Ach, we all put on different coats from time to time. I would hate to give you over to the authorities— on general principle, see. Me, I do not like the authorities. Besides, you are a good worker. Why is this man after you?"

Liam thought about that. The *hund* might have been sent by Clara's grandfather. Then again, he might have been sent by Maynard. Had it been playing on the warden's mind, what he'd seen at Sterling House? Had his suspicions been further raised by old Van Hamelin's agents asking questions at the jail?

It was worth Maynard's career, if not his life, to keep hidden what had been going on in the jail yard.

He said to Franz, "I have a past following me, one

I'd rather outrun."

Franz seemed to weigh that a moment before he said, "Most men have things they would rather forget. It is part of why we came to this country, *ja*? You are good with your hands, and I have many orders for customers who cannot wait long." He gave a grim smile. "And you have a wife to support, you say, and *kinder*?"

"Yes." At least one wife.

Franz shrugged. "Then you keep working. That coffin, it is done? Help me carry it out so Mr. Pfister can come collect it before dark. He wishes his wife to lie in his parlor this evening."

Liam nodded, and then caught the old man's arm. "You think he believed you when you said I wasn't here, this *hund*?"

Franz widened his eyes and spread his hands. "Do I look like a man to lie? You just wait until dark, William, before going home. You want to get there safely, *nein*?"

Liam did; he wanted to see Clara so badly he ached, longed to gaze into her eyes and take her in his arms.

He wondered what she might be doing now, whether she longed for him also, or thought of him. And he wondered, in despair, how he would ever make his future come right.

****

The interior of the hospital stank. As soon and Clara and Theodore left the front office, the odor assailed her nostrils, though the woman who led them—Mrs. Wright—did not even seem to notice.

Mrs. Wright had identified herself as the

administrator of the facility. She displayed no pride in doing so, nor should she; she did, however, seem curious about them.

"Mrs. McMahon has had no visitors since she arrived here—none, that is, except her husband."

Clara struggled not to look at Theodore. He, bless him, remained calm and businesslike, and explained, "We have only just discovered she is here. She used to be employed by my companion, Miss Allen, who has come out of concern."

Mrs. Wright turned dispassionate eyes on Clara. "Was she in your employ when she fell ill?"

"Yes."

"Then you are familiar with some of the details of her malady."

Clara was saved answering when Mrs. Wright unlocked a door and admitted them to what must be one of the wards. The malodor, much increased, struck her in the face in a wave.

The room—large and high-ceilinged—nevertheless had a stifling air. Tall, bare windows and a scuffed, ruined floor caught Clara's attention, all clotted with women—old, young, moving, motionless, babbling, silent, and in various states of dress and undress.

It looked, Clara thought, very much like a version of an all-female hell.

A woman with wild white hair stood at one of the windows—which was both cracked and barred—shrieking at intervals like an eldritch. Another paced like—well, like a madwoman—muttering words impossible to catch. A single steam unit, in worse condition than Dax when Clara and Liam first appropriated him, trundled about in a decidedly helpless fashion, one side of its chest caved in.

Clara's heart dropped like a stone. Which of these poor creatures might be Nancy McMahon? *Liam's wife.* The woman with a prior claim on the man Clara loved.

"Clean that up," Mrs. Wright said to the steamie, and Clara looked where indicated to see one of the patients, with a bare bottom, standing in a puddle of fresh urine.

She made a wordless sound of protest, and Theodore took her arm.

"There she is, in the corner." The woman Mrs. Wright pointed out had curled herself into a ball up against the scarred wainscoting, as if she wished to retreat as far as possible from her surroundings. And who could blame her? The very idea of existing here twenty-four hours a day turned Clara hot, sick, and desperate.

Mrs. Wright led them past a woman raving to herself and another who sat weeping. She called in a strident voice, "Nancy? Nancy McMahon?"

The woman huddled in the corner looked up, and Clara saw she was devastatingly pretty, despite the circumstances and the dirt and tears marking her face—with great, wide eyes and soft, fair hair.

Liam's wife.

The pain of it shot through Clara like a mortal blow. He had chosen this woman when he possessed the facility for choosing, before death stole his memory, before ever he knew of Clara, with her child's body and her unnatural ties, forged by whatever power she carried inside. This woman, mad or not, surely represented Liam's heart.

"Mrs. McMahon," Theodore said gently, "do you

remember Miss Allen? Your employer."

Bastard, Clara thought silently; she knew they played at a role, but how could he seek to deceive this poor creature whose confusion screamed aloud? The pools of her eyes, haunted and desperate and so utterly lost, reproached and accused Clara.

Clara said to Mrs. Wright, "Is she able to speak with us, to communicate? She looks…" Clara had no words to complete that thought.

Mrs. Wright cast a glare at the steamie. "Here, you—come and get her up." She herself swept her skirt away from Nancy as she might from the puddle on the other side of the room. "She has days when she is able to speak rationally. On others she retreats. But," Mrs. Wright added, as if proud of it, "she no longer screams."

"Perhaps there is some place better for us to speak with her?" Theodore suggested. "Somewhere private."

"Every inch of this facility is in use. We are severely overcrowded and understaffed."

"You might lend us your office for a few moments."

Mrs. Wright sniffed.

Theodore hastily drew his wallet from a pocket. "And you will allow me to make a small donation for the benefit of your patients—toward their holiday meal perhaps, next month."

"We don't celebrate holidays. They tend to bring back too many memories and stir up intense emotions. But I will put this in the clothing fund. We can't keep them in clean clothes."

Clara shuffled aside to let the servant, which leaked steam badly, in closer. But when it reached down to seize Nancy's delicate wrists, which Clara saw were already covered with bruises, she reacted involuntarily.

"No, let me—please."

She circumvented the steamie and bent to Nancy as she might to one of the children at home, Jimmie, perhaps, when he had one of his nightmares, or little Cassie. Nancy shrank from her, but Clara drew her up anyway, and into the circle of her arm.

"It's all right." A rampant lie—nothing could be right in this terrible place—but Nancy's eyes, with their wide, dark pupils, moved to Clara's and clung. She felt like skin and bone, fragile as a bundle of sticks. Clara's compassion rose in a staggering wave.

Nancy whispered something.

"What?" Clara bent her ear closer.

"She said 'Tommy,'" Mrs. Wright interpreted coldly. "It was the name of her infant son that died."

Chapter Twenty-Eight

Nancy clung to Clara with one hand and to the arm of the chair with the other, head tucked well down. If the woman had a third arm, Clara did not doubt she would have covered her head with it.

Mrs. Wright, who quite properly, so Clara had to admit, had remained in the room, now stood at the door. The office, not overly large, felt stifling.

Clara had looked once into Theodore's eyes when they sat down. Full of distress and uncertainty, their expression made it unsurprising when he said, "Clara, I'm not sure this is a good idea."

It would be difficult, Clara admitted, to have the conversation she needed, with Mrs. Wright present—or possibly any conversation at all.

She leaned toward Nancy and said, "Are you all right? Are they treating you well here?"

Mrs. Wright, her back against the door, stiffened in indignation, but said nothing.

Nancy looked into Clara's eyes, and Clara's heart clenched at the pain she saw.

"Want to go home."

Ah, and Clara should have anticipated this. Had she been bunged up here, it would be her first request also.

"Are they looking after you properly?" she pressed. "Giving you enough to eat?"

"Food is offered," said Mrs. Wright. "We cannot force her to eat."

"Please," said Theodore, "if we might have a few moments alone."

"So you can trump up allegations of abuse? We've had all that before. There is neither enough money nor enough staff. We do the best we can."

Clara asked, not without anger, "Then why is she covered in bruises?" She had not expected to feel protective toward Liam's wife, this woman whose loveliness cried aloud despite her stained clothes and tangled hair. But her every instinct now sat up and howled in defense.

Mrs. Wright replied waspishly, "The others do become violent from time to time, and they tend to bully her. She rarely fights back."

"Like hens in a henyard," Theodore contributed unexpectedly. "But, Mrs. Wright, it's your duty to intervene."

"Do not come in here and attempt to tell me my duty. We do intervene, of course, as soon as possible."

"She needs to be placed in another ward, then," Clara pressed.

Mrs. Wright gave a hard laugh. "All the wards are the same—overcrowded. They keep telling us conditions will be better when they open a women's ward at Mr. Richardson's new facility. But that may take years yet."

Years. Clara couldn't endure this place for hours.

Theodore got to his feet. When his chair scraped the floor, Nancy flinched. Clara tightened her grip on the woman's hand comfortingly.

Theodore said to Mrs. Wright in a low voice, "If I

make a larger donation to your clothing fund, perhaps we might prevail upon you to stand outside the door just for five minutes?"

Mrs. Wright took the money without protest and went out. Theodore nodded at Clara. "Go on, but for God's sake be quick."

"Nancy, dear, I need to ask you a few questions about your past."

Nancy looked at her from beneath the tangle of soft, blonde hair. Her lips, shaped like a perfect bow, parted, and she moaned.

"I am a friend of your husband's." Now, there was a lie. Friend, bed companion, recipient of pleasure. By some act of will, Clara held Nancy's gaze.

"Dead," Nancy whispered.

"Liam?" And how could she know that? She'd been locked up in this hellhole since before Liam was arrested, and surely Maynard wouldn't have put out word of Liam's demise.

But Nancy whispered, "Tommy."

"Tommy? That was your son? Liam's son?"

Nancy began to weep. The tears spilled over from agony-filled eyes, and she disregarded them. "Burned. In the fire. Ah, *ochone!*"

The lament, pure Irish, rent the stale air of the room, rampant with pain.

"I am sorry, so sorry." Clara was. She'd never birthed a child of her own, but she knew how she felt for those under her roof and her care.

"My fault." Nancy gasped it. "I tipped the lamp. Quarreled with my husband."

"Liam?"

"Yes, Liam was there."

"Liam—your husband, Liam McMahon." Clara needed to establish that; it was the whole reason she'd come.

"Out drinking. He was always out drinking," Nancy said earnestly, her tortured gaze clinging to Clara's. "Left me home with Tommy. I sat up, waited, with the lamp lit."

"Yes?"

"He came home drunk, drunk again. No money for food, and he drank what he earned."

Clara's heart sank like an anvil. Not her Liam, who was out working even now.

But he was not her Liam. He belonged to this poor woman.

"And you quarreled?" So might Clara have done, in the same circumstances.

Nancy nodded. "We quarreled, and he stormed out—left us again. I was so angry I followed him out into the night. But my elbow must have caught the lamp." She drew her fingers from Clara's and covered her face with both hands.

Clara shot a desperate look at Theodore. This was not the news she'd wanted. Better Liam not recall such a terrible thing.

"Tommy," Nancy moaned.

"Did he perish, then, in the fire?" But the ship's manifest said William and Nancy McMahon had sailed with an infant.

"His cot caught fire. So badly burned."

Clara turned sick inside.

"'Twas my fault!"

"No, Nancy, listen to me—it was an accident." Surely others had told her so. But she remained locked in a place no assurance could reach.

"My fault he's dead."

Clara fought the impulse to gather the poor, broken creature into her arms. "Nancy, listen to me. I need to know about Liam." Clara swallowed hard. "Your husband. He is your husband, is that right?"

Nancy lifted empty eyes.

"You sailed together from Ireland. From Galway. Before that you were in Dublin."

"He's dead, Tommy—"

"You'll get no sense from her," Theodore said softly.

Desperate, Clara clutched both Nancy's hands. "Is Liam McMahon your husband? Did you travel here, to Buffalo with him?"

"Liam? He's out working. Why doesn't he come home?"

Because he's been in jail, he's died, and come back again into my arms. Into my bed.

At that moment Clara thoroughly despised herself and all she'd done. Not that she could have prevented Liam's death at Maynard's hands. But she'd raised him for purely selfish reasons, and she wanted to keep him even now, even when she saw how terribly this woman needed him.

"When," she asked gently, "did your child die?"

And just like that, Nancy began to shriek. She withdrew her hands from Clara's, threw them in the air, and howled like a banshee.

Clara jumped. Theodore swore; the door flew open, and Mrs. Wright surged in.

"That's enough. You've upset her. It will take us hours to get her quieted."

"I'm sorry." Clara fought the desire to cover her ears.

The steamie came through the open door, puffing badly.

"Gather her up," Mrs. Wright told it. "Take her to the isolation room."

"What?" Clara began to question.

"You know what to do," Mrs. Wright told the unit.

Theodore tried to protest. "I must object."

"You know nothing about caring for these patients. And you've done enough harm. She'll get them all stirred up, and it will be nearly impossible to calm them again."

"I'm sorry." Clara looked at Nancy, whose face, now red, showed no signs of sanity. "Nancy, please listen—"

"I'll have to ask you to leave now." Mrs. Wright's tone brooked no argument. Clara felt Theodore seize her arm and urge her away.

They could still hear Nancy shrieking when they went through the outer door and, very faintly, when they stood in the street.

"My God!" Theodore breathed, heartfelt.

"What a terrible place, Theodore. What an awful, sinful, nightmare of a place."

"Yes."

Clara turned and looked at her companion. "I want to get her out of there, as soon as possible. I want to take her home."

Chapter Twenty-Nine

Someone trailed Liam through the newly-fallen late November dark—possibly two someones. He'd deliberately delayed leaving Hengerer's shop until he had some cover from the ensuing night, just in case a watch was being kept on the area, and he'd left by the back door through the alley that opened onto Fargo Avenue. Still he'd picked up company before walking half a block.

Now, heading down Fargo toward Virginia, he cursed the overcast, which seemed to smother the light cast by the steam lamps. On the corner of Hudson, he passed an upscale tavern and considered turning in—if those who tailed him meant mischief, he'd be safer in a crowd.

But the house on Virginia Street called him. Clara did. *Home.* Strange to say, when he had lost nearly all his past, but he did feel a sense of homecoming there—not from the place but the woman.

Clara's presence had become his home, and where he wanted—no, needed—to dwell.

He sped past the boozer and glanced over his shoulder as he angled across towards Tenth. The dark seemed to close around him, and the pursuing footfalls sounded louder.

Not steamies, then, not this time. Steamies rolled, though a well-constructed one had the ability to ratchet itself up steps. This sound denoted hard leather on pavement.

He walked faster, gauging the distance to decent cover and the best route. These could be common footpads. He had his day's pay in his pocket, and times in this city were lean for some folk. Or the pursuit could be far more sinister.

He quickened his pace to a half lope, and the pursuing steps sped up also. Definitely more than one man, and definitely not about to let him lose them. He ducked off Tenth and into an alley, heading for the west arm of Virginia Street. Still a good many blocks before home.

At the corner of Eleventh and Maryland, under a streetlight, they caught him and came at him from two sides. He didn't know how they'd managed it, unless they'd separated and one had sprinted ahead.

Both were out of breath now—big men with cloth caps pulled well down so he couldn't see their eyes. He didn't have to; their posture revealed their intent, and he braced himself, ready when the first fist came at him.

Ah, and his instincts took over then. His fists came up and his shoulders squared, and he went in swinging. Not averse to brawling, he knew to his soul every punch counted.

"McMahon?" the first fellow demanded even as Liam ducked his fist and got in a solid blow to the man's midriff.

The other man waded in behind, and there, beneath the dirty light of the steam lamp, an ugly battle began.

Liam used everything he had, from teeth to elbows, but these lads—two on one—didn't fight fair. One remained always at his back. Liam, delivering kicks and jabs as he could, knew that if once that man seized him from behind the other—with fists like iron—would pummel him until he was senseless or dead.

"Maynard send you?" he snarled as he landed a punch that hurt like hell but provided a satisfying crunch to his opponent's cheekbone. "The fecking murderer."

A foolish thing to say, he knew it the moment it left his lips. For it proved he had dangerous knowledge of Maynard's guilt. And he could no longer doubt Maynard had loosed these vicious hounds.

He shrugged the man at his back off yet again, turned, and caught a fist on the temple from his original opponent. For an instant the world around him, all dirty, garish light, blinked out, and he swayed.

If he fell, would these two drag him off to Maynard? Would he ever see daylight again, see home?

Clara.

The need for her flared so brightly inside him, it nearly consumed his doubt. He drew a mighty breath as she became his strength, and he kicked out with his heavily-booted feet. For one blinding instant he thought he would get away. Then a merciless grasp seized his arms from behind and wrestled with him, even as he saw the first man wind up for a blow meant to take him out.

"Liam McMahon? Is that you, Liam?" The eldritch screech tore through the gloom. A terrible figure emerged into the light; for an instant Liam could not tell it for friend or foe. Bulging with muscle and wearing a pair of blue coveralls, it had wild hair that flew as it tossed itself into the fray.

The next few seconds became very interesting.

Liam's newly-arrived ally waded in like a stevedore on a bender, and Liam picked up his own fight with a certain measure of enjoyment. Almost before he knew it, his first opponent lay senseless at his feet and the second man, at whom Liam had never really got a good look, fled unsteadily into the darkness.

Liam sucked in a painful breath and looked up into Ruella's broad face.

"To what," he gasped, "do I owe the pleasure of your presence?"

"To the luck of the Irish, no doubt. I was just on my way from my rooms on Palmer Street to Clara's to deliver some information."

"Can't say I was ever happier to see an Englishwoman. Thanks."

Ruella scowled and nudged the fallen man with her toe. "You know him?"

Liam had never seen the ugly brute before. He shook his head, which hurt.

"You suppose Maynard sent him?" Ruella asked. "He say anything?"

"Just my name."

"Help me drag him into that alley—he'll make an ugly surprise for some housemaid tossin' the trash if he don't come to before morning."

Ruella's muscles bulged as she bent to the task, and Liam eyed her with incredulous admiration. The Limey was quite a woman.

"Remember his face," she advised as they hauled the senseless lump from beneath the street lamp.

"I'm not likely to forget. Here, hang on a moment, lass." At the edge of the light, Liam rifled the man's pockets, came up with a number of coins, a lucky piece which he tossed into the shadows, and then a billfold stuffed with cash.

He squinted at the information within. "Name's Ignatius Krull. And this must be his pay."

Deliberately, he extracted the wad, divided it in two, and handed Ruella her half. "A profitable night's work," he said even as a large, unbeautiful smile split Ruella's face. "Worth a few bruises. This will pay for the rest of Clara's coal."

"Her welfare's all you think about, innit?" Ruella asked abruptly. "She's a lucky girl."

"She isn't," Liam said seriously. "I've a past following me, and those two lads were part of it. Worst part is, I don't even know what, though I can guess why."

Ruella thrust her cut into the pocket of her overalls and reached for Liam's arm, which she threaded through hers.

"That's what I've come to tell Clara, innit? Walk with me."

They set off like two drinking buddies, arm in arm, toward Clara's house.

"You've discovered something at the jail?"

"Friend of mine did, lad by the name of Fagan— new to the force. Wants to get into me knickers."

Liam drew away and shot her an incredulous look.

"Don't knock it," she scolded. "It's a fierce ride, one you might like to try yourself. But no; it's only Clara for you, innit?"

"Only Clara," Liam confirmed.

"I might give young Fagan a try," Ruella reflected. "Would have already, if he weren't Irish."

Liam stiffened.

"Now, don't go getting your arse up in the air. I have to be true to meself, see. But he does have a pretty pair of eyes. And he'd do anything for me. Loves me scones."

It began to rain, cold drops laced with sleet. Liam hunched his neck down into his collar.

"What did you find out?"

"That's for Clara's ears."

Liam squeezed Ruella's arm against his side. "But it affects me. It's a piece of my life you might give back."

Ruella said nothing.

"I want what's best for her." Liam drew a breath. "I love her."

"Think I don't know that? Think I'm simple or somefink?"

"I'm just not sure you believe it."

"Hard thing to believe. You're a man without a past; you could be anything. And I've a responsibility in this, as I'm the one dragged you to her door and all your complications with you."

"Then help me make it right."

"How?"

Liam shook his head. "Help me find a way. I'd feel better with you on my side and not against me."

"I'm not against you, despite everything." She began to recite, "You were arrested on October the eighteenth for battery on a man in the White Owl tavern. Hauled in and charged with drunk and disorderly—not assault, quite interestingly."

"Why's that interesting?"

Ruella stole a look at him. "Man you fought was also Irish, and you failed to kill him. They should have let you dry out and serve five days—that's the usual sentence for D and D. As it was, you never appeared before a justice for sentencing and, on the evening of November second, you were dragged into the jail yard and hanged."

A wave of black sickness washed over Liam; he fought it down.

Ruella went on, "Now, the motive's interesting. Damn me if I can think of a strong enough one."

"Maynard's addicted to the good life at places like the Sterling House—I saw him there."

"That's as may be. But he wouldn't receive enough for your keep to make it worth his while. There must be more to it. Anyway, Fagan's interested now. I kept as much of the story from him as possible, but he's a bright lad, and he's curious about the reason I'm chasing down an Irishman. A lot of Irish in the Buffalo police force—could have some possible allies there."

"You think they'd all rise up against Maynard? It would be worth their jobs."

"So it would, and decent, respectable jobs aren't easy to come by. There's a mystery here, right enough. But I did find out one thing."

"What's that?"

Ruella paused and dragged Liam to a halt. She peered at him through the rain and darkness.

"They wrote down your name on October eighteenth, when they dragged you in drunk. And that I can give to you now—Mr. William T. McMahon."

Chapter Thirty

"Liam, we need to talk." Clara dropped the words into the silence that filled the parlor even as Liam sat brooding into his glass of brandy. Ruella had gone, as had Collwys, who had been with Clara when Liam arrived. The children had been put to bed, and now Liam and Clara were alone with the knowledge Ruella had shared with Clara, over again.

Liam, sporting a whole new crop of bruises and abrasions from the fight on the way home, ached from head to toe and felt desperate to touch Clara—take her in his arms, draw her fast against his heart, and ease the great gulf of need that filled him. But Clara, tense as a fiddle string, paced the room. She'd perched nowhere since he reached home; her face looked pale and drawn.

Without waiting for him to reply, she went on, "What do you think it means?"

"Which bit?" Liam raised his eyes to follow her quick, fierce movements. The situation, prickly as a damned thistle, had too many points to grasp.

She paused long enough to return his look, her eyes burning. "Your name. The fact that you remembered your name. Are things beginning to come back to you?"

"I don't think so." She, after all, had come up with "William." The rest had just floated into his mind when she tried to label him a Fitzgerald. "I've recalled little else."

She resumed pacing. "That doesn't mean you won't." She drew a difficult breath. "Cassie—Cassie has stopped coming round so often. She's recalled some things—not her accident, but details of her life before it."

"That's good, surely?"

"It's not the way it's supposed to work." Clara's face twisted. "She's stopped needing me."

Liam did not know what to say. This, of all the tangle, worried Clara? Remembering?

Carefully, he asked, "How can you be sure how it's supposed to work? How many people did you say you've raised?"

"Two, you and Cassie."

"Me and Cassie."

"And now she's beginning to remember. Pulling away from me. Mollie never seemed to remember."

"Mollie was a dog. Could you ask her what she remembered?"

"No, but I saw her learn to love me all over again. She didn't pull away from me."

"She wouldn't, would she? For you put her back where she belonged. Clara, what is it bothers you so?" He could feel her emotion scuttling along his own nerves and skin. *Fear*. "Of what are you afraid?"

She stopped pacing abruptly and turned her eyes on him. "You will pull away from me too. I'm going to lose you."

"Is that it?" Hastily, Liam set his glass aside and got to his feet. He gathered Clara in with careful hands and drew her close against him. "Ah, lass." He crooned the words as he might to a child, but there was nothing childlike in the effect she had on him. He wanted to

223

bury himself in her, reach so far inside she'd never let him go. He wanted to pull her inside him also, engulf her in a place of safety where no harm—no fear—could ever touch her.

His pulse began to thud faster, and he pressed his lips against her temple. "No need to worry about losing me. I'm yours—yours forever, for better or worse. Isn't that the vow we made when we wed?"

She tipped her face up to look at him, great gray-green eyes swimming with tears. "But you made that vow first to someone else, Liam. And no matter how I want you in my life—in my bed—you belong to her."

Liam caught her face, framing it with his hands. "Listen to me, Clara: what I feel for you goes beyond the laws of man or even those vows we spoke to each other. It goes beyond all reason. I might be married to ten other women. By God, I want *you.*"

"Those feelings may pass, they may be a by-product of the raising. Once you remember your past, it may fade, just as it did for Cassie."

"Clara, no."

"Once you remember her." Pain flooded Clara's eyes. "And your child. I've seen her, Liam."

"Who?"

"Your wife."

Liam reeled. "What?"

"Theodore and I went today and saw her. She's in the women's hospital on Porter Avenue. It's an asylum for women."

"She—"

"Mad, mad with grief, I think, over the loss of your son."

Wildly, Liam shook his head. "I don't remember

her, or the child." But there'd been that dream of fire, grief, and darkness. *Nancy.*

As if to confirm his thought, Clara said, "Nancy. Her name's Nancy McMahon. Theodore's investigators found her. That means my grandfather's will, too, if they haven't already."

"Your—your plan…" he stammered.

"My plan is in pieces. It never was very good to begin with, was it? I should have known that. There were far too many factors I couldn't control. Like you. Maybe you were right about me, Liam."

"Right, how?"

"When you accused me of being like my grandfather."

"No."

"It was abysmally arrogant of me to think I could pluck you from the nothingness of death and use you to my own ends."

"I was wrong. You're nothing like that old bugger."

"And now just look where we are! You, pursued quite literally by your past. Me, pursued by the results of my ill-advised actions, and with poor Nancy to consider."

She looked him full in the eyes, her tears flown. Another bright emotion replaced them: determination. "I want to rescue her, Liam."

"Eh?"

"Nancy. I want to take her out of that awful excuse for a hospital and bring her here."

"What!" His wife wanted to bring his other wife to live with them? "Now, lass, think on this a moment."

"Do you suppose I've thought of anything else

since I laid eyes on her? You didn't see what it's like, Liam. I wouldn't leave a stray cat there. I wouldn't even leave my grandfather there."

"I see you're all fired up, and it's a kindhearted impulse, but—"

"I've already talked to Theodore about it. Once someone's committed to one of those wards, it's very difficult to get her out again. The doctors will never release her to me."

"So, then," Liam huffed, half agonized and half relieved.

"That's why you, as her husband, have to get her released."

"You're mad! I can't go walking in there. I'm supposed to be dead."

"But you are quite manifestly not dead, are you? And as you've said, my plan is already in pieces. I'll not put my welfare or happiness ahead of someone who needs my help."

"No?" Liam wanted desperately to step away from her, but couldn't let go of her even now. "And what about the welfare of all those already under your roof—those on whose behalf you were after acting in the first place?"

Her chin raised a notch. "I've already failed them."

"You want to bring a madwoman in here, as well? I suppose she truly is mad? With grief, you say."

"I fear so." Clara barely breathed the words.

"If I'm married to her"—this woman he couldn't even recall—"and if we were married in Ireland, it will be vows we took before a priest. There's no divorce in the Catholic Church. What does that do to you and me?"

"I refuse to put myself first."

"I've no need to put you first, Clara—you're already there. You're first and last with me, don't you see that? Vital as breath! Are you asking me to put you aside for her? For that I can never do."

"I am asking you to do what's right."

"And what's right about living beneath a roof with two wives? What of the fact that once your grandfather acts on what he's learned we'll be put out in the street—children, madwoman, and all?"

"I know I've made disastrous choices, but I can change none of that now."

The impact of her words went through Liam like a knife. "That's what you feel, is it? That 'twas disastrous to raise me? To kiss me, to lie with me?"

"I never said that."

Liam's emotions rose in a crashing wave. "You'd rather I'd gone in the river and you'd never known me."

"Not that, no. But I must take responsibility for what I've done. We don't know what kind of past you've lived, nor where your scruples lie."

"Oh, so now I'm beyond redemption, am I? Just some six odd feet of Irish you raised, with no morals and no expectation of them." Truly angry now, he lowered his voice. "Well, you didn't mind that when you had me between your legs!"

"I know, and you've every right to be angry with me. But I can honestly say taking you into my bed was the only time throughout this tangle I acted on my own behalf."

And even now Liam wanted her—even angry, more so because he was angry. The pure craving for her rode his blood like that for drink. He wanted his tongue in her mouth, tasting her sweetness. He wanted her heat.

"Come with me to the hospital and see Nancy," Clara beseeched. "If you can see her and leave her there, you're not the man I believe you to be."

"You don't know who I am. You've just said that."

"Perhaps not." Her eyes held him, inescapable. "But I've felt you in my soul. Despite all the evidence, I believe in you, Liam McMahon."

And, agonized, Liam bargained, "I'll go with you to see her tomorrow, lass, but you'll have to go upstairs with me tonight." He lowered his voice and whispered in her ear, making her shiver, "I can't go on living without a taste of you, and I'm your responsibility, after all."

Chapter Thirty-One

Clara lay staring up at the ceiling of her father's room, a broad expanse of shadowed gray, and marveled at herself. She could still feel the imprint of Liam's fingers all over her body, a wild tingle; the taste of him lingered in her mouth. Touching him solved nothing, and only made her want him more.

She'd never considered herself a stupid woman. Above-average intelligence, she would have said, without arrogance. But she'd been a fool in all this. Dead foolish, as Ruella would say. And the plan of which she'd initially conceived now lay around her in ruins.

She couldn't even walk away. As Liam said, she had responsibilities to him, to the children, and to Nancy now that Clara knew about her.

But she didn't think she could give Liam up. What had just passed between them proved that. She could try, but she'd suffer for it—they both would—and whatever this force that connected them, it would draw them together again.

So what to do? Abandon Nancy who, at best, could only be considered an inconvenient complication? No. Forsake the children who relied upon her? See them go back into service, where they would live perilous and miserable lives? No. The desire to protect them had got her into all this.

Was there any way to keep her grandfather from tossing them all out? He sometimes moved slowly, but always inexorably. She could go to the old man and beg; he'd enjoy that and might well string her along for a time, to savor her humiliation. But would that have an ultimate, beneficial outcome?

She'd go and efface herself in an instant, if she thought it meant she could keep Liam. Upon that thought, her fingers stole toward him, encountered his, and clung tight. He returned the pressure. So he did not sleep, then, any more than she.

"Liam, what are we to do?"

"I am going to meet Nancy McMahon, since I promised. And whatever you think of me, I'm a man of me word."

"I don't know what to think of you." She rolled on her side and looked at him. He lay like an effigy on a medieval coffin—a handsome effigy—his profile a dark outline in the dim room. Her heart twisted in her breast; she knew she might look at him forever, the proud prow of his nose, the pleasing sweep of his jaw, the black hair mussed from her touch, and not have enough. "My mind tells me you're a rascal. My heart…"

"Have I your heart, Clara?" He rolled toward her also, and his fingers threaded through hers with magical ease. "Do I possess you, or do you just possess me, a man you created on that table in your workroom where I awoke? Admit it—'twas what you wanted, an obedient creation."

"I admit it."

"Do I affect you one part the way you affect me? Only look." His fingers drew hers lower down to press against a pertinent part of his body. "I already want you again."

Clara freed her hand from his grasp, but only to caress him, helpless to prevent herself. She wrapped her fingers around the hot, great length of him, all velvet and steel.

"You affect me," she whispered. "Need you even ask?"

"Do I own you?" He leaned into her, and his breath caressed her lips an instant before his mouth found them. Lightning flared in the darkness as heat speared all the way to Clara's toes. "I want to own you, as you own me."

"Liam," she began, and got no further. His tongue filled her mouth; it wooed and danced and tasted so sharply of his essence all else fled her mind. For an instant she knew only existence, the two of them together, utterly complete.

This feeling she craved, this wild, hot, and sweet wholeness that came only when they joined. With a shuddering sigh, she guided him to the opening between her thighs. Pleasure spiked when he slid in, a knife going into its hilt, smooth and tight. She reached up to bury her fingers in the long silk of his hair then, and hung on for the wild, familiar ride.

When it was done she wept hot, inelegant tears for the beauty of this thing they shared, the impossibility of it, and the desperation. He cradled her against him in silence and let her cry as a child might, one with a broken heart.

After a long time, the light outside the windows began to gray. The new day approached, invading even this, Clara's one refuge.

"Now, now," Liam whispered then, his brogue a

soft, beautiful melody. "How can you cry when I love you so?"

Love. But it was so much more than that.

She splayed her fingers across his cheek, caressed the roughness of beard there, the soft strength of his lips, and the indent of a dimple beside them. Dead handsome, he was, but she couldn't say that was the only reason she loved him.

She certainly hadn't sought for love when she began all this. Neither had she sought this searing, scorching pleasure.

"I don't want to lose you," she admitted, giving him the truth.

"You won't, lass." He turned his face and pressed a kiss into the palm of her hand. "I go to meet this Nancy McMahon because you ask it. But she means nothing to me."

"She might, once you see her. It could all begin to come back to you." Clara added, though ashamed to, "She's very pretty."

"You think I want anyone but you?"

"You did want her once. She's your wife."

"Clara, ever since you kissed me on that work table I've been yours. Whatever else happens between us, don't you dare doubt that."

****

"We are here to see Mrs. McMahon. This man is her husband."

Clara spoke the words in a clear, firm voice. Was Liam the only one who could hear the terror hidden beneath them? She'd got herself up for this visit in her best frock, a high-necked garment of bottle green, and wore a hat that tipped over her brow. She'd insisted, also, that he don yet another suit from Miller's used clothing shop, bought with his hard-earned, or stolen, money. With Theodore Collwys once more in attendance, they made a small delegation.

The hospital, if such it could be called, stank inside like a daylight boozer. Women wandered everywhere in various states of dress and undress—staring, pacing, moaning, weeping, and even laughing—wild-eyed, wild-haired creatures Liam found it impossible to regard impassively. Which among these wretched souls might be his wife? How could he have wed the woman yet not remember?

He remembered everything about Clara—the curve of her calf, the soft yield of her thighs, the sweet mound of her breast. How she clenched around the length of him when he loved her. He eyed her now, admiring the delicate line her nose made beneath the brim of the hat.

The woman who received them—tall, spare, and gray-haired—regarded him unhappily. "I remember you. You came to see your wife twice after she was admitted, and then stopped coming."

Liam heard Clara gasp softly, and his stomach muscles clenched at the words, confirmation of his worst dread and nail in the coffin of his future.

The woman went on, "I was told upon her admission you were unable to care for her." She eyed him dispassionately. "You do not look unable."

Liam bowed slightly. "I suffered an injury and was incapacitated for a time." He dared not look at Clara. "May I please see my wife?"

Mrs. Wright, for such was the gorgon's name, narrowed her eyes. "You may, for five minutes, and on your own." She glared at Clara and Collwys. "These two upset her mightily the last time they were here."

Collwys stepped forward, brandishing a mitt full of papers. "Mrs. Wright, I do not think you understand. Mr. McMahon has come to take his wife out of this hospital. Here is the documentation authorizing you to release her."

Mrs. Wright accepted the papers, donned a pair of spectacles, and scrutinized them. Liam had no idea what words were written there, and he hadn't signed any authorization. His eyes stole away to the door of the office, which stood open. A woman hovered there, peering in at them, dressed in a long blouse and nothing else. When his gaze found her, she tore the garment open and bared her breasts at him.

A steam unit trundled forward and seized the woman, far from gently. She shrieked as it towed her away.

Mrs. Wright, still inspecting the papers, never so much as glanced up. *Jesus, what a place!* Clara might be right—if this woman, Nancy, had ever meant anything to Liam, he couldn't leave her here.

No matter what it might mean to his life.

"Well," Mrs. Wright said slowly, "this does seem to be in order. By rights I should consult with the hospital's board of governors before making any release."

Theodore bent forward and placed his hand on the desk in front of the woman. "On the other hand, you are terribly overcrowded, and you work very hard, Mrs. Wright. Surely you deserve a personal reward? And surely releasing a patient into the arms of a loving relation can only benefit everyone concerned?"

Liam saw a fold of money beneath Collwys's hand.

So did Mrs. Wright. Her eyebrows twitched, and she slid the money out from beneath Theodore's hand and into her own pocket.

"Let me take you to our Nancy." She glanced at Liam. "If she recognizes you after all this time, Mr. McMahon, then I'm sure I can see my way to placing her in your care."

"But what if she doesn't recognize him?" Clara objected. "She is very ill."

"Well, then we shall just need to think again."

And she'll require another bribe, Liam thought, not without bitterness, as Mrs. Wright stood up and briskly led them from the office.

Clara, head high, sailed after her, followed by Collwys and lastly Liam himself.

They walked into noise and chaos. It assaulted Liam from every side, along with a terrible barrage of emotions. The bare-breasted woman had been towed away, but her sisters all screamed in her stead, or moaned or wept. He thought of Clara weeping in his arms early this morning, like a woman lost. These, though, were truly lost souls.

They passed through one large room, beneath an arch, and into another. Clara reached for his arm and then caught herself; she wouldn't touch him here while she posed as Nancy's employer. But she whispered, "There she is."

"Where?"

Then he saw. The woman to which Mrs. Wright led them huddled in a corner, hunkered down on bent knees, her shoulder half turned to the room. A mass of yellow curls, that would have been pretty if not so tangled, clustered round her head, and Liam just glimpsed a pale, delicate cheek. Clara hadn't lied. Nancy was very pretty. But the sight of her stirred nothing in Liam's mind.

"Nancy?"

When Mrs. Wright called her name, she rose to her full height, and Liam saw she cradled something in her arms. No—she cradled the memory of something.

"These people have come to see you," Mrs. Wright said. "These two were here yesterday. But look at this man. Do you know him?"

Nancy raised pale, wide, empty blue eyes to Liam's face. Nay, but they weren't quite empty—it might have been better if they were. Even though he did not remember her, he could only sympathize with her pain.

"Hello, Nancy," he said, because Clara had told him to, because he must. "It's been too long. Do you not remember me?"

The creature drew a breath, and her hands flew out, releasing the imaginary bundle. A new, brighter spark entered her eyes.

"Liam!" she cried, and threw herself into his arms.

Chapter Thirty-Two

The summons came at dawn following an endless night. No one in the house had slept. Nancy McMahon wept and cried out endlessly. While Clara and Liam did their best to deal with her, Georgina comforted the children.

The steamcab puffed up to the door while Clara sat at the dining room table with her head in her hands, staring at a cup of tea she felt unable to drink. Liam remained upstairs with Nancy in the room Clara had assigned her, which was Clara's own. Nancy didn't want Liam out of her sight.

Neither did Clara, much good it did her.

"Two gentlemen to see you, Mistress." Dax hovered over her, looking worried—if a steamie could reveal emotions. He lowered his voice to a hiss. "I recognize them from your grandfather's house. You don't suppose they've come to take me back?"

They hadn't. As soon as Clara met them in the parlor, she knew trouble now lapped round her ears. Her grandfather had sent not just lawyers but bulldogs, the toughest in his pack.

"We have information," one of them began without preamble, drawing papers from an attaché case not unlike Theodore's, "that the man you are calling your husband, one William T. McMahon, was already married at the time you and he exchanged vows. The man is in fact a bigamist and a criminal. In effect, this violates the law, nullifies your marriage, and defies the terms of your bequest."

Clara accepted the papers and stared half unseeing at them. The one on top appeared to be a record of the ship's manifest on which Liam and Nancy were listed as having traveled to St. John's, Newfoundland.

"And this"—the second bulldog presented his own sheaf of papers—"will serve you notice to vacate this premises, since you are no longer entitled to reside herein. Because you are family, your grandfather will be merciful. He allows you five days."

"Five." Clara thought of everything—everyone—under this roof, and all requiring her protection. The children. Georgina. Now Nancy. What hope had she of re-housing them?

She raised her eyes to the faces of the lawyers, one after the other. "Is my grandfather willing to negotiate? Will he agree to meet with me?"

The man on the left bared his teeth in a smile that failed to reach his eyes. "Would you like to make an appointment? I believe he is free tomorrow afternoon."

"Are you saying I must schedule an appointment to see my own grandfather?"

"Mr. Van Hamelin is a busy man. I will carry your request back to him. Let's say you present yourself at three."

"There must be some way we can work around the terms of the bequest."

"I'm sorry, Miss Allen. You are now twenty-one and not in a legal marriage. You have violated the letter of the agreement. Your grandfather regrets..."

"I'm sure he does," Clara said bitterly. She looked

into the bulldog's eyes. "However, I'm sure this paper"—she rattled the record of the manifest—"is in error. Obviously my husband is not the same William McMahon as is listed here. My lawyer, Mr. Collwys, will file a paper with the court alleging that."

"Mr. Collwys is of course free to do so. I hope he will then explain to the court why, if the man now living as your husband is not the here-referenced William McMahon, he in fact claimed a woman named Nancy McMahon from the hospital for the insane on Porter Avenue yesterday afternoon, in your presence."

The second man said, "We have spoken with the administrator, a Mrs. Wright. She insists you had paperwork releasing the woman into her husband's custody and says she in fact recognized Mr. McMahon and reiterates she never would have been so neglectful as to release a patient to a man not her husband."

Clara's head began to pound. For an instant she thought she would be sick all over the bulldogs' highly polished shoes.

She thrust the papers back at them. "You may tell my grandfather to go to hell. We will not vacate this house. I have responsibilities—many of them."

"Then your grandfather intends to engage the police force to forcibly remove you and take your husband back to prison. We are still investigating how he came to be released and living here with you, Miss Allen."

"And there," Clara said, striving desperately for an air of insouciance, "is the heart of your error, sirs. There are obviously two William McMahons, whose histories have become entangled. My lawyer has told me the other man in question died in jail, while my husband is obviously very much alive."

They exchanged glances.

"The existence of a second Mr. McMahon will need to be proven, Miss Allen. Meanwhile, I suggest you begin packing."

Clara trailed them out to the front hallway where, from upstairs, the soft sound of hysterical weeping could be heard.

The first bulldog paused. "A truly curious thing, Miss Allen, how a woman claiming a man for her husband would then liberate his wife from a mental institution."

"It's called compassion, sir. Working for my grandfather, you've doubtless never before encountered it."

Dax rumbled up to open the door. The second bulldog shot him a suspicious look, but the improved, polished Dax bore little resemblance to the battered model Clara and Liam had brought home, and the men departed without comment.

Clara turned from the door to see Liam poised at the top of the stairs. Their eyes met for an instant before Nancy called his name, and he turned away.

****

"Five days. We have five days. Less than that now. Theodore, is there anything we can do?"

Theodore, a third of the huddle that included Clara and Georgina, frowned. "I must file a stay with the court on the grounds of hardship—given you've a madwoman upstairs." He shot Clara a careful look. "Does she ever stop wailing?"

"She hasn't yet," Georgina answered for Clara, who remained silent. "Not since you brought her into this house. It's stirred up all kinds of distress with the children. Bad memories."

"I'm hoping Liam will be able to calm her down, in time." Clara glanced toward the parlor doorway as if she might see through it. She ached for Liam's company as with a livid wound. She looked at Theodore. "What chance will a stay have, with the court?"

He shook his head. "Most of the justices are acquaintances of your grandfather, if not in his pocket. But I can try."

"Do so, please." Clara licked suddenly dry lips. "But I suppose we should have a contingency plan. What's to be done?"

"I'll tell you, if I may." Theodore drew a breath. "I'll try and secure another premises for you and as many of the children as possible."

"I've no funds to lease a place."

"I'll lend you the money."

"With no prospect of me being able to repay you?"

Theodore shrugged. "Liam is earning. If"—he scowled—"Liam does not end up in jail. I've no idea how that tangle is going to work out. Right now, Maynard is claiming the prison records are in error and he never housed a William T. McMahon, even though he took money for his keep. Frankly, I feel we need to interview the sexton—there must be more to this than meets the eye."

"Send Liam to see him," Georgina suggested. "That should shake him and loosen his tongue."

"Meanwhile," Clara said heavily, "I will go and seek mercy from my grandfather."

Theodore snorted. "Based on the likelihood of you

finding it, we'd better make whatever other precautions we can." His hand came out and covered Georgina's. "My dear, I suggest you bring whichever of the children can't bear to be parted from you, and come to me."

Georgina stiffened. "I beg your pardon?"

His eyes met hers, honest and intent. "This isn't the way I wanted it to happen—I wanted to woo and persuade you, give you flowers and all the other beautiful things you deserve."

"Mr. Collwys, I am a respectable woman—"

"Highly respectable. Georgina, I wouldn't ask you to marry me if you weren't."

Georgina sprang to her feet. Theodore rose with her, his hand clutching hers.

Beautiful eyes wide, Georgina breathed, "Is that what you're doing? Asking me to marry you?"

"In earnest. Georgie, dear, you know how I feel about you, and that's why I broke my engagement. I don't care if my family remains estranged from me—let them. I want no one but you. We'll start our family with the children we already have, and soon, please God, our own."

Georgina stood as if stricken, giving no appearance of a woman receiving an ardent proposal. "I told you before, your career—"

"Damn my career to hell! My heart's not in the big dollar cases. I'll be happy helping folks desperate for representation, and even happier if you're there with me. We may struggle a bit for money, but we'll make do."

"It's a pretty dream," Georgina said, "but I'm afraid the reality—the snubs, the insults and the hatred—would soon make you sorry."

"Nothing could ever make me sorry, so long as you're at my side. Do you want me to beg, Georgie? Because I will." Hastily, he fished in one pocket and brought out a small red velvet case. "When I broke off the engagement with Roanne, she insisted on keeping the ring. I wouldn't have wanted to give you that one anyway. Secondhand is not good enough for you. This isn't much—not as much as you deserve. But I chose it with all my heart."

He flipped the lid of the box with a thumb that trembled. Inside sat a dainty gold ring set with a cluster of diamonds in the shape of a heart, so perfect for Georgina's tiny hand that tears sprang to Clara's eyes.

"Oh!" Georgina breathed.

"If you accept this and the wedding band that goes with it, I promise I'll add a diamond for every precious year you give me, so long as we live."

Georgina's resistance crumbled. A beautiful, radiant smile came to her face an instant before she threw herself into Theodore's arms and held tight.

"Yes. Yes, yes, yes!"

Clara blinked back tears of joy, tinged with the faintest hint of sorrow. What would she do without Georgina's steady, gentle presence? They'd been together since the day Clara's father brought the girl into this house, frail, half-starved, and shattered. Yet this union felt right, and might be the one good thing to come of this awful situation Clara had wrought.

"Thank you," Theodore whispered into Georgina's ear, and kissed her. "I can face anything now." His eyes met Clara's over Georgina's head. "We can face anything."

Chapter Thirty-Three

"Listen to me, lass. You have to stop this weeping. You do yourself no good."

Nancy clung to Liam's hands and continued to sob. He wondered wearily where she got all the tears. Exhaustion nibbled at him; he'd been up with her all the night, and she drained his emotions the way a horsefly might drink blood. Add to that the emptiness he felt from Clara's absence—a debilitating loss—and he now struggled badly.

He knew Clara had acted out of mercy, but he began to wonder if it had been wise to take Nancy from the hospital. Sure and it was a terrible place where he wouldn't leave a diseased dog, but maybe they could have found somewhere better, somewhere she could get the care she obviously needed. He, dealing with his own demons, felt singularly unable to provide the right support.

He'd tried several times to explain to Nancy that he remembered nothing of the past they shared. She either refused to listen or failed to understand. Caught in a nightmare she continued to relive, she insisted on believing he shared it with her.

"Dead, he is dead." Her pretty eyes, awash with tears, reached for his. "I did love him, you know, so very much."

"Sure, and you did. Faith, who would doubt it?"

The "him" being her child. Their child. It still amazed Liam he could fail to remember his own son.

"I didn't mean for it to happen. 'Twas an accident. You were there; you saw. You know!"

"I do, Nancy. Quiet yourself now, or you'll become ill."

He ached to ask her questions. She was the one person from whom he might conceivably get the answers he needed about his past, their marriage, where he'd come from, and who he truly was. But the poor, mad creature remained so fragile he dared broach none of that. Just the sight of him sent her into this state.

"Where were you?" she asked piteously now. "Where, when I was in that terrible place?"

Ah, and this made a slight departure from the constant lamenting.

He resisted the impulse to smooth her fair curls. A bonny thing she was, right enough. But the woman he'd have chosen for his wife?

His heart hurt anew for Clara, who was just downstairs and who centered his life.

"I had a mishap. Remember I told you that? It's why I recall so little of what happened to us." He added very gently, "We sailed from Ireland, right? And before that we were in Dublin, but we're not from Dublin, correct?"

"We had Tommy with us then. So sore hurt! The fire! Oh, Tommy…"

The lamenting began again, a circle of the same sorrows Liam had heard all the night long. He sighed deeply and tried to ease his hands, into which Nancy's fingers had dug. Of one thing he could be certain: he had traveled with her from Ireland and was a firm presence in this nightmare she inhabited.

His head dropped over their joined hands, and despair flooded his heart. He ached to remember, but would remembering do him any good?

A whisper of sound from behind told him the room door had opened. Nancy hated the light, so he kept the drapes drawn and the lamp low, but he knew without seeing her that Clara stood behind him.

"Liam, if I might steal you for a moment—"

He got to his feet and strove to free himself from Nancy's grasp. She protested and began to weep harder.

"Just for a moment, Nancy, and I'll be right outside. Only give me an instant, love, before I'm back." He felt the impact of that word—love—go through the woman who stood behind him. Could Clara truly doubt his feelings for her?

Nancy wailed when he left her; Clara never looked at him as they stepped outside into the hallway.

He drew a breath. "Listen to me, Clara—that was an endearment, only."

"I know."

"The poor, pitiful thing—"

"You don't need to explain."

He lowered his voice and whispered fiercely, "She means nothing to me."

Clara did look at him then, a measuring glance. He wondered what she saw. His weariness? His desperation? "She's your wife. She should mean something."

"She should, but she doesn't. Christ, do you think I'm proud of that? I'm in there with her clinging to me as to a life raft, and all I can think of is you."

Compassion flooded Clara's eyes. Maybe that

made one of the things he loved best about her—her ability to not only sympathize with others but to act upon it. But no, he adored everything about her, each hair, each fleck of green in those great, gray eyes.

"Do you think you can persuade her to settle?"

"Cursed if I know—she hasn't yet. There's a good reason she was in that place, vile as it was. She blames herself for whatever happened to the child, though clearly 'twas a terrible tragedy." He remembered again the garish dream—Nancy coming out into the dark after him, arguing. Fire and screaming. "If only I could recall it. This wall in my mind is like a physical pain."

"But"—Clara voiced the truth that lay between them—"she remembers you."

"Yes." He couldn't deny it. "Have you something in your father's surgery that might calm her for a spell, just so I might catch my breath?"

"I'll look. But we can't keep her sedated long. It's what I came to tell you; I have news."

Liam had hoped she'd come to hold him in her arms, or at least touch him, and help to save his sanity.

Woodenly, she went on, "Georgina will be going to live with Theodore, and taking those of the children as will be happiest with her, such as Jimmie and probably the rest of the littlest ones."

"Eh? She's agreed to live in sin with the man?"

"No, they'll be married as soon as Theodore can wrangle a license. He's gone to arrange that now."

"Well, good for him. He's a man to stand by his principles, that I will say. And lucky to win her."

"She loves him, and he loves her. That's what truly matters." Disconcertingly, Clara's eyes filled with tears. "It won't be easy for them, but better, better than—"

"Than us? God, you're right."

Behind the closed door, Nancy called Liam's name.

"Please," he whispered at Clara, "please tell me we've some hope."

She lifted her hands. "Right now, it's hard to see any."

"Tell me you'll be with me tonight, so my heart may go on beating."

She shook her head. "Not a good idea. I must go and see my grandfather tomorrow—ask him for mercy." Her face twisted in repugnance. "I don't expect any, so meanwhile we plan. It will help to split the household. Theodore may be able to find us lodgings. He thinks I should set you, Nancy, and some of the older children up somewhere safe. He also thinks I should reside with him and Georgina."

"You won't do that." Wild denial arose in Liam's chest. "You won't leave me that way."

"It may be best. And"—she gestured at the door—"it's not as if you'll be alone."

"Ah, Clara!" He nearly fell to his knees. "You speak about responsibility—to the children, to her." He jerked his head at the door. "But what of your responsibility to me?" That wasn't fair, but he no longer cared. "You raised me from the dead; you can't abandon me."

"Do you think it's what I want?" Pain flared in her voice. "Do you think my agony is less than your own?"

"I don't know, is it?" He couldn't imagine anyone hurting worse than he did. "Tell me, Clara, tell me."

"I still love you." She confessed it the way a woman would confess to murder. "God help me."

He had to close his eyes for an instant; his relief felt so sharp it hurt. "Then there must be hope for us." He argued against her silence, "Love can accomplish most anything."

Clara nodded at the door behind him. "Have you remembered anything? I thought seeing her, being with her, might bring things back from behind that wall you say is in your mind."

"Nothing yet. Her sorrow is like a third presence in the room with us. I can barely think for it."

"Does she speak of your son?"

"Of little else."

"Yet you still don't remember him?"

"No, and how do you think that makes me feel? There was a fire—started by accident, so she says. The child must have been badly burned and died later, during our journey. She blames herself. She says we argued."

"About what?"

He shrugged. "Me boozing." He smiled bitterly. "You chose a real gem for your husband, didn't you, Clara? A drunk, a criminal, and already married."

Clara refused to rise to that bait. "You need to remember so we can get at the truth, all of it. Stay with her tonight."

"No."

"Lie with her, sleep with her, and perhaps then you'll remember."

"Clara, please." He did reach out then, seized her hands. Slowly he sank to his knees and pressed his forehead to her hands, like a man at prayer. "Don't turn from me."

"I'm not. But your wife—your true wife—needs

you now. And you need to find out who you are."

"Clara, take pity on me."

She bent to him then. He felt her lips on his hair, quick and fierce and, when he tipped his face up, on his brow, his cheek, his lips. Raw hunger ripped through him from her mouth to his, and the taste of her penetrated to his soul.

The fleeting taste. She drew him up by his hands onto his feet and backed away, pain, desire, and regret in her eyes.

"Find out what you can," she bade. "Do that for me."

Chapter Thirty-Four

"Well, Granddaughter; two visits in the space of a month. To what do I owe this unprecedented attentiveness?"

Clara regarded her grandfather with open dislike. She'd not slept all night, cold in her father's big bed and thinking of Liam across the hall in hers with Nancy. Torture, she'd reflected, would surely be no harder to bear.

She presented herself now, at the specified hour, filled with misgivings. This time tomorrow Georgina and Theodore would be wed. Clara wanted to be home with the friend dearest to her heart, planning the occasion. Instead she knew Georgina to be engaged in frantic packing while she, Clara, was here.

She tipped her chin up. "How are you, Grandfather? Well?"

His sharp gaze moved over her from head to toe. "I am dying. And I imagine you'll be glad to hear it." He smiled grimly. "But I have to admit, I wondered if you'd call on me before your allotted time was up. Come to beg, have you?"

In truth, Clara had. At home and desperate, she'd believed she could do or say whatever she must, and grovel if necessary. Now she did not feel so sure. "I have come," she said, "to ask you a question: why are you so determined to toss me and my entire household out into the street? How will it benefit you to have that house standing empty?"

He twitched a thin eyebrow at her. "What makes you truly think the place will remain empty long? I have a prospective tenant, a doctor. He wishes to use the surgery."

That knocked Clara back on her heels. Her grandfather smiled wryly. "What, girl? Did you think your father the only doctor in the city? He wasn't even the best but made a poor excuse for a professional, giving his services away more than half the time."

"My father championed something of which you have clearly never heard: mercy."

"He was a soft fool. I told your mother so before she ever married him. Would she listen?"

"She chose for the sake of another commodity to which you are a stranger, Grandfather—love."

"Ah, and now we get to the crux of it, do we? The heart of the discussion." He waved a hand so frail Clara could almost see through it. "Will you sit, or would you rather do your begging on your knees?"

Clara experienced a sharp, painful flashback to Liam on his knees before her in the hallway outside her room. She struggled to dismiss it and then decided not: what she did now, she did for love, for him. He would be her strength.

She sat very carefully on the edge of a chair, her chin still high.

"Now, I imagine," her grandfather said, "you will reproach me and cite your adherence to your father's supposed high morals—you who took for husband a man straight out of the county jail, a common street brawler, a bigamist, and Irish to boot, and presented him to me."

"I do not believe all of what you say about him is true."

"Then you're as much the fool as your father."

"The information you have about my husband is not complete."

"If you suppose that, you're a silly chit." Van Hamelin's gaze prodded her cruelly. "I expect you are going to say you love him."

Clara hesitated. How many weapons did she want to place in this old man's hands? Instead of answering, she asked in turn, "Did you love my mother?" Was he even capable of the emotion?

Van Hamelin sat back. "Of course I did, at least until she defied me."

"Not much strength in a love that could be destroyed by so small a thing as defiance."

"Would you love a dog that bit your hand?"

"My mother was not a dog. She was a good and honorable woman."

He sneered. "What is honorable about tossing away the excellent opportunities I worked to provide her? I came to this city, girl, with nothing. I struggled, bargained, and yes, lied and cheated, to gain what I now have."

"You must have wished for her to have the house on Virginia Street, despite her defiance, or you wouldn't have entailed it to her—and me. Why take it from me now?"

"This isn't about the house."

"It most certainly is, and it's about my responsibilities. I've a dozen people under that roof."

"Including your bigamist and his mad wife?"

Clara swallowed hard, then leaned forward and fixed him with her gaze. "Listen to me. You can fault me all you wish for failing to toe your line and grovel at your feet. But if you've one jot of honesty in you—*honesty*, for I don't expect love—you'll see that what I've done is bargain, lie, and, yes, cheat, to hold what I need." She sprang to her feet. "And if you can be proud of that, so can I!"

For the first time her grandfather looked taken aback. He stared at her with cold blue eyes, and his spotted hands clutched the arms of his chair.

Clara turned to the door, then paused and lifted her chin another notch.

"As for begging—I'd rather do my begging on the streets with my bigamist husband."

She sailed out of the room and through the big foyer with its marble floor, propelled by something beyond anger. The steamie sprang to open the door for her, and she went through it. Not until she stood on the front walk facing Delaware Avenue did the trembling in her knees catch up with her and make her pause.

She'd done it now. She'd truly cooked her goose.

****

"Tell me where I can find the sexton, Old Tim."

Ruella, sleeves rolled up and arms buried to the elbows in bread dough, looked up, startled, when Liam spoke. She blinked at the sight of him leaning in through the door of her kitchen and said, "You shouldn't be here. By gaw, what if you're seen?"

Liam tugged the brim of his cloth cap lower over his forehead, though he already had it pulled well down. He'd walked here from Virginia Street, wondering if he retraced the path along which Ruella had trundled him the night he died, and reconnoitered well around the building that stood at the corner of Delaware and Eagle. He'd circled around back and through the jail yard, trying to ignore the prickles that crept up his spine at being where they'd hanged him that night, and waited till a tradesman came out the back door to slip in and find Ruella's kitchen.

"Had to see you, lass," he said simply. "It's desperate."

He doubted many men called Ruella a lass, unless her pretty-boy copper did. What had she called him? Fagan.

She straightened and scraped the dough from her muscular arms and hands. "Dangerous way to go about seeking my help, innit? Couldn't you have sent a messenger? One of the kiddies?"

"No." He shook his head. "I don't want Clara to find out."

"Get in here, then, and shut the door."

Liam obeyed, his nose twitching at the scents that filled the kitchen, of new-baked bread and rolls.

Ruella fixed him with a stern eye. "I'd never lie to Miss Clara."

"I'm not asking you to lie. Just keep your trap shut."

"My what?"

"Your lovely trap."

"She's been a good friend to me, Clara has."

Liam grimaced. "And you've been a good friend to her, dragging home dead men."

"Just the one."

"You think you're not involved in this? Listen—we're out of the house on Virginia Street in five days."

"What?"

"Four, now. Clara's gone to see her grandfather, but you can guess how much kindness she'll win from him."

"None."

"None," Liam repeated. "She's breaking up the household. Wee Georgina's going to the lawyer, Collwys."

"Bloody hell! To live in sin?"

"No, they'll be married."

"Well, well."

"And Clara wants to set me up in another, smaller household with me wife."

"Your what, then?"

"We liberated her yesterday, from the hospital for the insane."

"You have brought some news, haven't you?" Ruella studied him frankly. "And what of Clara?"

"What, indeed? She's planning on going with Georgina." Liam swallowed a lump of raw, hot pain. "I can't live with that, Miss Ruella. I have to be with her."

"Quite the pickle, innit? What do you want from me, big Irishman?"

"Clara told me to find out who I am. Not until I break down this wall in my head and remember will I be able to set Nancy aside."

"The wife, you mean? Is that what you want to do?" Ruella clicked her tongue. "And her mad."

"I'll provide for her any way I can. But I can't live like this, without Clara. Better I'd ended out there in the yard."

Ruella's eyes narrowed. "Have you remembered anything?"

"Snippets here and there, as well as a few things seen in a dream. Clara believes I will remember, because Cassie did, or seemed to."

"Cassie wasn't dead as long as you were, though, was she? Minutes, as I understand it, rather than well over an hour. What do you want with Old Tim?"

"I want to find out what Maynard's about with these hangings, and why he chose me. There must be a reason, but so far it makes no sense. I've seen what Maynard gets up to at Sterling House, and I understand his need for the ready. But taking pennies for my keep won't finance those habits. I'm missing something."

Ruella shook her head. "That's as may be, but you won't get much from Old Tim. He's confused on his best days."

"Still, I've nowhere else to begin."

Ruella chewed her lip. "Look—you're in a bit of luck. Me boy Fagan's just come off a shift, and he's hanging round cooling his heels till I'm done here, so we might…" Incredibly Ruella blushed.

Liam blinked at her.

"Don't go looking at me that way. A woman's entitled to a bit of a tumble, and he's a fine, big lad even if he is Irish. And why should Miss Clara have all the fun?"

For the life of him, Liam could think of nothing to say.

"Brendan's looking into what's been going on here," Ruella confided. "And he can take you to Old Tim. You just wait out in the yard, and I'll send him." She eyed Liam sternly. "That's the best I can do."

Without a word, Liam went.

Chapter Thirty-Five

Liam cooled his heels in the jail yard far too long, and as he did he thought about dying. His eyes, quick and careful, moved around the space: perhaps forty by thirty paces, it opened onto Eagle Street, was paved in brick, and surrounded by brick walls on three sides. The building at back had no windows, the jail kitchen but one. Not many eyes would see what happened here on a cold, dark November night.

He tried to determine just where the noose had been rigged and at last decided it must have hung from a supporting beam high on the brick wall next to the kitchen. No hint of rope betrayed the spot now, but it would be a shadowed corner at night, and a box made of rough wood had been shoved against that wall.

He closed his eyes and struggled to remember what he didn't want to recall—rain pissing down and a torch thrust through that bracket there, casting a garish, smoky light that reflected off the wet brick. Hard hands forcing him, well-bound, up on the box, and the harsh rasp of the rope at his throat. The terrible sound of wood scraping brick as, without ceremony, the box got kicked away. Then pain, pain, *pain*.

A utilitarian death, it had been. But did he remember, or just imagine? His skin pricked all over his body, and he broke into a cold sweat. No way to tell, but he wanted out of this place, and now.

"McMahon?"

Ruella's voice brought his eyes open and banished the terrible scene from his mind. She stood before him with a fine, strapping lad at her side. Nearly as tall as Liam himself, the fellow had to top six feet, with sturdy limbs and a deep chest, light brown hair, rosy cheeks, and eyes so blue they shone in the dingy yard.

"This is Brendan Fagan. I had to fill him in on who you are. He's been looking into what's been happening here, and he'll take you to see Old Tim."

Liam eyed the lad frankly. "Glad to meet you, Fagan. Not the superstitious sort, are you? Not afraid of meeting a ghost out here in this yard?"

"I am that," Fagan replied, "and a bit put off by the idea. But Miss Ruella can be very persuasive. And I'll admit I'm after wanting to know just what's going on. A mystery, it is."

"Good man."

"Miss Ruella says you survived the hanging that night, but no one knew?"

Liam glanced at Ruella, who winked at him. Ah, so she hadn't betrayed Clara's confidence by telling the lad the whole story.

"Something like that," he said. "I want to know what's going on here as badly as you. That bastard, Maynard, is nothing but a base murderer, and I don't even know the why of it."

"You don't remember much, then?"

"Nothing, before they wrestled me up on that box, gave me the noose, and kicked the crate away."

Fagan shivered. "I've just come off duty." He indicated the street clothes he wore. "So I've some time on me hands."

"Get out of here, the both of you, before you're seen." Astonishingly, Ruella leaned in and planted a generous kiss on Fagan's lips. "I'll see you later, lad. Our usual time?"

"Aye, Ruella."

Liam's senses reeled. Ruella went back inside, and he followed Fagan from the yard.

Of all the things he wanted to ask the lad, he chose one. "So—you're tumbling Ruella? By God! What's it like?"

Fagan gave him a speaking look. "With all due respect to your recent near death, sir, I hardly think it proper to discuss the nature of my relations with Miss Ruella, and perhaps besmirch her virtue."

"Her what, then? Come lad—the mind boggles. And she's scarcely a delicate flower, is she?"

The intense blue eyes regarded Liam a moment before Fagan inclined his head and leaned a bit closer. "I'll say only that her favor's strong. Bruising, in fact, but well worth the effort. Anyway, us Fagans can take our knocks."

"And give them, by the sound of it."

Fagan grinned. The light that appeared in his eyes looked wicked, for a copper.

Liam asked, "How long you been out of Ireland?"

"Ten years. Me mummy, pa, and I all came, with six brothers and sisters, when I was eleven."

"Ah. And what made you choose the copper's life?"

"Respectable trade, sir, and steady." Fagan's face clouded. "But I have to say I've little liking for what's gone on at the jail. I've been looking into things on the sly, like, taking peeks at the records. You're not the only one to be strung up in that yard."

"So Ruella said."

"There are great gaps in the records. Come, sir, walk this way. Old Tim has a room down on Georgia Street, off Niagara."

"Aye, lad. What kind of gaps in the records are you talking about?"

"Men who are processed in and put on the books, their keep charged to the county, and then just disappear. Some have trumped-up sentences, some just a word or two after, saying 'released for time served.' "

"Which was I?" Liam matched his steps to Fagan's without difficulty.

"Released, sir, after time served for D and D."

"Ah."

"Yet Mr. Maynard kept charging the county for you. Still, sir, do you know what bothers me most?"

Liam nodded. It bothered him too. "It's not worth Maynard's time—or worth committing murder."

"Right, sir. 'Tis a bad proposition. Miss Ruella says Mr. Maynard's a big spender at the gentleman's club."

"He is that."

"Yet he's not making big money charging the county for prisoners who are no longer there. Must be more to it."

"Indeed, there must. I'm hoping Old Tim will have a clue." Liam slanted a look at the lad. "Of course, the last time Old Tim saw me, he believed I was dead."

"Might shock him a bit to see you now. Though," Fagan added judiciously, "you're pretty lively, for a dead man."

****

Clara heard the screaming the moment she came up Virginia Street from the direction of Delaware. She hadn't wanted to spend the money for a steamcab and hoped the exercise might calm the anger she felt. But it hadn't, and now her nerves, already unbearably stretched, tightened another notch.

She glanced at the children—all hers—gathered in a knot on the doorstep. "Why aren't you at your lessons?" she asked the younger ones. They all stared back at her. Woodrow and Fred, already back from work, shifted from one foot to the other uneasily.

"We're wanting our dinner, miss," Fred replied. "But Georgina has her hands full with that up there." He nodded toward the upstairs and made a face. "Can't stand the noise inside."

"You say Georgina is looking after our guest? Where's my husband?"

Fred shrugged. "Not here."

"Is he at work?"

"Don't know, miss."

Clara's heart thumped in her chest as she went inside, and the screaming increased in volume. Liam wouldn't desert her. He wouldn't abandon Nancy—again. She didn't know how she felt so sure of that. He'd buggered off on her before, hadn't he? In truth, she barely knew the man even though she loved him to the root of her soul. And she *had* given him something of an ultimatum.

How could she have been such a fool?

She climbed the stairs on legs that trembled and found Georgina in the hallway, leaning against the door of Clara's old bedroom as if keeping it shut by force.

"What's going on, Georgina?"

"Oh, thank the sweet Lord you're home. I can't get her calm, Clara, no matter how I try. She wants Liam."

"Where is he? Why did he leave her?" Clara's heart pounded in her throat.

"Said he needed a break, and who could blame him? I got the idea he was going to walk down to the coffin shop."

"How long ago was this?"

"Right after you left." Georgina's eyes revealed her doubt. "You don't think…"

"That he's ducked out?"

"I was thinking more he'd been snatched. You know how he was attacked before."

"I do." Clara's anxiety increased.

Georgina jerked her head at the door. "You must do something."

"I'll bring a draught from the surgery and see if I can get it into her."

"Did you have any success at Mr. Van Hamelin's?"

Clara shook her head and went back down to search out a soothing remedy. Her father had left a few mixtures, and as she began to prepare one with trembling hands, she faced the very worst of herself. That creature upstairs, living through this hell, deserved a full measure of peace. What would happen if Clara poured a double dose into the glass? Would poor Nancy just fall asleep, forget her dead child and her husband, and slip into the arms of eternal rest?

And, Clara asked herself sternly, was her motive truly to afford the woman mercy, or to be rid of her? Was she truly so much like her grandfather? And could she be honest enough to admit the truth?

She could: she wanted Nancy's agony to cease, but

she also wanted Nancy gone so Liam could be hers, *all hers*.

She set the glass down and rested her forehead against the door of the cupboard while emotion surged through her—desire and shame in equal measures. How could she ever give him back to Nancy? How hope to live without him? And this thing would be so easy to do, merely empty a second packet into the cup. Make the screaming stop, and the pain.

But, but, *but*. Her father had been a healer, a good man. How could she use a remedy he had concocted in such a way? How so betray his legacy? She might carry a full measure of her grandfather in her blood, but she carried Anson Allen, as well.

And what of that other gift—or curse—she carried, the talent passed on by all those who had come before her—some outcast for it, some honored, some feared and burnt as witches? It granted life. It didn't take it.

Could she, even for the love of Liam McMahon, go against who she was?

Almost. Almost she could. She needed him so very badly, his strength and heat, the taste of him, and that indefinable something that joined them.

Her fingers crumpled the packet in her hand. She swirled the contents of the cup till the powders dissolved, and bore it up the stairs.

Chapter Thirty-Six

"Here?" Liam asked in disgust. "This is where the old man lives?"

Somberly, Fagan nodded.

The rooming house—if such it could be called—wouldn't make a decent kennel. Whatever money Maynard was wrangling, he clearly didn't share much of it with the sexton.

The building, grim and narrow, shed flakes of paint the way a leper might shed skin, and the wood beneath looked dark with damp. It seemed to lean like a badly constructed chimney in the direction of the river. An evil smell emanated from it—or from the garbage in the adjacent alley.

"Followed him home one afternoon," Fagan said. "He's a room round back. Come on."

Access was found through the alley which, upon closer acquaintance, boasted not only the smell of garbage but piss and worse. Somebody had been using it for a toilet, and both men picked their way with fastidious care.

"So," Fagan asked as they did so, "what's it like to nearly die?"

Liam slid his gaze to the lad's face. "Not very pleasant. No white light, no angels, to my recollection. Not a glimpse of the pearly gates. Take my advice and keep alive a while."

"I mean to. A great deal I want to accomplish yet, including a wife and children."

"Ruella?"

Fagan rolled his eyes. "Don't be daft. Ruella's just—well, an exercise in daring. Though I confess, I've no notion how to break it off with such a woman."

"She'll hurt you, lad."

"I know. Whisht, now—there he is."

Liam's eyes opened wide. A door opened off the end of the alley, and on its step lay what he might have taken for a pile of dirty laundry. When Fagan spoke, though, Liam realized it had a shock of white hair up top. He hissed between his teeth.

Nearby against a wall leaned a large wheelbarrow. He realized with another jolt it must be the same in which Ruella had brought him to Clara's house.

"Come on," Fagan bade.

An empty bottle lay beside the old man. He snored softly, face turned to the overcast sky. A miasmic smell rose from him, nearly as bad as that of the alley.

Liam pushed the cloth cap to the back of his head and then, on second thought, pulled it off completely; he wanted Old Tim to recognize him. He nudged the old man with his toe.

No response.

"Drunk as a skunk," Fagan said.

"Look, lad, you might not want to be seen here."

"Not planning to harm him, are you? 'Cause I'm still a policeman, even off duty."

"Just going to ask him some questions. You wait at the other end of the alley."

Fagan wrinkled his nose. His bright, blue eyes slid over Liam with interest. "Maybe I'd better stay."

"You might hear some things you don't like."

"Still, I think I should keep an eye on things."

Liam plunked his own cap on Fagan's head and pulled it well down over the lad's face. Then he nudged the old man again. "Tim!"

The bottle slid away and clunked against the wall.

"Don't know as you'll be able to rouse him, if he drank all that," Fagan said.

As if on cue, the old man groaned. Liam hunkered down and, with distaste, shook the bony shoulder.

"Tim, come awake—I've a drink for you."

Fagan snorted. The old man opened foggy eyes, still focused on the sky, and lay for several moments looking uncannily like one of his own customers. Then he fixed on Liam hovering above him, blinked, and drew breath. His eyes grew painfully wide, and his lips moved, forming a word that might have been, "You!"

"I've some questions—" Liam got no farther. The old man drew a deeper breath, filled his lungs, and shrieked.

"Jaysus, Mary, and Joseph!" Fagan exclaimed as the old man scrambled away backwards, trying to put distance between himself and Liam, yelling all the while. His cries echoed off the bricks and the walls of the shabby rooming house, his horror amplified.

"Whisht now!" Liam told him. "Listen to me."

"A ghost! You're a ghost! Dead!"

"I'm not, then." But Old Tim never heard Liam. He'd gone white as his hair, face frozen in a terrible rictus. Liam's thoughts flew desperately.

"Aye, then," he said, "I'm a ghost, come to avenge what was done to me."

Fagan swore an oath shameful to a good Catholic

lad. Liam shot him a warning look.

"I was murdered in the jail yard and," Liam accused, "you were there. You saw it done."

"I wasn't!" Tim had backed himself against the door and could retreat no further. "It all happened before I got there. They just told me to come and collect the body."

"They—who?"

Old Tim went suddenly silent.

Liam scowled at him. "If someone besides you is guilty in this, name him. Otherwise, I'll avenge meself on you, for your part in it."

"The message always comes from Mr. Maynard, by a runner. Or one of the two guards brings it to me at the tavern."

"Which guards, ask him," Fagan hissed. "Which guards?"

"Not sure of their names, only that they come from Mr. Maynard. Are you going to kill me?"

"Maybe, unless you answer all my questions. Why's Maynard after killing his prisoners, do you know?"

Tim gave an odd little shrug. "Must be for the money. How is it you came back?"

"Ghosts can go anywhere, can follow you even to the gates of hell. Why's Maynard murdering Irishmen?"

Old Tim spat, a shocking gesture in one of his decrepitude. "Don't matter, do they? He says it's like puttin' down stray dogs."

Fagan growled and shifted on the balls of his feet.

"Wait, lad," Liam cautioned. He wanted very badly to choke the life out of the old man, but not yet. Fear seemed to have loosened the sot's tongue, and he ran on.

"Or like rats—river rats. Mr. Maynard says there's just too many of them in the city, with the way they breed. Might as well make a bounty on them."

"Bounty? What the hell are you talking about?" None of it made any sense. Maynard simply couldn't earn enough off falsified records to make the foul deed worth his while.

"No one follows up on missing Irishmen—or if they do, if some drab wife comes asking, no one cares. Easy to make them disappear."

Liam could now feel the horror streaming off Fagan, at his back, and strove to ignore it. His mind beat at the riddle.

"So an Irishman gets arrested, booked, put in the cells. Then the records get falsified, saying he's been released for time served, but he's not released. Instead he's hauled into the jail yard and hanged, and you dump him in that river with your barrow, there. Tell me, where's the money in that?"

Tim's eyes were now so wide Liam could see white all around the brown. But he buttoned his lip.

"Tell me," Liam threatened, "or I'll strip the skin from your bones by inches."

"Don't drop them in the river, do I? What'd be the point of that?"

Aye, what?

"When Mr. Maynard gets a good, healthy Irish bugger like yourself, he sends him to the Cuttery." Tim's face crumpled. "Only they said they'd kill me, if I ever told."

"Cuttery? What the hell's the Cuttery?"

Tim, blubbing now, lowered his voice. "They do

terrible things. I've never seen…"

"They? Who?"

"The Steam Company," Tim whispered in a low tremor. "That's what they call themselves. I've only seen the two of them. I think the rest are mechanicals."

"Mechanicals? You mean steamies?"

Tim nodded. "The two men I saw, both were young and… Don't make me tell!"

"Listen to me, old man. As far as I'm concerned, you had a hand in me death and the deaths of me brothers. You think I don't want revenge for that? I can take it out on you or on these men to whom you've been delivering corpses. I want names."

"Don't know them!"

"A direction, then. Where's this Cuttery?"

"Down the waterfront," Tim gasped. "At the foot of Perry Street."

"Descriptions. Come on, you already started to tell us."

"No, it's too horrible. And I barely saw them. I just dumped them bodies—"

"And these men paid you?"

"Must have paid Mr. Maynard direct. I only ever got money for booze."

Liam reached down and hauled the old man up by his collar. "Know what I could do to you?"

Fagan never protested the threat of violence. Liam could feel the lad's anger, a presence at his back.

Old Tim promptly pissed himself; the smell arose into the already miasmic air. He whispered, "Both young men, as I say, not above thirty. One has a terrible white face and hair stark black. His eye—" Tim broke off again.

Liam shook him, but he remained silent.

"And the other man?"

"Red."

"What? Red-haired, you mean? Ginger?"

"No. Red. Skin and all."

"He's dreaming it," Fagan whispered. "A whiskey dream."

"No." Liam looked into Old Tim's eyes and believed him. "There's something quite horrible going on, lad." He let Old Tim drop onto the doorstep and arose to Fagan's side. "Happen we need to go down to the waterfront and find out what."

Chapter Thirty-Seven

It took both of them—Clara and Georgina together—to get the draught down Nancy McMahon's throat. Even as they coaxed and persuaded her, Clara asked herself if she'd mixed the right dose. This whole twisted tale had begun with murder, after all.

Nancy slowly quieted, and Georgina, who knew nothing about Clara's inner battle, breathed a sigh of relief.

"Thank the Lord! I'm sure the neighbors must have been ready to call the police, and we don't want that, do we?"

"No." Clara's nervous energy had her dancing from foot to foot. She stood watching as Nancy eased back into the pink upholstered chair that had been Clara's since childhood. She glanced at Georgina. "Go see if the children are all right."

"Are you sure you want to be left alone with her?"

"It's fine now. She's calming."

Georgina hurried out and shut the door firmly.

"All right, then." Clara pulled up a second chair from the desk and sat. "It's just the two of us now, Nancy. Let's talk until you get sleepy."

"I want my husband."

So do I. Clara longed for him—body and soul—with an intensity that shocked her. "He's not here, but I'm looking after you. You can confide in me."

Nancy began to weep, but without the previous intensity. The sad tears merely seeped from her eyes. "I hate it here. I want to go home."

"To Ireland?"

Nancy nodded. She truly was a lovely thing, despite the wild hair and tearstains. Clara's heart clenched in her chest. No wonder Liam had married her.

"Will you tell me about your home, in Ireland?"

A faint smile chased the tears. Yes, Clara thought, the draught she'd administered had been a powerful one. Her father had possessed rare skill at compounding remedies.

"I was once happy there with Tom."

"Your son?"

"Aye, wee love. My beautiful boy!" Tears filled her eyes, and her face crumpled.

Clara leaned forward and covered the woman's hand with her own. "Nancy, tell me what happened."

In a whisper, Nancy replied, "I was angry that night, so very angry. He'd gone out drinking again and taken the last of our money for whiskey and beer. Stealing food from our bairn's mouth, that was. And the bairn had greeted for hours—I had the devil's own time settling him. It wasn't fair."

"No, it wasn't." Clara could not help but agree, ruing Liam's behavior in her mind.

"When I heard them coming, I got up and swung wide the door."

"Them?"

"My husband and his brother. My man was so drunk he could barely stand. His brother had to lug him home. I flew at him—I couldn't help it—and he turned his back on me, walked out. Would not even listen! I went after him, thinking only how angry I was. My elbow must have caught the lamp as I went past. I didn't see—I was outside arguing with him all the while, and I didn't see! My fault!"

"Nancy, no." Clara took the woman by the shoulders. "It was an accident."

"The cot—my wee son's cot was right beside the chair. I'd put it there whilst I tried to quiet him. The oil splashed everywhere; it must have caught his blankets. We didn't see until the flames leaped high—and then I screamed, and my man flew in, he flew in—snatched our son, but the thatch started to fall before they could get out again. So badly burned! Both of them badly burned, and the smoke... Wee Thomas never recovered. He took terrible sick on our journey, after, and died on the way."

"What did you say, Nancy? Your husband was burned when he rescued your child?" But Liam bore no scars on his body. Clara had seen every inch of him. His big hands were calloused, yes, but showed no burns.

"The whole cottage went up like a haystack. I lost everything that night, everything."

"Your son's name—it was Tommy?" The pieces began to fall into place in Clara's mind. "And what's your husband's name? Tell me, Nancy."

"Thomas McMahon." Abruptly, Nancy's eyelids fluttered down as the strong draught began to do its work. But Clara needed answers from her yet.

"Nancy, listen to me. Liam—was he your husband's brother? So you were never married to Liam, not then or ever?"

"Married to Liam?" Nancy's eyes flashed open in a shocked gleam of blue. "Why would I wed with Liam, when 'twas Tom I loved? Loved him, for all his sins. But 'twas my fault, what happened, and I lost them both…"

Clara's heart, already much abused, bounded in her chest. "Your husband died saving your son from the fire?"

"Tom didn't die in the fire, nay. That came after. Couldn't forgive himself for what happened to Tommy, no more could I. He took a gun…took a gun and shot himself."

By God. Clara knew a rush of compassion. Little wonder the poor woman couldn't live with her grief, and no wonder she had been out raving in the street. "I'm sorry, Nancy," she whispered. "So very sorry." What had Liam done? What could he do, in such a case?

"I couldn't stay there any longer," Nancy continued brokenly. "Liam took me to Dublin…had some relatives there. They gave us enough money for our passage, said we could have a better life in Canada. But Tommy died on the way, my wee angel went to join his Da, and I couldn't outrun the pain."

"But Nancy, on the ship's manifest you and Liam were listed as man and wife."

"Better that way. Liam said 'twas not safe for me to travel without the protection of a husband." Nancy's eyes closed. Clara clutched the woman's fingers still more tightly. She had to be sure.

"Nancy, please—can you assure me Liam's not wed, has never been wed?"

"Never. Swore to be a bachelor all his life, he did."

Clara's treacherous heart bounded again, with hope this time. Liam had acted in good faith, lent his protection to his brother's grieving widow. And the fault, if anyone's, belonged to Thomas McMahon. A tragedy all round, but at the heart of it, Liam—Liam was hers, hers, *hers*.

Gently she released Nancy's hands and got to her feet. Nancy slumped to one side, drew a deeper breath, and subsided into sleep.

Thank heaven Clara hadn't given her the double draught of sedative. She'd be a murderess, and for no good reason. She marveled at what the love of Liam McMahon had almost made her do, and she acknowledged the deep flaws in her own soul. Perhaps she truly was more like her grandfather Van Hamelin than she wanted to admit.

Because only her reluctance to betray the man her father had been by misusing the medicine he'd compounded had kept her from a very foul and ruthless deed.

And now—now she had to find Liam and share the truth with him.

****

"That's the place."

The afternoon had grown late, and at this time of year dark came early. Liam and Brendan Fagan huddled together in yet another alley, this one fortuitously stacked with a screen of empty crates, and looked at the warehouse directly ahead of them. The place was the only one at the foot of Perry Street, as Old Tim had described. It looked like an ordinary warehouse, but Liam sensed something different about it that he couldn't quite identify.

"Someone inside," said Fagan, who proved a very sharp lad indeed. "See? Those are steam-powered lights."

So they were. And steam billowed from a number of vents set along the roof of the building in addition to the brick chimneys that belched smoke—coal smoke, from the smell of it.

"They make the steamies here?"

"No." Fagan shook his head. "Those are turned out in a big operation south of Ohio Street. This is something else. See—they're drawing water straight from the lake."

"How d'you know?"

"Those are pipes, there." Fagan waved a hand at plumbing barely seen. It grew darker fast, and the windows glowed more brightly.

"Come on." Liam grabbed Fagan's arm. "Let's see if we can peer in."

"Careful. There may be guards."

There were. No sooner had Fagan spoken than someone appeared around the corner, coming from the harbor side. A steam unit it was—a big one and, from its silhouette, armed.

Liam swore bitterly. "I need to get inside."

"No."

"I need to know, Fagan, need to face these bastards. They're killing our countrymen. Don't you care?"

"Aye."

"Don't you want to know what the hell's going on?"

"I do, but I'll not be stupid about it." Fagan drew a breath. "I wonder if we can take that steamie, the two of us." He swore. "Och, damn. There's another one."

The two steam units met on their patrol and appeared to confer together. Just like the building, Liam sensed something different about them: they didn't move exactly like steamies and must be very advanced models.

"Something not right here," he muttered. "Those windows—they're painted over." He narrowed his eyes. "White paint. We'll not be able to see in."

"You want to get inside so badly?" asked a voice behind him. He felt the muzzle of a pistol bite the back of his head. "I think we can oblige."

Chapter Thirty-Eight

"Our Liam's in danger. Him and my Brendan, both," Ruella gasped the words, breathless. She must have run all the way from the county jail, and Ruella hadn't been built for running. Now she stood on Clara's doorstep struggling for air, even while Clara's stomach dropped.

"Come in." Clara drew her friend into the foyer and looked at her in concern. "What kind of danger? Where are they?"

"Liam came to the jail earlier, looking for me. Said he wanted to talk to Old Tim, get some answers from him."

"Oh, no."

"I hooked him up with my boy, Fagan—you know how I'd asked him to look into the records at the jail."

"I do."

Ruella raised agonized eyes to Clara's. "Maynard must have had some suspicions. As soon as the big Irishmen left the jail yard, I saw two of the jail guards leave and go after them. I think they're the same two who were in on hanging Liam that night."

Clara's heart thudded. "Where were Liam and Brendan headed? To Old Tim's, you say? You know where he lives?"

"Yes, but, Miss Clara, it's dangerous, innit? No place for you."

"Wherever Liam is, that's the place for me. Listen to me, Ruella." She seized the woman's beefy arms. "I've just calmed Nancy enough to get some sense from her. She was never married to Liam but to his brother. My marriage to Liam's legitimate. That should put a spike in my grandfather's wheel. But I need Liam safe."

Before Ruella could speak, Clara turned and bellowed up the stairs, "Georgina?"

When Georgina tiptoed down, Clara bade, "I must go out. Watch over Nancy for me, will you? And send a message to Theodore—better yet, get him to come here and wait with you. Tell him Liam's never been married—so the bequest is in force."

"But where are you going?"

"To find my husband." *Her husband.* "Do you remember where Liam put my father's pistol?"

Georgina's dark eyes widened. "Why? You don't mean to—"

"I may need it. I'll take Dax, as well. Dax—" The steamie, having opened the door to Ruella, stood by silently.

"What is it, miss? What's wrong?" Fred and Woodrow, having arrived home from work, appeared from the direction of the kitchen. Clara realized it was already very nearly dark out.

"Nothing for you to worry about, lads."

"Is Mr. Liam in trouble?" Woodrow puffed himself up. "I'll help him."

"And I'll protect you," Fred added.

"Not a good idea, boys. You stay here and guard the household."

"Beg pardon, miss, but we're too old for you to tell us what to do anymore. We're out earning a wage.

And," Fred added, proving they'd been eavesdropping, "I can handle a pistol."

Clara exchanged looks with Ruella, who shrugged. "Appears we have a delegation."

****

The windows of the warehouse had, indeed, been painted over, and the interior was brightly lit, making Liam blink after the dusk outside. The place smelled of hot metal and steam, with an underlying scent of something far less pleasant. Liam saw Brendan, hustled in beside him, wrinkle his nose as he caught it also.

It smelled like a slaughter yard. Or a charnel house. Somewhere beneath all the bright lights, death lingered here.

Yet at first glance, the open space looked almost too clean. A raft of white globes, powered by a steam turbine, hung in a row from the high ceiling, and Liam could just see the great furnace half way down the room.

In truth, he barely noticed it; all his attention had been caught by the occupants of the place.

For a man hurried out when their captors shoved them in—another followed quickly from the direction of the furnace. Both took Liam's breath away.

The first—surely he whom Old Tim had striven to describe—had skin of a dead, chalk white, and long black hair worn loose on his shoulders. Everything about him seemed elongated—face, neck, body, features—Liam's mind stuttered as he looked into the fellow's face, and his stomach turned over. The man had but one eye, his left. The right socket held a metal contraption very like Dax's joints but much more complex. It whirred and ratcheted and adjusted itself as the man regarded them.

A mechanical eye, grafted to flesh.

"Well, what have you brought us, gentlemen?" The monstrosity's voice sounded in a thin whine like the buzz of many bees. For an instant Liam went dizzy, and he heard Fagan draw a breath.

"These two were poking round where they shouldn't at the jail, and at Old Tim's, as well. We followed them here."

Stupid, stupid, stupid, Liam chastised himself, and could almost feel Brendan thinking the same. But the gun still pressed against the back of Liam's head, and the steamies who had been on guard had joined the forced escort. Fight appeared futile, but now he wondered if a quick death outside might not have been preferable to whatever might happen in here.

"Who are you?" he asked. "And what's going on here?"

The man ignored the questions as he might the yapping of a hound. "Ah—Irish! What a gift. This will make up for our inventory shortage earlier in the month."

"He *is* your inventory shortage." The fellow with the pistol pressed it harder. The as-yet-unseen man went on, "Two birds with one stone, you might say."

"What goes on here?" The approaching man reached them. Liam took one glance into his face and could not make himself look again. The fellow had brown hair, somewhat mussed, and mild brown eyes—two of them—but his skin was red as if he'd been dipped into a vat of boiling oil. Burns, surely, and no doubt caused by steam in some terrible accident. Liam's gaze dropped to the fellow's body, and his stomach clenched once more. The man had no hands. That was, no flesh and blood hands. Instead, mechanical devices had been grafted to the flesh half the way up the forearms, gleaming metal far more sophisticated than what Liam had ever seen on any steamie. The skin that met the metal, seamed and deeply scarred, red and purple from burning, looked so painful Liam flinched inwardly.

"Jaysus, Mary, and Joseph," Fagan breathed, and took a hasty step backward, bumping into the steamie behind him.

"We have been brought a bounty," the black-haired man told his fellow. His lips pulled back in a snarl, revealing long teeth. "Two of them—Irish."

"Ah." Liam felt the second man perform a visual inspection, measuring his arms and legs, and the width of his chest. "Just what we need." He, like the other, spoke as if Liam and Fagan were insensate. "A long night's work ahead, it seems."

"No matter, Charles. Pay the men, and they can be on their way."

"Wait just a minute." Fagan drew another deep breath. "I am a member of the Buffalo police force. I'm arresting you for—"

He got no further. Black-hair leaned toward him, the mechanical eye adjusting for closer inspection. "You *were* a member of the Buffalo police force," he corrected. "Now you're just a lump of Irish flesh. Useful flesh, at that." He looked at the guards, and the eye adjusted with a series of audible clicks. "Tell your boss we'll count these two toward his quota."

The man with the mechanical hands, whom the other had called Charles, reached into his waistcoat and extracted a billfold. Liam could not help but watch in fascination as the fingers, moving with delicate precision, counted out two lots of dollars. The arms moved so smoothly they barely made a sound. He passed the money over, and the hard mouth of the pistol withdrew from the back of Liam's head.

He tensed himself for fight or flight. But a number of steamies had moved in, gathering so close around him and Fagan he barely noticed the two jail guards slip back out into the night.

He cast a desperate look at Brendan, who had turned white with fury.

"Strip them down," Charles told the steamies. "And if they struggle, try not to damage anything too badly."

****

Clara wished Dax didn't make quite so much noise when he moved. The lads had done a fine job with his overhaul, but he definitely revealed his age as he trundled along and emitted regular puffs of steam. At least she didn't have to worry about him running out of coal. Woodrow and Fred had stoked him well and filled his reservoir before they left the house.

Like a ragged, ungainly band of gypsies, they'd followed Ruella through darkening streets under an overcast sky, west along Georgia Street almost to 4th, a most unsavory part of town. Fred had appropriated the pistol and stayed close to Clara's side.

Now, at the mouth of a noisome alley, Ruella paused and said over her shoulder, "I think it's down here."

Clara stiffened with distaste. From the little she could see, the alley lay cluttered with garbage. But she'd venture into far worse for the sake of Liam.

Liam. The very thought of him called to her and raised a longing she had to tamp down in order to think clearly.

"Dax, you go first," she bade the steamie. She didn't want to sacrifice him, but heaven only knew what lay down that dark chute.

The steamie rolled forward willingly. The rest of them pressed in behind.

"Ugh, what a stink." Ruella fairly gagged.

Ahead lay a rooming house, only one window lit against the gloom. No sign of movement or human habitation, though Clara would be willing to bet rats abounded.

"Nothing here," Dax said. Was that relief or disappointment Clara heard in his voice? Was he capable of either emotion?

"Let me knock. The rest of you hang back." Ruella pounded a large fist against the door, with no immediate effect.

She raised her arm to knock again, and the door swung open.

"What do you want? I've a pistol and no money in the house, so look sharp." The woman revealed by a dim light from behind looked every inch the slattern. Brown hair straggled over her neck, and her ragged dress appeared far from clean.

"You the landlady here?" Ruella asked.

"Who wants to know?"

"We're from the jail, looking for Old Tim. Have a job for him." Ruella nodded at the wheelbarrow leaning against the outside of the house, and Clara realized with a shock it must be the one in which Liam had been brought to her.

The landlady snorted. "Right, but you'll get little sense from him. He's so drunk I had to drag him up the stairs to his bed when I got home." She swung wide the door. "Come on in."

"You wait here with Dax," Clara told Fred and the pistol. "Woodrow, you come with us. We may need you."

They trooped into the house, only marginally cleaner than the alley, and up a dim, narrow, creaking set of wooden stairs to an equally narrow hallway faced with doors, one of which the landlady indicated.

"In there."

She went back down the stairs, and Ruella pushed the door open into darkness. Woodrow pulled a box of matches from his pocket, flicked one with his thumb, and located a candle fixed on the wall, to which he placed the flame.

Like the rest of the house, the room stank. Sparsely furnished, it contained only a washstand and a narrow bed on which a man sprawled in an attitude of utter senselessness.

Woodrow leaned forward to peer at him. "Damn! Is he dead?"

"I hope not." Ruella stepped forward and prodded the old man's shoulder. "Tim? Tim!" She prodded him still harder, but he did not stir. Mouth slightly open, eyes wide, he stared at nothing. Clara, striving to see, could detect no sign that he breathed.

"Looks dead," Woodrow opined.

"Well, we need to know what he knows." Ruella bent closer to Clara, so close Woodrow couldn't hear. "Guess you'll have to revive him, won't you?"

Chapter Thirty-Nine

It seemed to Liam he'd begun this wild nightmare just this way—strapped naked to a table and damned well helpless. The table to which he now found himself bound wasn't scrubbed wood like the one in Clara's workroom but a smooth expanse of steel that burned his bare back with cold. And the straps weren't leather but some metallic fabric no doubt impossible to rend. He and Fagan had been stripped and pinned by the steamies with ruthless efficiency.

And that made another difference. When he'd awakened at Clara's, Fagan hadn't been strapped to a second table beside him, beneath blazing lights.

He turned his head now and scrutinized his companion. The lad looked terrified, and with good reason. His broad chest rose and fell, fighting against the straps, and his eyes were wild.

"Steady, lad," Liam told him, though he himself felt far from it.

"What are they going to do with us? What goes on in this place?"

Liam hated to think. The area where they were now confined lay separated from the rest of the warehouse by the great steam plant, which he could still hear hissing and rattling behind a big pair of wooden doors. He'd caught glimpses of other things as the steamies hustled them in, things that would give him bad dreams for years—if he survived that long.

Fagan gasped, "I smell blood."

So did Liam, and worse. The charnel reek that colored the place definitely originated somewhere close by.

He closed his eyes for an instant against a staggering wave of horror. He'd wanted to know what happened to his fellow prisoners. Now he feared he did.

The table on which he lay was grooved, and when they wrestled him down, fighting every inch of the way, he'd caught a glimpse of channels on the floor underneath, stained dark.

Men had died here before him. Those channels had carried Irish blood.

"Courage," he told Fagan, speaking as much to himself as the lad. "We're not done yet."

"Oh, but I think you are." The black-haired man appeared at the side of Liam's table. He now wore what looked like a rain slicker that covered him from the neck down. The black hair had been covered by a crude sou'wester that, in any other circumstances, would have looked ludicrous.

"Coward!" Liam tossed at him, and bared his teeth. "'Tis easy enough to face men who can't fight you."

The man leaned in, and the mechanical eye adjusted disconcertingly. But Liam had passed far beyond being disconcerted.

"You're a fine specimen," the man said. "I'm pleased."

"What are you going to do with us?" Fagan croaked the words as if he couldn't prevent them. The man's head swiveled to face him.

"Nothing very pleasant, I assure you," he said

without much emotion. "But comfort yourself with knowing you'll be part of a grand and important experiment, and significant portions of you will live on."

"Jayus," Fagan wailed.

The black-haired man advised, "I really shouldn't bother calling on *him*, if I were you. He never comes here, though many have called."

"Do you have a name?" Liam snarled. "Your buddy there is called Charles. But are we not to know the name of the man who murders us?"

"You may call me Master Mason, since I am a member of that noble, ancient, and venerated society. And I'm no murderer."

"Right. You usually have your meat brought to you fresh hanged."

"Usually, and only the finest. You should consider yourself honored to be amidst an august company. The Irish have many faults—many—but they do grow fine examples of manhood, strong and tall. And, so very often, dispensable."

"He's not dispensable." Liam jerked his head at Fagan. "A policeman—"

"Unfortunately, a victim of a tavern brawl while off duty. Someone saw him going into the river. Lost."

"Get on with the job." The steam-burned man, Charles—he with the horrific hands—appeared at Mason's side. "Must you toy with them? Just end it, and let's get to work."

"Me? Why me? You do it."

Liam bared his teeth again. Aye, they had no liking for the ugly deed Maynard usually accomplished for them.

"You're the man who's so good with the saw," Charles said.

Fagan moaned.

Even though he knew he shouldn't, Liam taunted their captors, "Afraid?"

The mechanical eye clicked as Mason regarded him. "Afraid of a little blood? On the contrary, Mick, I'm just unwilling to monopolize all the pleasure. Always eager to share with my partner."

Charles waved a metal hand. "Be my guest. Just get on with it and shut them up."

"To be truthful"—Mason struck a pose—"I'm wondering what the effect might be if we kept them alive throughout the procedure. We've never before had this opportunity; I hate to waste it. Think, Charles—living flesh grafted to metal, just like your arms, only amplified a hundred times."

"They'd never endure the pain. Just kill them. Cadaver flesh has always served before."

"Ah, they're fine, strong lads. They can withstand a great deal of pain, right, boys?" Mason turned to Fagan. "You want to live a while yet?"

"What goes on here?" Fagan hollered.

"Do you want to see? Do you really want to know the reason you give your bodies and perhaps, indeed, your lives?"

"Just get on with it," Charles reiterated.

"Not so fast, Master Grasp—we so seldom have living guests, and I want to see if they're impressed. Bring out some of our creations and show them."

Creations? Liam swore to himself as every wild and terrible idea that had been kicking about his fevered brain developed into hideous images.

"It's too dangerous," Charles objected. "And we're not ready."

"Ready enough. Anyway, these two aren't going to tell anyone."

Fagan shut his eyes tight. "Just kill me now. I don't want to see whatever you've created—monsters like yourselves, no doubt."

"Oh, no, Irish, not like us but much more exquisite. Charles, here, and I honed our skills not through choice but necessity. Charles lost his hands in an industrial accident. He would have died, but for me. And I lost the sight in one eye when acid was flung at me by a disgruntled worker—an Irishman." Mason smiled, a terrible rictus. "He later served as the first of our experiments."

"How do you know to do such Godforsaken things?"

"Building world-class steam units teaches you a great deal. People who've owned them a while say they acquire a kind of rudimentary intelligence—even personality. Why not foster still more of that tendency with the contribution of human elements? So you see, lads, you really will live on. Oh, not your minds, of course. Those, I am afraid, must be sacrificed."

He turned to his companion. "Trot out Unit 59. Show them."

Charles hesitated but a moment and then went as bidden. Liam cast a desperate look at Brendan, whose blue eyes were once more stretched wide. What chance had they?

Mason stepped to Brendan's table, where he parted the lad's eyelids with relentless fingers. The lad fought and thrashed but could not move far enough to escape.

"Very pretty. These will look fine in our next unit. We've found that's what bothers people most about the mechanicals—their eyes. I'll be able to charge extra for these."

"You sell the monstrosities you build?" Liam gasped.

"Don't call them monstrosities—you haven't even seen one yet. And yes, they're selling well on the black market. You've probably even walked past them on the street. You just can't readily tell. Ah—here we are."

He turned as Charles and another man joined him.

No, not a man. Liam looked at the thing, and his stomach heaved, making him sure he'd projectile vomit. He fought the sickness down.

The thing was tall and broad, with a build like Fagan's, fully clothed. Impossible to say what parts beneath the clothing might be mechanical. But the portions that showed were at least part flesh. Its eyes… A rich, lively green, they dominated the broad face beneath a thatch of auburn hair. The hands, unlike Charles's, looked normal. It truly would pass as a man, on the street.

Mason waved a hand. "The framework—or skeleton, if you prefer—is steel alloy. The steam chamber's concealed in the thorax. When it expands, it appears he's breathing. Vents draw air through the nose passages to feed the coal fire in the bowels. Certain organs—harvested from our donors—keep the mortal portions alive. The eyes, the hair, and the main organ— that's the skin, including the scalp and nail beds—are all from donors. They'll be harvested from you, including a certain, for lack of better wording, 'human essence' that makes these automatons what they are, and far superior to regular steam units."

Fagan gagged and retched. The thing looked at him with what almost appeared to be concern.

"They have emotions?" Liam asked, his voice a hoarse rasp of horror. "You trap the spirits of dead men in there, after murdering them?"

"I've murdered no one, as yet."

"You have, in your dirty deal with Maynard, as surely as if your hand was on the rope."

"Don't be a fool, Mick. What I'm doing is important. And, technically, no one's died if—as you say—a little of the dear departed's spirit has gone on in these units." Mason concluded by pronouncing, "I've made those Irish sinners immortal. I doubt even God would have consented to go so far, for the sake of scum."

The mechanical man's eyes jerked round to Mason. It appeared to consider what he'd said.

"How many of these do you have?" Liam asked, still hoarsely.

"On the premises? Nearly a dozen. We've already sold almost half as many again. I'm considering perfecting the design and then approaching the military. Imagine an army of these! The skin overlay can be cut, but everything else is protected within the frame."

"You're going to do that to us?" Fagan sounded ready to snap. "Put my skin—my eyes—on a metal puppet?"

"Good thing you're such a big lad, isn't it, Mick? I build my units strong."

Liam watched as 59's eyes twitched again, at the word "Mick."

"I won't have it!" Fagan raged. "It's an

abomination against God and all the saints. I'll die first."

"As you wish." Mason called to his partner, "Bring the saw. We'll start with this bog-jumper, and cut into his cranium while he's still alive."

Fagan bellowed. Under cover of the racket, Liam said to 59, "What's your name, lad?"

The thing looked at him in confusion, an expression with which he could identify. Liam himself had waked not knowing who he was. But on some level, he'd recalled his name.

Just what made a man human? He prayed he was about to find out.

Chapter Forty

Clara regarded Old Tim with horror. The last thing—the very last thing—she wanted to do was place her mouth on his and breathe life into him as she had Liam and Cassie. Even for love of Liam she didn't know if she could.

Woodrow leaned closer and held his hand near the old man's mouth. "He's still breathing, barely."

"Thank God." Clara sagged with relief. "Get him up, Woodrow, if you can. We must have some sense out of him."

Not unkindly, Woodrow hauled Old Tim upright and rested him against the spattered wall. The old man gasped and choked.

"Leave me alone!"

"It's me, Tim—Ruella. Mr. Maynard has a job for you, an important one."

"Eh?" Tim pried one eye open and then the other. "I need a bottle."

"Smells like he's just had one." Woodrow muttered and nearly gagged.

"You'll get your bottle," Ruella said. "Soon as you give us some answers. Two men came here looking for you not long ago, young Fagan from the force, and another man. What did you tell them?"

"Sent them to the Cuttery, didn't I?" Tim mumbled, and closed his eyes again.

"The Cuttery?" Woodrow repeated, mystified. "What the hell's that?"

Clara did not even bother to scold him for his language. "I have no idea. Ruella?"

Ruella shook her head. She reached out and grabbed Tim by his filthy collar, then shook him till his old teeth rattled. "What's the Cuttery?"

Tim muttered something Clara did not catch. She stared at Ruella in frustration. "He's not making any sense."

"Listen to me, old man," Ruella said through gritted teeth. "What's this Cuttery place? Is it where you've been taking the bodies? Those of the men killed in the jail yard?"

Tim rolled his eyes till only the whites showed. "You're in on that?"

"Sure I am. Didn't I give you that bottle from Mr. Maynard, and take one of those bodies meself? But see, I didn't do the job right. Mr. Maynard wants me to train as your backup in case you're ever indisposed, because he trusts me, see? So you just take me wherever you sent young Fagan, so long as it's the same place you take those bodies."

"Don't think he'll be able to walk far," Woodrow put in.

Neither did Clara. She doubted the old man could stand, at this point.

"Doesn't need to—just give us the direction. I'll get us there." Ruella squared her beefy shoulders in resolve. "If my lad Fagan's gone off into trouble, I'll rescue him."

"Tim." Clara leaned down and engaged the old man's eyes. "You need to tell us how to find this

Cuttery, please."

He considered her hazily and then grinned. "What'll you give me if I do?"

"What do you want?" she returned, praying it mightn't involve physical contact.

"That bottle the lass promised."

Clara glanced at Ruella, who winked. "I just happen to have a small measure, here, of gin." She drew a bottle from the pocket of her coat. "Now, Tim, start talking."

****

The saw, unlike any Liam could have imagined in his worst nightmares, proved to be mechanized and steam-powered. Charles brought it in his metal hands and fired it up with a roar that sounded like the whine of a giant hornet.

"Take his scalp first," Mason insisted, "but try to do as little damage as possible. I'm eager to see what happens when we harvest the vitals from a live subject."

Fagan went abruptly silent, either with fear or because he'd passed out, as the buzzing tool approached his head.

Liam, knowing he had only seconds to save the lad, began to sweat. "Wait!"

"The second Mick speaks!" Mason said, and held up a hand. Charles paused with the whirling blade of the saw mere inches from the top of Brandon's head.

"You'll kill him."

"Inevitably, but not right away. A man can survive scalping. You'd be surprised—will be surprised—at what a man can survive."

"Best to be careful, though," Liam gasped. "You

don't want to waste him. And I'm not convinced you're as skilled at this sort of thing as you claim."

59, still standing by, turned its head and followed the conversation. It—as much as Brendan—was Liam's reason for talking.

"That's a ridiculous statement," Mason snapped.

"But if you're so miraculously good at all this, why not give him new, real hands?" Liam jerked his head at Charles. "Why not give yourself a real eye? Then you could go out into the world without frightening children."

That seemed to snag all Mason's attention. He gestured at Charles, who lowered the saw, and swung round to face Liam.

"You think I want to be like other men? You think I want to associate with the scum that fills this city, garbage like yourself, like that used to be?" Wildly, he indicated 59. "People are ignorant. You should understand that, bog-jumper, for your kind are the most ignorant of the lot, fit only for drinking, fighting, and spawning more like yourselves under the auspices of your church. I am superior. I needn't hide that superiority beneath a harvested skin. And I certainly wouldn't contaminate myself by placing one of your eyes in my head."

Deliberately, Liam looked at the steam unit. "You see what he thinks of us, lad. Shameful, that. What are you going to do about it?"

Mason appeared momentarily taken aback; then a smirk twisted his lips. "Don't bother, Mick. They're completely loyal to me."

"Are they, then? Even though you don't bother to hide how you despise them?"

"I do not despise it, I despise *you*. This unit is a brilliant piece of work."

"Despite the fact that it's a lowly Irish Mick bog-jumper?"

"It is not, not any longer. Portions of it were merely harvested from criminals better dead."

"Irishmen."

Brendan was aware and following the conversation now, staring at Liam, his eyes painfully wide.

"You said yourself," Liam pressed, half his attention on the unit, "they carry the essence of real men. Irishmen."

Mason's single, dark eye glowed; the mechanical fitting in the other socket adjusted wildly. He said to Charles, "I've changed my mind. Bring that saw over here; we'll start on this one."

****

"Can't see inside," Fred grunted. "Windows are all painted over."

The five of them huddled in a clump, concealed by shadows and the cold mist that rose from the water, and regarded the warehouse. A brick structure, its walls perhaps thirty feet high, it seemed to waver before Clara's eyes in time with her heartbeat. If Liam were there, she wanted to rush in impetuously but dared not.

"Steam units," Woodrow muttered. So there were—two of them on patrol, fine, big, new-looking machines.

"Whatever's here wants guarding," Ruella whispered. "We need a look inside."

"I will go." Dax rattled and puffed as he rolled forward. "No one will suspect me."

Clara and the others stared at him. Could a steamie

show initiative? Courage?

"No, hold on." Fred put out a hand. "I have a better idea. Woodrow and I will get in a scrap and distract those two. The rest of you try to sneak inside."

Deliberately, he handed the pistol to Ruella and said to his friend, "Come on."

"All right," Woodrow agreed, "but watch out for my nuts. Last time we did this, you planted your knee square on 'em."

"Sorry about that." Fred raised his voice. "You dirty, filthy cheat! You took my money! Give it back!"

As easily as that, a fight erupted. The two lads, hollering and swearing most convincingly, rolled and scrapped together, kicking and pushing, out from the cover of the shadows.

Clara stared in amazement. Through the fog that hung in the air like a chilly blanket, the boys thrashed and bellowed. Ruella seized Clara's arm and urged her through the dark perimeter toward the building. Dax rattled behind, his clatter well covered by the fracas.

The two steamies on patrol reacted immediately to the erupting brawl and moved in the boys' direction.

Clara took a deep breath and reached for the handle on the tall door. She didn't know what lay within, but at this point she was willing to brave whatever she must.

"Miss, let me." Dax barred her way. Half-started, she looked into his metal face. The eyes, mere depressions in the polished surface, should have revealed no emotion. But she saw determination there, and a certain measure of gallantry.

Her hand dropped from the handle. "Very well."

Dax pushed against the door. Behind them, the lads were howling like two tigers in their death throes, keeping the guards distracted.

The door resisted—locked or barred from the inside. Dax pushed harder and made a sound surprisingly like a grunt. Steam poured through the joints at his neck and shoulders, and his chest creaked alarmingly. He pushed still harder, and his elbows jittered.

The door flew inward, and the three of them stumbled through.

"Shut it quick," Ruella gasped, "before they notice."

"The lads—" Clara protested.

"They can take care of themselves."

"Dax"—Clara laid a hand on the steamie's arm—"please keep a watch for Fred and Woodrow."

Dax slipped back out even as Clara raised amazed eyes to survey the interior of the warehouse. Large, high-ceilinged, and blindingly bright, it contained absolutely no one. Steam billowed from a large plant some eighty feet distant, and equipment lay everywhere, very little of which she could identify.

"No one here?" Ruella asked in a whisper.

As if in answer, a bellow came from beyond the great furnace, quickly followed by a high, angry whine like that of the drill Clara's father had sometimes used on his patients' teeth.

"That's young Fagan's voice," Ruella declared, and took off down the room at a heavy gallop.

Clara followed and, seeing Ruella take the pistol firmly in hand as she rounded the furnace, prepared herself for anything.

But not for what she saw.

The space beyond the furnace had been partitioned.

A gray wall equipped with doors faced Clara as she skidded to a halt, leaving a space about thirty by twenty feet, brightly lit.

"Well, now," Ruella gasped, her eyes bulging, "there's a sight you don't see every day, innit?"

Too true. For Liam and a young man—Fagan?—both stark naked, were strapped to metal tables, while three men stood over them, one with a whirring, whining tool in his hands.

Clara gulped and stared. In his *mechanical* hands.

She screamed, and everything froze as five faces turned toward her. The buzzing tool swung and wavered, mere inches from Liam's head.

"Stop right there," Ruella croaked, "or I'll shoot!"

They'd already stopped, but Clara felt it a moot point. Her gaze reached for Liam's and his for her, as a drowning man for rescue. The breath surged in her lungs.

Ruella said, "Put the contraption down."

It did seem the most pertinent point. The thing whirred above Liam's ear, ready to bite. The man who held it—he with the horrific metal hands and, Clara now saw, livid steam burns—stared and sneered, and one of the other two whirled to confront them.

He had long, black hair and only one eye. The other—but Clara's mind stuttered over it, refusing to accept the truth.

What monstrous place was this?

"Put it down," Ruella commanded again, and raised the pistol in unsteady hands. "I will shoot!"

"Take care of them, 59," the black-haired man ordered.

The third man—the most ordinary looking of the

lot—moved to obey.

"Don't do it, lad," Liam gasped. "Don't abet the enemy."

The tall man with the auburn hair hesitated. He looked at Liam, and Clara felt something pass between the two of them.

"I am not your enemy," the black-haired man keened. "I'm your creator, and you will obey me! Damn it, I didn't construct you to have free will."

"Maybe not," Liam retorted from flat on his back. "But neither do I think you constructed all the Irish out of him."

Created? Clara blinked at the auburn-haired man and then blinked again. He couldn't be an automaton, if that was what the word implied. But was he entirely human? Her stomach wobbled.

"Bloody hell!" Ruella gasped, tumbling to the truth at the same instant as Clara. The pistol shook so badly she almost dropped it.

"So!" The black-haired man seized the terrible tool from the other's mechanical hands and glared at the steamie hybrid. "You have loyalties I didn't manage to bleed out, do you? Well, my friend, that's the trouble with being human: loyalty can so easily be used against you."

And he thrust the whirring machine at Liam's head.

Chapter Forty-One

Several things happened at once. Liam jerked his head as far across the table as he could, given the strap across his chest. The blade of the saw hit the metal table and spewed sparks. Clara screamed, a crash came from beyond the furnace, and the gun went off, knocking Ruella back a step. The mechanical man—Liam corrected himself—the mechanical *Irishman* gave a sound like a factory whistle marking the end of a shift.

Mason swore and whirled toward 59, the saw still in his hand. It skittered across the steel of the table top beside Liam's ear, and then 59 tackled Mason, and they both went down.

The doors in the gray wall at the rear of the warehouse opened, and Liam, still breathless at his near-miss, blinked and stared. A small army of what could only be others like 59 emerged.

They looked very like a stout company of Irishmen, tall and hearty, for the most part, all wearing human eyes, hair, and skin. Had they come in response to 59's terrible battle cry? Or did they answer the demands of their creators?

If the latter proved true then he, Brendan, Clara, and Ruella were all lost.

Ah—and what was this? From around the furnace raced Fred and Woodrow, looking like they'd just been in a fierce fight. Fred raced to Ruella and took the pistol from her hands.

"Stop right there! Everybody stop!" Charles, too, had a weapon in his hands, one such as Liam had never seen. Long and black, with a twisted muzzle, it looked like nothing so much as an overgrown licorice stick.

The melee ground to a gradual halt. Liam could only assume Mason and 59 still grappled together on the floor, for he could not see them. Nor could he see Clara, and his heart seized in his chest. Had she been hit by Ruella's shot? Had she fallen?

Charles pointed his weapon at Brandon's head. "Anyone moves, and he dies." Contradicting his own instructions, he added to Fred, "Drop the weapon."

"Do it, lad," Ruella begged.

With a grunt, eyes fixed on Charles's hands, Fred obeyed.

"Now, 59, get up. Obey me!" Charles roared when 59 did not immediately comply. "Or this piece of Irish meat dies."

The automatons standing in a line shifted uneasily. Liam tried to count them, but they wavered too badly before his eyes.

59 arose slowly and stood balanced like a dancer, all his attention on Charles.

Charles hollered, "Help your master up."

59 stiffened. He threw back his head and spoke in a deep voice. "I am an Irishman. I have no master."

Liam wanted to shout in pure delight at that, but Charles's face darkened with anger.

"You," said Charles, clearly enraged, "are an amalgamation of the parts from which you were made—the fact that most of them came from Irish corpses is purely incidental."

"You call murder incidental?" Liam croaked. "Look at them, man! Haul up your partner and make him look also. These aren't your creations. They're your victims!"

For an instant the great, echoing room went still. Then Liam's ear caught a faint hum—no, a rumble— no, a roaring moan. It came from the throats of all the hybrid steamies at once, up from the fires in their bellies, through their steam chambers, to their throats.

"Murder," said one.

"Murder."

"Murder."

The word repeated again and again. A hand grasped the edge of Liam's table and Mason pulled himself up. He had no attention for Liam, though, and stared at the ring of metal and flesh that surrounded him.

"Stand down!" he commanded.

"Murder, murder, *murder*." It became an accusation, like a rising tide, mobile and restless.

Mason shrank toward Charles, his eye adjusting frantically.

Another hand appeared, this time on the other side of Liam's table—fingers he recognized and knew right well. Clara scrambled up until she could touch him. Her fingers closed on his bare shoulder, and he felt his breath come easier.

"You shouldn't be here," he whispered at her.

"Yes, I should." Her eyes were all for the circle of automatons, but her love flooded Liam as she concluded, "Because you are."

"Drop the weapon," 59 told Charles. He gestured at Brandon. "He, like this other man, is our brother. If you harm him, we shall tear you limb from limb."

"And maybe," said the tallest of the lot, who had flaming red hair, "even if you don't."

Charles jerked the black gun round and aimed it at 59. "Perhaps I'll just shoot you, instead."

"No, Charles!" Mason cried. "They're too valuable. We've worked too hard, for too long—"

He got no further. Charles's finger spasmed on the trigger of the weapon. What looked like a beam of fire took 59 square in the chest and knocked him over backward. Before Charles could even attempt to shoot again, the circle of automatons closed on him and formed a knot between the two tables, absorbing Mason as they came.

"Damn, damn, damn!" Clara struggled with the metallic straps that held Liam to the table, finding them stiff and difficult. The one across his chest suddenly came loose, and then that which bound his arms. He seized her head and pressed it into his neck.

"Don't look," he bade her.

But neither of them had to look. The sounds of tearing flesh conveyed exactly what took place on the warehouse floor.

****

"So," Liam said, marveling over it, "Nancy and I were never married? She was my brother's wife?"

"Yes," Clara assured him with considerable satisfaction. "Which means our marriage is perfectly legal, and we've successfully spiked my grandfather's guns. Everyone under this roof is safe."

They sat in the parlor of the house on Virginia Street with Georgina and Theodore, Fred and Woodrow, and Brendan and Ruella, sharing a drink.

Theodore and Georgina had needed to be filled in on just what had occurred at the warehouse. A certain amount of disbelief needed to be overcome, even among those who had been at the Cuttery. Liam, like the others, could scarcely assimilate what he had seen.

Like a mad dream it all seemed, and had been ever since Clara breathed life into him. He quivered at that thought and threaded his fingers through hers still more securely. She perched on the arm of the chair in which he sat, virtually in his lap. He wanted her even closer, needed to go upstairs with her so badly he shook with it. But first this stout company had to talk through the horror they had shared.

"And what about Dax?" Tears flooded Georgina's eyes as she looked at Fred and Woodrow. "You say he sacrificed himself?"

Fred raised the glass he held to his lips before he replied. No one had objected when the two lads requested a small measure of whiskey—they'd earned a man's portion this night.

"We'd never have got past those guards if he hadn't come back looking for us," Fred said. "I've never seen steam units as advanced as those two, and I've worked on my share. They were miles beyond Dax, yet he threw himself to them the way a mama cat throws itself to the dogs."

"Impossible to claim steamies aren't capable of loyalty," Clara said fiercely. "That's the mistake those horrible men made, isn't it? Mason and Charles, you called them. But oh, I could weep for Dax."

"Don't, miss," Fred hastened to assure her. "I think Woodrow and I can rebuild him, maybe put in a few improvements of our own."

Clara raised her eyes to the lads. "But will he still be Dax?"

"I don't think we can doubt that, given what we've seen this night."

"What will happen to those super-units in the warehouse?" Fred wanted to know. "They're not really steamies, are they? But they're not quite men."

Fagan, whose hand rested on Ruella's knee, spoke. "That will be a decision for the powers that be, won't it? For now, they've been taken into custody for their own safety. I know what I'd like to see happen—they should be offered jobs on the police force. I'm thinking an all-Irish division."

"A fine idea, that." Liam quirked an eyebrow at the lad who had now become more than a friend. "I'd be willing to join that force meself, if I weren't such a reprobate."

"Irish reprobate," Brendan corrected, lifting his glass of whiskey. "Don't forget the Irish—it saved our skins this night."

"Nearly morning, now." Georgina glanced at the windows, where a faint radiance gathered. "Come on, lads—finish your drinks. You need to go to bed."

They all needed to go to bed, Liam thought, desire racing through his blood.

Theodore looked at Georgina. "You do recall this is our wedding day? That is, if you still mean to marry me now you don't need a roof over your head."

She gazed into his eyes, and Theodore returned her look with a seriousness that stopped every tongue in the room. "Of course I mean to marry you," Georgina told him. "Unless you've reconsidered our perilous position."

"Perilous?" Theodore waved a hand at the rest of them. "The term pales, in light of what's occurred tonight. All you and I do, sweet love, is take a step into a future I hope will one day become commonplace, wherein people judge each other not by the color of their skin but by what lies beneath." He shot an ironic look at his listeners, and smiled. "And the spirit within. Even if that spirit's trapped in the framework of an automaton."

"Amen," Fagan agreed, and they all drank again.

Chapter Forty-Two

"Alone at last," Liam breathed into Clara's ear, making her quiver with incipient delight. "I thought they'd never leave. And Nancy, by a miracle, is quiet. Come upstairs with me, Mrs. McMahon. I don't think I can bear it if you deny me."

Clara turned her face so her lips brushed his tenderly. They still sat in her father's armchair, but the others had departed, citing various duties and exhaustion. Brendan and Ruella had gone off in the direction of the jail, hand in hand, Brendan eager to lay charges against Maynard.

Theodore, wearing the stunned look of a man in love, had stumbled off, and Georgina had gone upstairs to check on Nancy. Fred and Woodrow had ostensibly gone to their rest, but they'd taken their whiskey glasses with them, and Clara doubted they slept.

"We've a few things to settle before we go to bed," Clara said.

"Have we?" His lips returned her caress with lingering sweetness. Desire leaped inside Clara, raw and fierce. She seized his shoulders in an attempt to hold him—or herself—down.

"Yes." Clara gazed into her husband's eyes and lost her breath. She fought to think clearly. "What's to be done about Nancy? She may not be your wife, but we clearly have a duty to her, if only in your brother's memory."

Liam's eyes clouded. "I wish I could remember him, but don't know as I ever will. You say he took his own life?"

"Out of guilt and remorse. He blamed himself for the fire and little Tommy's suffering, even as did Nancy."

"No wonder the poor lass was raving. Still—suicide. It's a terrible sin." Liam's black lashes dropped and concealed the depth of his sorrow. "I do feel I have a sacred obligation to her, Clara, if only for his sake."

"Of course. I'd love to have her live here, once she's well enough. But I do think she needs some intensive care first. If we budget my allowance carefully and you keep earning, we should be able to afford a private hospital for her."

Liam smiled slowly. "Your grandfather will not be best pleased that you're getting the house and money after all."

"My grandfather will be furious. He'd better take care apoplexy does not carry him off, old and frail as he is."

"You've a nasty streak, Mrs. McMahon."

He would have kissed her again, but she held him off, sudden doubt possessing her.

"Yes, Liam, there's that to speak of, as well."

"Eh?"

"Look at me," she urged. "Tell me what you see."

The black lashes swept up, revealing eyes deep and blue like sapphires. "I see a beautiful lass, a warrior pixie with magic in her—old magic—and a giving, compassionate heart. I see the woman I love. I see my whole world."

"You're wrong."

"I beg pardon?" He crooked an eyebrow.

"I'm serious, Liam. Before we go any further, this must be aired between us. Those men—Mason and Charles, you called them—they did some terrible things: had men murdered. Harvested parts of them for their creations. They were ruthless and without conscience."

"Agreed."

"Agreed. And I am not so very unlike them."

"Eh?" Liam exclaimed again. "You? Tell me how! You spend your concern on everyone you meet—take in abused children like stray cats, worry yourself into a frazzle over them. You've even offered a home to Nancy. How are you anything like those bastards at the Cuttery?"

"They had men killed for their own purposes. I waited for a man—you—to be killed, and did the very same. As I've said before, there was little compassion in my raising you from the dead, Liam. I did a dreadful thing. I'm ashamed to say it, but I truly am more like my grandfather than I care to think."

"You did a dreadful thing, did you?" Very gently he tipped up her chin so she once more had to meet his gaze. "Bringing me back to life. Giving me an opportunity to live again as a finer man. Would I really have been better off cut up into one of Mason's automatons?"

"No. Not that. But I fear it's the motivation that matters, Liam—not so much the *what* as the *why*. It scares me to think Roderick Van Hamelin's blood runs in my veins." And Liam did not even know about the battle she'd fought over her temptation to end Nancy's misery…

"Yet it does, as does that of your father, who was clearly a merciful man. If this terrible night's work has taught us anything, Clara, it's that we can't deny our blood—it will out. Thank God! Blood colors the spirit, Clara, but the spirit's our own. And," he told her devoutly, "your spirit is beautiful."

She said, with tears in her eyes, "I'll never be perfect, I fear."

"Nor will I. Do you think I want you perfect? No, Mrs. McMahon, I want you complete with all your faults—impatient, bossy, enraged, and ruthless. I want you wild in my bed, crazed with desire, and very, very naughty."

Clara told him, her heart bursting, "I think I can manage that—if only because you're so dead handsome."

"Then," he whispered seductively, "come upstairs to bed and prove that you love me."

And, most gladly, Clara did.

A word about the author...

Born in Buffalo and raised on the Niagara Frontier, Laura Strickland has been an avid reader and writer since childhood. To her the spunky, tenacious, undefeatable ethnic mix that is Buffalo spells the perfect setting for a little Steampunk, so she created her own Victorian world there. She knows the people of Buffalo are stronger, tougher, and smarter than those who haven't survived the muggy summers and frigid blasts found on the shores of the mighty Niagara. Tough enough to survive a squad of automatons? Well, just maybe.

Thank you for purchasing
this publication of The Wild Rose Press, Inc.

If you enjoyed the story, we would appreciate your
letting others know by leaving a review.

For other wonderful stories,
please visit our on-line bookstore at
www.thewildrosepress.com.

For questions or more information
contact us at
info@thewildrosepress.com.

The Wild Rose Press, Inc.
www.thewildrosepress.com

Stay current with The Wild Rose Press, Inc.

Like us on Facebook

https://www.facebook.com/TheWildRosePress

And Follow us on Twitter
https://twitter.com/WildRosePress